Tortured Souls

The Orion Circle Book 1

Kimber Leigh Wheaton

Published by
Sea Dragon Press

Tortured Souls
Copyright © 2014 by Kimber Leigh Wheaton
ISBN 0990402614
ISBN 978-0-9904026-1-9

Library of Congress Control Number: 2014910565
Sea Dragon Press, San Antonio, TX

Cover Art Designed by AM Design Studios

To everyone who has ever felt misunderstood or like they didn't quite fit in. And to everyone who has taken a leap of faith to try to understand them.

Table of Contents

1
Something Wicked

Deafening music shakes the walls, vibrates the floor, and pounds a rhythmic beat in my skull. Gyrating bodies turn every bit of space into a dance floor. Sweat breaks out on my forehead, and my heart races. Strobe lights flash, teens dance with wild abandon. Shrieking laughter bubbles around me.

"Gotta take a leak!" my dance partner shouts over the music.

He races off, weaving through the thick wall of bodies. Mike or Mick or something—I didn't catch the name he yelled when he asked me to dance. Doesn't matter, he wasn't my type at all. I mean, the guy guzzled beer while dancing. After grabbing a diet soda from a nearby cooler, I'm about to search for my friends when a dark feeling washes over me. My feet refuse to move, and I stand rooted in place.

The once loud music is now hollow in my ears. I gasp for breath, choking on the lack of air around me. Tiny hairs on the nape of my neck rise to attention. Something wicked is behind me. I know I'm the only one here who feels a difference in air pressure. An oppressive weight presses against my skin, making me feel as though I'm underwater. I blink a few times, watching the people around me continue their manic dancing—oblivious to the bogeyman that just entered the room.

Afraid to turn around, I stand my ground, sipping my soda. I pretend I'm unaware of the shuffling noises behind me, sounds I shouldn't be able to hear over the blaring music. Swaying my hips, I hum along with the music, trying to ignore the ominous presence crushing me.

Whatever it is, I can't let it know I sense it. Evil pours off it in waves, blanketing the entire room. I close my eyes, willing the creature to go away, return to whatever mausoleum or grave it calls home. Malevolent spirits feed on fear. I must control mine at all costs.

When I open my eyes, I'm gazing into the face of an angel. Not literally, but he may as well be in my book. Logan glances behind me, and I know he sees the spirit. He doesn't gasp or scream or faint dead away. His golden eyes narrow as though he's in a staring contest with the specter.

"You're not welcome here," Logan says to the presence behind me. He meets my gaze again. "You know it's there."

It's not a question but a statement. I nod, a weak bob of my head, unsure whether this intimate moment with my dream guy is a good thing or not. Meeting over a nasty phantom is not my idea of romantic. And yet I can't stop staring at the way his blue t-shirt hugs his broad shoulders and chest—how his light brown hair curls around his earlobes. I don't know whether to laugh or cry. For six weeks I've wanted out of the friendship box with Logan, but I was hoping for girlfriend, not *crazy girl*.

"Kassandra," a voice rasps behind me.

Bitter cold lances through me, raising goosebumps all over my body. Cold liquid spills over my fingers from the soda can as I crush it in my fist. Logan places his hand on my shoulder, the simple gesture driving away the biting cold. He pries the can from my fingers, dropping it to the floor. I take a step closer to him, desperate for comfort, still too scared to turn and look upon the evil presence. Everyone in the room continues to go about their business, dancing and laughing. Logan and I are the only ones aware of the evil presence affecting the entire room.

"Who are you? Why are you here? What do you want?" My voice rises with each question until it reaches the point of hysteria.

A rush of frigid wind buffets me on all sides. Logan takes my hand, squeezing it in his firm grasp. My strawberry blonde hair whips around my face, and I close my eyes, trying to prepare my mind for an attack.

"Saint Michael the Archangel, defend us in battle. Be our protection against the wickedness and snares of the devil," Logan yells into the raging wind. "You are not welcome here. Leave Kacie alone!"

"For now," the voice rasps.

A sharp, stinging sensation on my back makes me gasp. My eyes fly open and I whirl around to face the source of my pain. The specter disappears in a flash of light so bright I'm blinded for a moment. Music blares in my ears, and the oppressive weight lifts from my body. I stare down at my pale hand clasped in Logan's, unable to look up to meet his eyes.

"It's over," he shouts over the music. "Whatever it was is gone. The spirit called you Cassandra."

"Yeah, my full name is Kassandra, with a K." My heart hammers in my chest, but I don't want to let on how much the ghost scared me. "My mom named me after the Trojan oracle."

"Oh, the one who had the gift of prophecy but was cursed to never be believed," Logan says as he scans the room.

Everything is back to normal, like the ghost was never here at all. The pain in my back, though, is enough to remind me.

"Yeah, ironic, huh…"

"How so?"

I take a breath to reply, but my best friend, Celia, races over before I can say anything. She opens her mouth to speak but stops when she sees my hand in Logan's. A knowing smile lights her face.

"Jake has to leave," she says while bouncing in place like she might erupt into a cheer at any moment. "He's got a test tomorrow. If he doesn't pass, he'll get suspended from the team. I mean, I know Mandy's parents are out of town and all, but who throws a party like this on a Sunday night? Especially when half the junior class has a history midterm tomorrow."

Celia sways a bit on her platform heels. Height has always been a sore spot with Celia. I'm three inches taller than her petite five-foot-two. In her towering sandals her dark brown eyes are level with mine. They twinkle as she stares at me, waiting for an explanation she won't be getting tonight.

"I'm ready to go anyway," I say, rubbing at my lower back trying to ease the sting.

My other hand is still nestled in Logan's warm grip. Do I pull away or wait for him to do it? It feels so nice—I don't want it to end.

"Besides, I don't want to be here when the cops arrive," I add, babbling a bit as I tend to do when I'm nervous.

"I'll take her home," Logan says grinning. He releases my hand, brushing my fingers with his thumb as he pulls away. "She lives a few blocks from me."

"I do?" I ask, wondering how Logan Finley could possibly know where I live.

"Yep," Logan replies. "I don't want to be here when the cops arrive either. Not with the amount of pot circulating this place."

"Great, I'm gonna go find Jake," Celia says, jumping up to see over the crowded living room. "See y'all tomorrow."

She races off, bouncing like a hyper Easter Bunny, her long blonde hair swaying with the motion. I love Celia, but sometimes her perkiness is more than I can handle.

"You ready to go?" Logan asks.

"Not yet," I reply, scoping the room for a blond head. "I need to remind Dave to study for his test or he can kiss his football scholarship goodbye."

When I spy Dave's wavy hair over by the wet bar, I breathe a sigh of relief. His girlfriend, Rachel, is nowhere in sight. What Dave sees in that stereotypical blonde bimbo cheerleader is beyond me.

"I don't think he sees anything past her chest," Logan says laughing. "I take it you don't hang with Rachel much?"

"Oh my God, I said that aloud didn't I," I say cringing. "Yeah, Rachel hates me, calls me a buzz-kill. She's more concerned with the next party than Dave's future. But it's A&M for Christ's sake."

"I'm pretty sure the only person Rachel cares about is her reflection," Logan says with a disgusted snort.

The moment I open my mouth to speak to Dave, Rachel appears with a vicious scowl marring her red painted lips. She drapes her body across Dave, a living fashion accessory. If I didn't know better, I'd swear she was marking her territory.

"What do you want, drama queen?" she asks in a high-pitched whine.

"Baby, be nice," Dave says while groping her chest right in front of us. "Kacie's my friend. She's cool."

"She's so far from cool she's… uh, she's…" Rachel trails off, unable to finish her thought.

She looks so perplexed that I have to bite my lip to keep from laughing. One hand rakes through her platinum blonde locks while the other taps a beat on Dave's chest. Her pale blue eyes are almost crossed from thinking too hard. I somehow manage to hold my tongue. While I don't care what Rachel thinks of me, I also don't want a war with one of the most popular girls in school.

"Hot?" Logan suggests.

"Yeah, hot," she says, nodding her head a few too many times. "She's so far from cool she's hot."

"I couldn't agree more," Logan says, grinning at me.

"Honey, how much have you had to drink?" Dave asks, peeling her arms away from his body. "Go lie down for a while, sleep it off."

"I'll lie down if you come with me," she says giggling. "And by come I mean—"

"I'll meet you upstairs in a few," Dave says, cutting her off with a lewd grin.

He turns her around by the shoulders, giving her a little shove toward the stairs. She teeters away on her three-inch heels, and somehow makes it out of the room without knocking into anything. I don't know how girls like Celia and Rachel manage to walk in those things without breaking an ankle.

"I'm on my way out," I say, returning my attention to Dave. "Test tomorrow. You asked me to remind you to study tonight."

"Thanks, Kacie," Dave says, draining his beer in a few gulps. "I'll see ya in the morning."

"See ya," I call out to his retreating figure.

"Well, that was rather amusing," Logan says, not bothering to hide his smirk.

"That's one word for it," I reply with a deep sigh. "Sometimes I wish I didn't care about Dave's future either. Let's get out of here."

We walk outside, leaving the deafening noise of the party behind. Out here, the bass from the music is a droning thump I can feel like a second heartbeat. I take a deep breath of fresh air, sighing as the tension leaves my body. Parties are just not my thing. I always seem to run into ghosts. Perhaps they're drawn to the noise or excitement. As we walk away from the party, we pass several cars with couples making out in the backseats. A black pickup has some girl's legs dangling out the passenger window.

"It's a truck," Logan says, shaking his head. "Something wrong with the bed?"

I snicker at his remark, and glance up at him from the corner of my eye. He's staring right at me, his eyes sparkling in the dim moonlight. My eyes dart around, looking for something to comment on, something to say. We pass a bouncing sedan.

"Really?" I mutter under my breath. "You're doing it parked in front of someone's house..." A light flickers on downstairs in the house we're passing.

"Crap, we need to get out of here," Logan says, taking my hand and jogging down the street.

"Where's your car?" I ask, glad I wore hiking boots rather than heels to the party.

"I walked," he replies as we round the corner. Halfway down the street he slows to a walk. "I think we're far enough away, don't you?"

"We're walking home?" I ask a bit surprised.

Granted it's only about half a mile away, but my friends drive everywhere, even down the block. When he drops my hand, my heart falls just a little. Well, maybe a lot. But I continue walking alongside Logan, casting surreptitious glances whenever he isn't looking. He's tall and lean with broad shoulders that would suit a football player. But Logan runs cross country with me. His long legs are covered in torn jeans, faded to a light blue. I wonder if they're as soft as they look.

"It's not far, Kacie," Logan says chuckling. "It'll give us a chance to talk about what happened at the party."

"What do you mean?" I ask, trying to appear perplexed.

My hand moves to my stinging lower back like it has a will of its own. I gasp in pain when my shirt scrapes across the skin.

"Let me see your back," Logan says, stopping to face at me.

"Nothing's wrong with my back," I mutter, staring at the ground.

He grabs my shirt, lifting it to bare my lower back. He hisses. "Damn, you've got three deep scratches."

"Crap," I cry out, jumping away from him. "Must've been a cat or something."

"I know you felt the presence," Logan says. He crosses his arms over his chest. "The spirit attacked you. I was there. Now tell me what's going on."

"I, uh…" I try to think of something, anything. But I freeze under his knowing gaze. "I think I was a bit sick."

It sounds lame, I know. But I learned a long time ago never to reveal my abilities. Regular people don't understand. They think I'm lying, or worse crazy. Old habits die hard.

"I was there, Kacie," he says in a soft, gentle tone. "Please don't pretend you don't know what I'm talking about. Besides, Mandy doesn't even have a cat. And those scratches are fresh."

"I don't want to talk about it," I say before walking away down the street.

My footsteps become faster as my feet slam against the concrete. Whether I'm running from Logan, the ghost, or myself, I don't know for sure. My lungs burn, but not from exertion. I run track and cross country... no my endurance is fine. Fear prickles the back of my neck, shooting a cold chill down my arms. The last time someone I cared about discovered my ability they left and never looked back. I like Logan too much to allow that to happen.

"Kacie, wait," Logan says, jogging beside me. His stride is much longer. I'm running and he's barely loping. "Please, just talk to me. I can help you."

"Look, just drop it, okay?" I blurt out after skidding to an abrupt stop. "I need to get home. I'm sure everything will be a distant memory by morning."

"Are you sure this is what you want?" Logan asks with a scowl creasing his forehead.

"It's for the best," I reply as I start walking again.

Wow, I ran farther than I realized. I make a right turn onto my street, Logan following behind. Why did this have to happen? I really like Logan, and now my stupid abilities have messed it up just like they mess everything up. He walks me to the front door.

If I hoped for any privacy, I blew it big time. The front of the house is ablaze with lights. I think Dad turned on every downstairs light as well as the porch light. After digging out my key from the front pocket of my jeans, I turn to face Logan.

"Thanks for walking me home," I say while twisting my fingers together. "And thanks for dropping it too."

"Sure, Kacie," he replies, tipping his head to the side. "You wanna go running with me tomorrow morning? I go every morning before school since afternoons are still too hot."

"Um, yeah, what time?"

"I'll come by about six," he says, his lips curving into a smile.

"Don't knock or ring the bell," I warn him, cringing at the thought of Logan waking my dad or brother.

"You got your phone with you?"

With a sigh, I pull the iPhone from my back pocket and hand it over. He programs his number into my contacts and sends himself a text.

"I'll text you in the morning when I get here," he says before waving goodbye.

Standing at the door, I watch him jog down the street and disappear around the corner. Somehow I manage to keep from banging my head against the front door. In all my daydreams about Logan, not once did I imagine this night's events. Sometimes I think fate hates me.

2

Can Nightmares Become Reality?

Horrifying broken pictures shatter the tranquility of my once pleasant dream. Though I scream in my mind to wake up, I know I won't be able to. I'm captive in my own head while the gritty scenes play out in stark black and white, flickering like an old silent movie. I run from the phantom chasing me. When I slip in a dark gray puddle, my body collides with the ground, my hands slapping into the viscous liquid. Blood. The sharp, pungent odor assaults my nose, telling me this is no ordinary dream.

I stare into the sightless eyes of a teenage girl sprawled across the grass like a broken, discarded doll. Her legs bend beneath her at impossible angles, the bone poking through the shin of one leg. Blood seeps from her shattered skull, flowing to the grass in rivulets to pool around her lifeless body. As I try to crawl away from the broken girl, I sense the approach of a monster, the man responsible for this gruesome display. With a tiny whimper I surge to my feet. He's on me in a flash, and I scream a wordless keening cry before my airway is forced closed. My sanity begins to shatter then everything goes mercifully black...

Somehow I manage to tear myself from the gut-wrenching dream. I bite my lip to keep from screaming. Blood pours into my mouth, and I gag on the metallic taste. As my heartbeat begins to return to a normal rhythm, I untangle my body from the sheets holding me captive on the floor of my room. Lurching to my feet, I try to comfort my mind, ease my quaking nerves. This is the fifth night in a row I've had this dream. It's always the same, always in black and white, gritty, the images jerky.

I haven't seen the attacker, the monster responsible for the grisly murder. The faceless phantom hides in the darkest recesses of my mind. He chases me for several minutes in the dream, but I never turn to face him. Deep down I know if I face this dream monster, something awful will happen.

Leaving the sheets on the floor, I move back to sit on my bed, staring into the room, but only seeing the dream. Vision, my mind insists—it was a vision not a dream. My gaze falls on the red numbers on the digital clock resting on the nightstand. Five twenty-seven in the morning, just three minutes before my alarm would have jarred me awake. With a resounding sigh, I turn off the alarm and switch on the light. Logan will be here in half an hour.

Crossing the bedroom, I pull some shorts and the Aggies jersey Dave gave me from my dresser. After tugging on some socks and tying my running shoes, I run a brush through my long hair before braiding it in pigtails. I check out my reflection in the mirror. Dark circles stain the skin beneath my eyes. Though I could try covering them with makeup, I'd rather not wear makeup jogging. Some of the girls on the cross country team run with full makeup covering their faces. By the end of a run they all look like scary clowns with smeared, sweaty streaks. No thank you. Logan will just have to accept me *au natural*. I do look quite adorable in the twin braids. Those and the dusting of freckles across my nose give me an innocent farmer's daughter look.

Creeping from my room, I tiptoe down the carpeted stairs. Dad hates it when I go running before dawn, though I'm sure any dangerous criminals must be asleep by now. The last thing I want to explain to Dad is why I'm running before dawn with a boy he hasn't met.

Kodiak prances in his kennel when I enter the kitchen. I release our faithful Goldendoodle and attach him to the jogging leash around my waist.

The eighty-pound white dog is ecstatic for a morning run and tries to drag me across the room toward the front door. He stops when I murmur a sharp command to heel. I disarm and rearm the security system before heading out the door.

Outside, the October morning air is pleasantly cool, the humid heat of the San Antonio summer giving way to autumn. The soft glow from the first rays of sunlight creates a beautiful orange tapestry across the eastern sky. Taking a deep, cleansing breath, I stretch my muscles while casting surreptitious glances down the street. Most Cedar Bluffs residents are still fast asleep in their beds, leaving the neighborhood quiet. Dawn and late night are my favorite times to run, much to Dad's chagrin. He doesn't like me being out in the dark alone, but I crave the peace and quiet I find when everyone else is sleeping.

Logan appears at the corner, running at a steady pace, much faster than I want to run this early in the morning. My heart hammers as I watch his approach. Now that he's here, my palms sweat, and I almost shake from nervous energy. This moment is straight out of my daydreams. I wipe my hands on my shorts.

Straightening up, I can't help but stare, lost in his rhythmic strides. His mop of light brown hair is darkened with sweat. The curls at his nape, sagging under the weight, still bounce a bit with each step.

He slows to a stop within inches of me, giving me a lopsided grin.

"Love the braids," he says, picking one up and twirling it between his fingers. "Though I think the jersey's gotta go."

My breath catches in my throat, and my eyes narrow. He didn't just... as my mind processes his words, I notice his t-shirt—UT Longhorns. So he wasn't trying to undress me. Is he one of the rabid football fans who despise anyone rooting for the opposition?

"I mean, uh," he stammers, his face turning pink. Perhaps he just realized what his words could have implied. "Aggies..." he croaks.

"I'm neutral," I say, biting my lip to keep from smirking. "Dave gave me this 'cause I help him remember to study. See, it has his name and number for next year on the back." I turn around so Logan can see. "My brother goes to UTSA, so he's a huge Longhorns fan by association. It makes football season more interesting in my house if I root for the Aggies."

"Sorry, that whole thing just came out wrong," he says with a shy smile. "My mom's A&M and my dad's UT. The whole family's divided. Isn't most of Texas?"

"So you're okay running with a girl wearing an Aggies jersey?" I ask chuckling under my breath. It seems my nervousness has faded in the face of his own.

"Yes, though I can understand now why Rachel hates you," he says, motioning to the jersey. "I've never seen her wearing one." His eyes sparkle with mischief. If it was possible, I think I might drown in the liquid gold of his eyes.

"I'm sure it's a fashion *faux pas* of some sort," I choke out through laughter when I picture Rachel in a football jersey paired with a miniskirt and heels.

"Who's this?"

"This is Kodiak." Kodiak inches closer to him, his nose scenting the air.

"He looks like a polar bear," Logan says, holding his hand out to the dog. "What kind of dog is he?"

"Goldendoodle," I say, trying to hide my snicker behind my hand. "He's half poodle, half golden retriever. A good breed really, even if they do have a dumbass name."

When he reaches out to pat Kodiak, his hand brushes mine lying on top of the dog's back. A tiny jolt of electricity travels up my arm, and I snatch my hand away.

"What was that?" I ask gasping.

"I'd say static electricity but that would be a lie," he says. He gazes at me in silent speculation. "You really are clairvoyant."

"What would give you that idea?" I ask, trying desperately to play it down.

Having learned the hard way long ago, I'm not about to reveal my abilities to a relative stranger. Especially one I've had a crush on since last year. I was hoping last night was a distant memory, maybe even my imagination.

"That spark occurs when two people with talent connect. I'm guessing you didn't notice it last night when I grabbed your hand," he replies, still gazing at me with those knowing eyes.

"I was a little preoccupied," I say, wringing my hands together.

"You're running from a disturbing vision," he says, closing his eyes and releasing me from their spell. When he opens them he says, "You can't run forever, eventually it'll catch up. If you aren't ready it could overpower you, perhaps even harm you."

"I'll be fine," I say, shrugging my shoulders. "I'm sure it's nothing but a recurring nightmare." Deciding it's time to escape before he asks any more uncomfortable questions, I walk to the end of the driveway. "Are we going to run or not?"

"Sure. Think you can keep up?" he asks with a chuckle.

He takes off at a brisk jog. Kodiak trots at my side, not pulling on the leash, just content to follow my easy stride. As we turn right at the first intersection, I pick up the pace a bit, pushing my legs to take longer strides. I catch up to Logan and we run side by side. My mind begins to clear, and I settle into a comfortable jog, my breathing easy this early in the run. Another quick right followed by a left turn and we're running past the gate and down the main road toward the park.

"I'm a member of an exclusive club at school, the Orion Circle. Perhaps you've heard of us?" he asks, cocking his head to the side.

My eyebrows shoot up at his admission, and I stumble a bit on a crack in the sidewalk. He grabs my elbow to steady me. Not trusting my voice to work, I nod in response. Of course I've heard of the secretive Orion Circle—everyone has. Speculation as to the nature of the club runs the gamut from academic to secret society.

The moment we enter the park, Kodiak prances in excitement, eager for the wild trails up ahead. This time of morning wildlife sightings are plentiful. Kodiak lunges at a squirrel crossing our path. I make a clicking noise with my tongue, and the dog reverts to his obedient behavior. Pavement gives way to a dirt trail, forcing me to slow my pace due to the uneven footing.

"I think you should come to our meeting this afternoon. I'll find you later today and give you an invitation."

His offer blindsides me, and I nod like an idiot, my head bobbing a few too many times. Somehow I manage to smile at him before returning my gaze to the trail. Wow, the Orion Circle and Logan in one day. I feel like I'm floating on a cloud until a rock brings me back to Earth. After stumbling a few steps, Logan's hand on my arm is the only thing that keeps me from falling.

If I continue to run down this dirt trail, I'm afraid I might fall to my death. It seems I'm having a hard time seeing anything other than an image of Logan's handsome face. I glance up at him, surprised by the concern etched across his face.

"Are you okay? You didn't twist your ankle, did you?"

"No, I'm fine, really," I reply as a hot flush creeps from my neck to my face. "But my mind is a million miles away, and I'm afraid I'll break a leg on this trail if we keep going."

"We'll head back, then," he says before turning to walk back to the park entrance.

"Thanks for understanding," I say, relieved we are walking rather than running.

"I only got a glimpse of your vision," he says in a soft voice. "It was bad. Real bad. Don't worry, I'll help you, I promise. I think you'll feel a lot better after the Orion Circle meeting."

His words fill me with warmth along with a feeling of contentment. Perhaps this vision isn't so bad. I mean, it brought me closer to Logan, after all.

3
Home
~

When I throw the front door open, I notice the alarm is off—someone other than me is awake. I release Kodiak and wander into the kitchen for a much needed cup of coffee. Feeling the need to relax frayed nerves, I choose the green tea pod instead of my usual French roast and push it into the Keurig machine. As the machine dumps the tea into the coffee cup, I open an English muffin and place the two halves into the toaster. By the time my breakfast is ready, Dad comes down the stairs dressed for work.

"Morning, pumpkin," he says as he pops a pod into the coffee maker. "Saw you were out before dawn again this morning. Now you're drinking coffee? You know it's not good for a young body."

Concentrating on buttering my English muffin keeps me from fighting with Dad. When he joins me at the table, I glance up at him.

"This is green tea, not coffee," I say, blowing my bangs out of my eyes. "I took Kodiak with me this morning. No one will attack me with a large dog at my side. Besides, I met up with a friend so I wasn't really alone." After the words leave my mouth, I realize my mistake.

"Who's this friend who can drag herself out of bed before dawn?" he asks, curiosity lighting his face. "That's a rare trait among teenagers."

"Just a guy from school. He's on the cross country team too," I say in a breezy tone, before changing the subject. "I have a meeting after school today so I'll be late getting home."

Dad's dark eyes meet mine with a skeptical look. "You aren't failing any classes are you?"

"No, of course not!" I bite back. "It's an afterschool club. I've been invited to attend a meeting today."

"By the boy you met this morning," he says between sips of coffee.

"What makes you say that?" I ask, staring at the table.

"You didn't mention this club last night at dinner," he replies still eyeing me. "Therefore, I assume you got the invitation this morning." He rises from the table, grabbing his wallet and phone from the drawer. "Look sweetie, I have to get to work, important meeting this morning. Have fun at school, call if you'll be later than eight tonight."

I nod my agreement as he walks out into the garage, locking the door behind him. With a heavy sigh, I take my dishes and Dad's coffee cup to the sink and wash them out before heading upstairs to shower.

As I enter my room fresh from the shower, my cell chimes signaling the arrival of a text. Picking up my iPhone from the nightstand, I groan, realizing I left it behind this morning when I went for my run. Ten missed texts from Celia, none important, the last five all asking why I'm not responding.

Out 4 run 4got cell my bad, I quickly text back before heading to the closet.

The cell chimes again as I'm pulling on my gray jeans. Deciding to ignore it, I dig through my dresser drawer trying to decide on a top, selecting a long-sleeve black and gray t-shirt. I love the black lace sleeves and the way it hugs my curves. It's perfect for today. I look nice, but not like I went to any real effort.

Grabbing the blow dryer, I turn it on high and dry my hair for a couple of minutes, leaving it a bit damp. By the time I get to school it should be dry, and I'll brush it before I go inside. Celia would kill me if she knew, but I'm pretty low maintenance—a brush is the only styling implement my hair will see today. I line my upper eyelids with a charcoal liner followed by a light coat of mascara on my lashes.

Another chime from my phone, Dave this time, saying he'll pick me up at eight. It leaves me fifteen minutes to finish getting ready. Sitting on the bed, I type a quick reply to Dave before pulling on some black socks and lacing up my black hiking boots. These boots are fantastic, black leather with a black Sherpa lining on top of a two-inch stacked heel. Whoever thought of these is a genius in my book, comfort and style in one adorable boot.

Rifling through my black leather backpack, I check to make sure all of my books and notebooks are packed within. After slinging the backpack over my shoulder, I walk down the hall, stopping to pound on my brother's door. Gavin is nineteen and attending UTSA. His commute is twenty minutes. He'll miss his first class if he doesn't hurry. When he finally shouts that he's up, I head down the stairs to wait for Dave. Knowing Gavin will forget, I feed Kodiak even though it's his chore. I'd hate for the dog to go hungry all morning until the pet sitter arrives for his daily walk.

While the dog devours his food, I prepare Dave's bribe—a travel mug filled to the brim with French

Vanilla coffee. His mother is dead set against him drinking coffee, and I managed to snag a ride to school every day with the senior in exchange for his morning hit. The heavenly aroma of fresh-brewed coffee fills the kitchen. I lean forward breathing in the calming scent.

A car horn blares outside. I grab my backpack and the coffee, locking the door behind me. Dave is in his cherry red pickup, windows open, with the satellite radio blasting Octane. There's nothing like a little hard rock music to jolt you awake in the morning. As I get into the passenger seat, I toss my backpack in the tiny backseat and hand Dave his bribe. He greets me with a half-smile. His eyes are puffy with dark circles under them.

"Damn, Kacie," he says in a raspy, sleep-deprived voice, "you have no idea how much I need this right now."

He runs a hand through his disheveled, blond hair before backing out of the drive. After taking a large gulp of coffee, he tears down the street. I grab the door frame as he whips the truck around the corner.

"Didn't get any sleep. Rachel kept me busy all night," he adds, in a lewd tone. "Only got in a half hour of study time for the midterm. Coach says I'll get suspended from the team if I don't pull my average up to a C."

"Probably should have taken a break from Rachel last night, Dave," I reply, looking away so he doesn't see me roll my eyes.

"Easier said than done, I'm afraid," he says with a deep sigh. "You know anything about the War of 1812?" he asks, his voice full of hope.

"Sorry, no clue," I reply, looking back in time to see his huge yawn. "Skip first period and go to the library to study. Don't you have Mrs. Callahan? She's blind as a bat, she'll never notice if you sneak out."

"Good advice, Kacie," he says, ruffling my hair with his hand. "I can always count on you for coffee and ideas."

Yep, good old Kacie, so many guy friends but no boyfriend. Sometimes I get so sick of being one of the guys. As Dave pulls the truck into the school parking lot, big fat raindrops splatter against the windshield.

My great-aunt Rosemary used to say: *If you don't like the weather, wait a minute*—her tribute to the quickly changing San Antonio climate. When Dave picked me up sunlight was shining through the clouds. I was hoping we'd skip the rain today.

"I'll drop you at the theater entrance, Kacie," Dave says, veering away from student parking to head to the theater.

"Thanks," I reply, sighing in relief.

I don't know why Dave is acting so chivalrous today, but I won't complain. Had he dropped me off at our regular location, I'd have been soaked by the time I ran across campus to the theater building. He pulls alongside the curb next to the theater. I hop out, grab my backpack, and race through the pelting rain to the sanctuary of the theater.

4

Not Your Average School Day

By the time third period rolls around, the rain has slowed to a light drizzle. The quad outside the Arts and Humanities building is empty—tables and benches all drenched from the morning downpour. My view from this window is normally much more interesting, diverting me from the tedium of English class. How can a teacher take something as interesting as reading and turn it into mindless torture?

We just started Hamlet, a wonderful play full of intrigue, love, murder and insanity. Instead of an open discussion about the play, Mr. Farlow has us taking turns reading it in class. Listening to my classmates stumble over the archaic phrasing in a dull monotone is enough to lead me to fantasies of breaking a window and fleeing into the misty morning air. The bell finally rings, releasing me from my torment and silent vigil over the courtyard below.

My classmates fall over each other in their desperation to escape, while I hang back, still eyeing the silent quad. Once the crowd has fought their way out the narrow door, I follow with ease, a tiny smirk on my face at the absurdity of it all.

Sometimes you've just gotta laugh lest you end up crying in your cereal. Another of my late great aunt's many bizarre sayings. Though, now that I think about it, she may have been onto something. The family wrote her off as senile at worst and eccentric at best. Perhaps she was merely wiser than the rest of us.

The bright hallway is filled with eager students rushing past loitering delinquents. I have yet to understand the propensity to hang out by the lockers since so many have a tendency to leak foul odors. More than one of my friends has left a lunch to rot in the confines of the metal cage. Perhaps they couldn't bring themselves to toss it away even though they had no desire to eat it. A single row of lockers is a microbiology science fair project all ready to go, only the colorful poster board and labels missing.

Making my way down the staircase to the first floor, I head out the door and into the quiet quad. The rain has stopped, leaving the outdoors feeling clean, the fresh scent of ozone permeating the air around me. Spreading the dingy white towel I nabbed earlier from the locker room on a stone bench, I sit down and pull my script from my backpack. Fourth period would normally be PE, but I'm exempt due to my stint on the cross country team.

As I try to concentrate on learning my lines for the fall play, other students trickle outside now that the rain has stopped. Ignoring the incessant chatter surrounding me, I lose myself in my *Anything Goes* script. I'm playing the lead, nightclub singer Reno Sweeney, and I have nine songs along with what seems like hundreds of lines to learn before our performance in eight weeks. My mind is so wrapped up in the script I don't notice the person who sits down beside me on the other end of the towel.

"Kacie, are you in there?" a male voice asks, making me jump in surprise. "I saw you sitting alone and thought you might like some company, but you seem busy so I'll go."

When I glance up, warmth rushes not only to my face but all over my body. Logan scoots closer, his leg brushing against mine. His cheeks flush an endearing shade of pink. My gaze moves to his lips, and I can't help biting my lower lip as I watch him speak. I've never felt like this before—this strong almost uncontrollable desire to lean forward, close the small gap between us, and press my lips to his.

"Kacie?" Logan calls out, snapping me from my thoughts. "Should I go?"

"No don't go," I say as I stuff the script back into my bag. "I'm sick of reading this script anyway.

So what's up?" I ask, my heart fluttering a bit when he rewards me with a brilliant smile.

He pulls an envelope from his backpack and hands it to me. The envelope is heavy ivory stock, very formal in appearance, with my name written across the front in elegant calligraphy lettering. *Kassandra Ramsey.* I don't see my full name often. Curiosity wells within as I release the seal on the back, careful not to mar the ivory stock. There's a notecard inside, also written in calligraphy.

Dear Kacie,

Congratulations on your referral to the Orion Circle. We would like to extend an invitation to attend our meeting on the ninth of October, at fifteen thirty hours in the loft of the Sciences building located at the top of the eastern stairwell. You will be asked to take a formal vow of silence in regards to anything you see or hear at the meeting today. Please RSVP to your courier.

Orion Circle

"Vow of silence?" I ask a bit dumfounded. "No wonder your group gets compared to a secret society."

"It's not like that," Logan says with a wink. "I think you of all people understand the need for discretion when it comes to certain talents." He gives me a knowing look. When my hazel eyes widen at the realization, he nods and his lips curl into a serene smile. "I'll meet you at your locker after school if you'd like an escort," he offers in a rather casual tone, though if I'm not just reading things into it, his gaze is anything but casual. His fingers rake through his curly hair in what almost appears to be a nervous gesture.

"Sure, Logan, that'd be great," I reply, trying not to blush. My heart races, the beat rattling my chest. He flashes another killer smile before he stands.

"I'll see you after school then," he says before turning and walking away.

A tiny sigh escapes me as I watch him walk away, unable to ignore how his jeans cling to his long legs. I'm so enrapt with Logan's retreating figure that I jump and squeal when Celia plops down beside me. She's dressed to perfection as usual, her denim mini-skirt hugging her tanned legs, adorable black ankle boots adorning her feet. A green and black varsity jacket covers her body, dwarfing her. Her boyfriend du jour is a fullback on the football team and built like a tank.

"Logan Finley, huh?" Celia says, tossing her long, blonde hair. Her dark eyes twinkle with a knowing look. "Holding hands at the party last night and now making googly eyes at each other."

"He invited me to a club meeting today," I say, trying not to sound as interested in him as I feel.

When Celia lets out a tiny gasp, I realize my mistake. She knows the basic stats on every cute guy in school—guess she'd have to considering she has a new boyfriend every month or so.

"The Orion Circle," she breathes in wonder. "I can't believe it. You have to tell me everything that happens!"

"Can't," I tell her. "I have to take a vow of silence."

"No way," she says. Her eyes narrow in suspicion. "Wow it really is a secret society." When she begins to pout I have to stifle a giggle. "So you're into Logan?" she asks, the beaming smile returning to her face. It's sometimes exhausting to keep up with her mood swings.

"Well," I say ready to defer, but then I realize I have to get it out or I might explode. "He's gorgeous, I'm totally into him. I could get lost in his eyes," I admit in a whisper as my cheeks heat up. "Do you think I have a chance?"

"Of course you do!" Celia all but squeals. "We need to make a detour to the bathroom, get your hair fixed, get some more make-up around your eyes, you know really make them pop…" She trails off, digging through her backpack.

Anxiety eats at me as I consider the awful things she might subject me to. When she pulls out a lash curler I cringe.

"That thing looks like some kind of medieval torture device. Put it up, Celia," I say in exasperation.

There's no way she's putting the metal monstrosity anywhere near my eyelashes. "If he doesn't like me the way I am why would I want to be with him? Besides, I'm already wearing make-up."

"Oh, Kacie, you're so naïve. It's cute, really," she says looking at me like I'm a poor lost child. "Fine," she sighs when I continue to glare at her. "Have it your way. You're gorgeous so you can probably get away with it." As she's stuffing the eyelash curler back in her make-up case the bell rings signaling the end of fourth period. She leaps from the bench. "Let's go, I'm only two tardies away from detention."

I jump from the bench, grab the damp towel, and follow her back into the building.

When the final bell rings, I bolt from my desk and rush from the classroom. Pushing my way through the throng of chattering students, I arrive at my locker to find Logan waiting for me. He's talking to Celia and her boyfriend, Jake, but when he notices my approach, his gaze moves to me as if the others have ceased to exist. His lips curl into an adorable smile, making my belly flutter in response. Celia and Jake step back so I can reach my locker, but Logan doesn't move.

I brush up against him when I open the locker. Another tiny spark passes between us, causing me to shiver in response. The initial spark is followed by a very pleasant warm feeling, though I don't know if the warmth is caused by my attraction to him or our shared psychic bond. It's not like I can ask him yet.

"Well, I have to get to the theater for rehearsal," Celia says in a bright chirp. She is Juliet in the fall production of Romeo and Juliet. "Call me later tonight, Kacie," she calls over her shoulder while leading Jake away by the hand.

As I watch their blond heads disappear into the crowd, I realize her relationship with Jake has lasted six weeks, heading to a new record since she still seems infatuated with him. She's not the only one with ammo for a phone call tonight. With a chuckle, I turn back to my locker and remove several notebooks, stuffing them into my backpack.

"Are you ready?" Logan asks in a soft murmur.

Closing my locker, I nod and smile at him, trying to hide my anxiety. Why did I agree to go to this club meeting? What if they sacrifice goats to some pagan god or something? Laughter wells up within at the absurd image of an animal sacrifice occurring on the third floor of the Sciences building. Besides, it couldn't be a goat—it would have to be a cat or a fetal pig since that's what the AP biology class is dissecting this year. I guess it could be a crawfish or an earthworm since the regular biology classes dissect those.

My laughter finally bubbles out when I picture figures in black robes sacrificing an earthworm to their pagan god. I feel Logan's eyes on me. When I glance at him, he has a strange, indecipherable look on his face.

"Are you alright?" he asks, concern clouding his features.

"Yeah, just a little nervous," I reply, fighting another blush that threatens to form.

He walks down the hall, navigating through the maze of students, checking back every so often to make sure I'm still following. When we pass through the doors leading out into the damp autumn air, he surprises me by heading over to a bench rather than continuing to the Sciences building.

He sits down and motions for me to join him, so I lower myself to the gray stone bench. The stone soaked up the chilled rain today, and the cold passes through my jeans up into my body. I've always enjoyed cool weather, probably a tribute to my Norse ancestry. Though I shiver a bit, I feel exhilarated as a slight breeze ruffles my hair, making it dance around my head.

"I'm gonna break the rules and give you a heads up about us," Logan says in a very low voice.

My eyes fly to his in surprise. He moves closer to me on the bench so our legs are touching.

"We are a paranormal research group. Hunters you might say, hence the name Orion. I know you're already aware there's more out there than meets the eye, but you'll be surprised by just how much more there really is."

He's speaking in a very low voice, obviously not wanting to be overheard. I use this as an excuse to lean a little closer to him.

"So you investigate hauntings?" I murmur, intrigued by the idea.

"Not just hauntings, anything supernatural," he replies. I wait for him to elaborate, but he doesn't. "I can't go into more detail until you're a member. But don't worry, Kacie. I'll be right beside you today, and by tonight you'll be a member, then we can talk."

He stands and extends his hand to me. Taking his hand, I allow him to pull me from the bench. There's no spark or jolt this time, just pleasant warmth that permeates me.

"It appears our powers are adjusting to each other," he comments, a smile lighting his face.

"You know, my Dad always told me to hide my abilities," I admit with a resounding sigh at the pain deeply ingrained from such a young age. "He said people wouldn't understand. It embarrassed him when I'd talk to someone only visible to me. I've never had anyone to talk to before, you know about when things get scary."

The last part comes out a whisper as images from my recurring dream surface unbidden. *VISION*, my brain shouts, making me cringe. *Fine vision*, I accede, trying to mollify my volatile powers.

"You're not alone anymore, Kacie," Logan says as he leads the way to the Sciences building, glancing at me from the corner of his eye. "You can talk to me whenever you want, even two in the morning if needed."

A smile lights my face at his generous offer, and for the first time since my mother walked out on us six years ago, I feel as though a great weight has been lifted from my shoulders.

5

The Orion Circle

The rain begins again as I follow Logan up the eastern stairwell of the Sciences building. It turns from a drizzle to a deluge, creating a loud roar all around us. Cold shivers race through my body by the time we reach the third flight of stairs. A giant skylight covers the ceiling above us revealing the darkened sky through the sheet of rain running across the glass.

Thunder sounds in the distance, a low rolling rumble. Logan pauses at the top of the stairs right in front of the door that must lead to the loft area. He grins at me and gives my shoulder a reassuring squeeze before opening the door and ushering me through.

The room beyond is enormous, a wide open space that covers at least a third of the building. Floor to ceiling windows span the length of the room revealing the fierce flood of rain outside. In a way, the space reminds me of a loft apartment. There's a small kitchenette in one corner beside a cozy nook featuring a table and six chairs.

Bookcases cover the wall across from the expanse of windows, filled with an amazing array of books—some so old they look like they might crumble if touched by a rough hand. Two sofas and several plush chairs flank the bookshelves creating a pleasant sitting area. Following Logan across the large room, I see our destination before we arrive. On the far end of the room there's a long conference table surrounded by numerous black leather chairs.

Most of the chairs are filled, some by students I recognize and a few by adults I don't know. As we approach I count eight students and three adults. My stomach clenches as nervousness sets in. I really have no idea what to expect, but the eleven pairs of eyes staring at me are disconcerting to say the least. When we arrive at the conference area, Logan stops and places his hand on my back in a reassuring gesture. A rather timely move considering I was contemplating my chances of escape. I glance at him, and he flashes a serene smile at me.

"This is Kacie Ramsey," Logan addresses the group. "She's here at my invitation as a potential initiate to the Orion Circle."

An adult stands, I recognize him as the AP physics teacher though I can't remember his name.

"Welcome, Kacie, I'm Roger Kincaid, the faculty advisor for the Orion Circle," he says, crossing over to shake my hand. "We have a few tests for you before we vote on whether you shall be admitted into the Circle. Michelle, you can go first."

One of the students rises from her chair and beckons at me to follow. She leads me away from the conference area to several closed doors I hadn't noticed before. One has a sign showing a man and a woman, a bathroom, leaving four other doors a mystery. She opens the farthest door and ushers me into a small conference room. I watch her sit at the table, my heart hammering in my chest. My body is frozen by nerves as I stand rigid, my eyes darting around the small room. When she motions for me to join her at the table, I hesitate.

"Logan has told us about you," she says, folding her hands on the table. "It's okay. I just want to talk."

Blowing a breath out in a long sigh, I sit in a chair across the table. Her brown hair is tied in a short ponytail behind her head, though stray hair has fallen out to frame her face in frizzy curls. San Antonio humidity can be murder on hair. My hand passes through my hair, and I cringe when I feel the tight waves.

"Although all Logan really knows is that you're a clairvoyant of some sort having disturbing visions.

And visitations…" She pauses and gazes at me with her chocolate brown eyes as if sizing me up before continuing. "I read people. I have no connection with the dead, only the living. With your permission, I'd like the chance to read your aura and discuss your abilities."

She pauses again waiting for my response, not looking at me but rather studying her bright red manicured nails.

"I'm not really sure what you intend to do, but I suppose it's okay," I say in a hesitant murmur.

She glances up at me with a calm smile on her face before placing her hands palm up on the table.

"Place your hands in mine. I need a physical connection to do a reading."

There's no spark like there was with Logan—her hands cool to the touch but nothing more. She closes her eyes and appears deep in thought. Seconds creep by while she sits, eyes closed, unmoving. As more time passes I become anxious, squirming in the plastic chair from both mental and physical distress. I never was good at sitting still for any length of time. When her dark eyes open again, she regards me in silence before releasing my hands.

"Let's head back to the conference table," she says, lurching to unsteady feet. "You'll want to hear about what I sensed."

As we near the long table, all conversation stops. Michelle takes her prior seat on the far side of the table. When Logan motions for me to sit beside him, I'm grateful. The idea of standing in front of this group is mortifying.

"Your report, Michelle," Mr. Kincaid prompts.

"Sorry, just organizing my thoughts," Michelle says, rubbing her chin with her fingers. "Kacie appears to be a very strong psychic medium. I really don't think any additional testing is necessary. But she dammed up her talent behind a massive wall in her subconscious mind. Her power is so strong it trickles out around the barrier. This is incredibly dangerous since the power that leaks out is uncontrolled. It acts almost like a beacon to the supernatural world. Why did you do that, Kacie?"

All eyes turn to me, and I can't help but squirm under their stares. This is a difficult subject for me. I always felt responsible for my mother leaving. My powers annoyed and scared her. She hated them and by association hated me. Tears blur my vision, threatening to spill over my eyelashes. Logan places his hand on my arm.

"It's okay, Kacie," Logan says, running his hand up and down my forearm. It has the desired effect and I relax under the soothing contact. "You can trust us, I promise. You'll feel better if you tell us what happened. Believe me, the people at this table will not only listen but understand."

I watch entranced as his fingers run a light caress up and down my arm. After a few deep breaths, I glance up at him, expecting to see the scorn and disbelief I always saw on my parents' faces. Logan gazes back, his brow creased in worry—but not about me embarrassing him with what I might say. No, he's worried about me, about my feelings. With a gentle tug he pulls my arm down over the armrest, lacing our fingers together under the table. I look at our clasped hands then back up at his face. He gives a little nod, urging me to tell my story.

"When I was young, I didn't know I was different. My parents assumed the people I talked to were imaginary friends. They were busy—no they were oblivious really. I'm sure if they'd paid attention, they would've noticed how strange the conversations were."

I pause when my throat closes up, overcome by the guilt and the heaviness in my chest. Had I known I'd be sitting here telling strangers my darkest secrets, I doubt I would've agreed to come to this meeting. Taking a deep breath I continue, clinging to the hope that telling my story will help ease the pain.

"When I was nine my parents decided I was too old for imaginary friends. They sat me down and ordered that I stop talking to people who weren't there. I tried to explain that the people were real, but my father was furious. He thought I was lying. I started ignoring the spirits. By this time I knew they were ghosts, and I was starting to realize most if not all people didn't see them."

The blonde lady seated next to Mr. Kincaid rises and strides over to the small kitchenette. When she returns, she places a bottle of water on the table in front of me.

"Thank you." I crack open the bottle and take a long drink of the cool liquid, allowing it to soothe both my nerves and my dry throat.

"Take your time, Kacie," the blonde lady says when she returns to her seat, "I'm Anna Kincaid, and I really do understand what you've been through." She gazes at me through soft blue eyes full of understanding. If only my mother had been so open and eager to listen.

"I continued to ignore the spirits for several months, but they were making it increasingly difficult. It seemed the more I ignored them, the more they craved my attention. We were at the park one day and a particularly pesky spirit wouldn't leave me alone. I finally gave in and started talking to him to the utter mortification of my parents. I was grounded for two weeks." I pause again, taking a sip of the water as I try to prepare myself to tell the rest of the story. "A week later I was alone at the kitchen table when the spirit of a woman appeared in the chair across from me. She was an older woman with such a comforting presence. She told me not to worry, that everything would be okay. For some reason I believed her. But she was wrong, very wrong."

My breath catches. Painful pressure spreads across my chest. A burning sensation in my nose lets me know tears aren't far behind. The girl seated next to me places her hand on my arm.

"I don't have any abilities," she says in a soft voice. "I can only imagine what you've been through. But I will say it's not fair the way some people treat mediums. People are so willing to accept a God they can't see who can work miracles, but tell them ghosts exist and the shit hits the fan."

Quiet chuckles and a few snickers draw my gaze to the group. For years I prayed to find someone who understood. Now I have a room full of them. I can do this.

"My mother walked in while I was talking to the spirit. Her eyes grew wide, and it seemed like she could see the spirit too. I felt so betrayed. She yelled at me for lying along with my father. If she could see ghosts then how could she not stand up for me, help my father see that I wasn't lying, help me understand why I could see them when others couldn't? How could she not be there for me when I needed her so badly? I asked her if she could see the ghost..."

Closing my eyes, I swallow around the lump in my throat. Something cool touches my hand. When I open my eyes, I see the girl next to me pushing the water bottle into my palm. I drain the remaining contents of the bottle before I'm able to continue.

"My mother backed out of the room and fled upstairs without answering. She packed her bags and left that night, filing for divorce a few weeks later. I haven't seen her since. She calls once in a while but only talks to my brother. It's as if I ceased to exist in her mind at all."

I pause again, blinking my eyes in a failed attempt to keep the tears at bay. Several tears trickle down my cheeks. The room is silent, everyone waiting for me to finish my story, though I have a feeling they already know the outcome.

"Dad blamed me for the divorce. My mother filed for joint custody of my brother, Gavin, but didn't even want visitation rights with me. One night when Gavin was away, Dad got drunk and finally told me how much he hated me for ruining his marriage. He apologized for weeks afterward, said he didn't really mean it. But I know somewhere deep down he really did. He did mean it."

More tears fall and I'm unable to continue the story. Logan squeezes my hand, trying to offer comfort. When I look into his eyes, they contain such sorrow and a flicker of anger. Just knowing he was affected in such a way by my story fills me with warmth. It feels so good to have someone listen and not judge, not immediately call for a straightjacket.

"Your wall is crumbling, Kacie," Michelle says, her voice ringing in the quiet room. "We can teach you how to control your abilities so they don't over-whelm you. You need to learn control before the dam bursts."

"Is that acceptable, Kacie?" Mr. Kincaid asks, "Will you allow us to help you with your abilities?"

"I'm sick and tired of running and hiding from my abilities," I say, somehow finding a well of courage within my heart. "I'd like to learn how to live with this, maybe even find a way to help people with it."

"All those in favor of initiating Kacie into the Orion Circle?" Mrs. Kincaid asks the group. 'Ayes' resound around the table. "Opposed?" Her question is met with silence. "Welcome to the group, Kacie," she says with a brilliant smile. "We'll continue the meeting now and introduce you to everyone later. Rebecca, I believe it's your turn."

The brunette girl beside me shuffles through her notes, separating several from the pile and passing them to Mrs. Kincaid. Her brown hair is pulled back into a messy ponytail. She pushes her glasses back up the bridge of her nose before speaking.

"Carl and I performed an investigation last weekend at the new bed and breakfast in the Queen Anne District. The owners were ecstatic to have us visit. They're currently hyping their inn as one of the most haunted in Texas. We set up the equipment, did EVP sessions in every room and did client interviews. After careful review of the video and EVPs we have absolutely nothing, zip, nada."

She rises from her chair, placing her palms on the table. A bundle of nervous energy, she makes my pulse leap. After slapping the table she stalks over to the sitting area and grabs a leather messenger bag. The contents spill onto the table, papers flying everywhere.

"The owners had an amazing amount of stories for such a brief ownership of the place. My research indicated they bought the place two years ago and took over a year to renovate. So they've only had guests for a few months. These were all written by Mrs. Anders. I haven't read more than a few. There's enough here for a series of novels, and they read like a script for a paranormal movie. They refused to provide any past guest info, stating privacy as the excuse. Our take is that it's a complete sham. Not haunted in any way, shape or form. Before submitting the final report to HQ I'd like a medium to do a walkthrough."

"This is a good opportunity for you, Kacie," Mrs. Kincaid says. "Logan, I'd like you to take this assignment along with Kacie. Call and make the arrangements with the owners for one night this weekend. Full written report by next Monday—don't slough the report off on Kacie. Though I think my concern may be misplaced," she adds with an innocent look on her face.

"Daniel, your update on the chupacabra," Mr. Kincaid prompts.

I know Daniel, he's in drama with me, though I had no idea he was into this kind of thing. Then the words sink in and I let out a small gasp. Chupacabra? Surely this must be a joke!

"We investigate all manner of supernatural activity and encounters, Kacie. There is so much more out there than meets the eye," Mr. Kincaid says.

He must have noticed my utter disbelief. Daniel snorts before dropping his papers on the table.

"Well, this one was a case of mistaken identity," Daniel says, shrugging in what appears to be disappointment. He runs a hand through his short, messy black hair before continuing. "It turned out to be a cross between a pit bull and a coyote. Not sure how they managed that but the reports came back from Texas A&M this morning. DNA results show canis latrans and canis lupus, specifically the American Pit Bull Terrier. I will admit it was one ugly, mean-looking sucker though. Can't blame the poor guy who shot it through the head for thinking it was some sort of monster. It was attacking his cattle—guy lost two calves to that beast."

"We've been invited to participate in a hunt for a possible rogue werewolf this weekend by the UT Austin chapter," Mr. Kincaid says as he glances around the table. *Werewolves too?* "This will be a potentially dangerous assignment. Any volunteers?" Daniel's hand flies up along with a girl I haven't met yet. "Daniel and Yolanda see me after the meeting for your assignment details. Unless there is any other new business, we are finished for today." He pauses waiting to see if there is any objection. "Alright then, meeting adjourned."

Everyone stands and begins talking among themselves leaving me feeling a bit uncomfortable. Logan jumps up and beckons for me to follow him.

"Come on, Kacie," he says, leading me across the room. "It'll be more comfortable to relax in the sitting area by the library than to stay here. We'll keep the introductions brief so you don't feel overwhelmed."

6
New Friends

The storm continues to rage outside as I follow Logan over to the large sitting area. So much for weather reports—they said a thirty percent chance of rain today. A quick glance outside shows a one hundred percent chance of flooding based on the deluge striking the windows.

Setting my bag on the floor, I join Logan on one of the two brown leather sofas. My hand strokes the buttery soft leather, cool to the touch in the warm room. It's a nervous gesture, I'm well aware of that but one I can get away with given the circumstances. As I try to calm my frayed nerves, Mrs. Kincaid walks over and settles into the chair adjacent to my seat on the sofa. She gazes at me for several seconds before giving me a serene smile.

"I'm so sorry about what happened to you, Kacie," she murmurs, sorrow reflected in the depths of her eyes.

Calmness settles over me. I lean into the arm of the sofa, resting my head on my hand. Her voice is soothing, wrapping around me like a fluffy blanket. It makes me feel at ease.

"I'm also a psychic medium with parents who didn't understand my gifts. It can be very hard for some people to accept anything they can't see with their own eyes. My adolescence was fraught with conflict, but I'm happy to say I have a good relationship with my parents now."

She leans forward in her chair before continuing. "I'm Anna Kincaid, married to Roger Kincaid who is a psychic null. He does, however, believe strongly in psychic ability, living proof that some people are able to make the leap of faith to accept what they themselves can't experience. Of course he's a physicist so I suppose his whole career revolves around particles one can't see with the naked eye, if at all." She pauses, glancing over at Mr. Kincaid with so much love in her eyes. "I'm the president of the Orion Circle, San Antonio chapter. We have hundreds of chapters across the United States, most are at universities but some are at high schools. We're short on time today so I'll spare you the history lesson. I want you to have a chance to meet everyone."

Giving me one last smile, she rises from the chair and walks away. Her spot is taken by Rebecca. I already like her due to her kindness during the meeting. The brunette girl stares at me for a moment before pushing her glasses back up her nose with her index finger. Now that she's closer, I can see her eyes are an odd shade of green, almost yellow green, very striking.

"I'm Rebecca, I'm a lead investigator and researcher for our chapter," she says, extending her hand in greeting. Her grip is firm as we shake hands. "I have no psychic abilities just an insatiable thirst for knowledge of anything paranormal. I'm especially into cryptozoology and mythological creatures, several not quite as mythological as you might think."

As a child I always had a penchant for unicorns, dragons and mermaids. My pulse jumps a bit, and I take a breath to ask the first of dozens of questions.

She laughs. "You look excited, perhaps we can get together next week, and I'll fill you in on what you've been missing."

"Sounds great, Rebecca," I reply, eager for the knowledge she possesses.

Cryptozoology is fascinating. Searching for and maybe even discovering a new animal species no one has ever heard of would be amazing.

She nods before vacating the chair for the next person. Daniel walks over and plops down into the chair before propping his feet up on the coffee table.

His black bangs cover one eye while the other gray eye stares at me with undisguised interest. A smile lights his face, and I see what makes so many girls swoon in his presence. This guy owns the room. His jeans are covered in artfully placed holes—something I would have sworn was against our dress code. He's wearing a black t-shirt that hugs his lithe torso.

"No introductions necessary, huh, Cici," he says with an expression somewhere between a smirk and a leer.

I cringe a bit at the nickname. No matter what I say, he refuses to call me Kacie. Daniel plays Billy Crocker, the male lead, in our production of *Anything Goes*. He's been calling me Cici since the first day of drama class my freshman year. The idiot spilled coffee all over my brand new shoes. His utter lack of concern made me furious, embarrassed, you name it. I remember exploding—yelling something like, *Look what you did! See? See?* I've been Cici ever since.

Daniel has an ego the size of Alaska along with his very own set of groupies. He was an enigma I was determined to solve. Last year, I swore I'd get beneath his veneer. Didn't happen. My crush on him faded pretty fast after that.

"Had no idea you were clairvoyant. You always seemed so normal," he adds with an amused snort.

"I'm clairsentient." When I stare at him with a blank look he decides to elaborate. "My psychic ability stems from touch. Objects or people, I can get readings from both. You'd be amazed at what gets soaked up into the walls of some places. It'd blow your mind. Remind me tomorrow morning and I'll give you a reading."

He takes my hand and kisses the back before rising in a fluid motion. My guess is this gesture is meant to be endearing, but I find it rather annoying. I somehow manage to resist the urge to wipe the back of my hand on my jeans. As he walks away, I hazard a glance at Logan and notice he's bristling from Daniel's behavior. I offer him a smile and his entire face lights up in response. Hearing someone move to the chair next to me, I manage to pull my eyes away from Logan's golden gaze to give the new arrival my undivided attention.

The rest of the evening passes in a blur as I'm introduced to everyone in the group. When the final introduction is over, I pull out my phone and stare in shock. Twenty-five text messages and six voicemail messages are waiting for my attention. It's already six-thirty, guess I'm not cooking dinner tonight. It's about time Dad and Gavin learned to fend for themselves.

Ever since my mother left when I was nine, I've taken care of the house and cooking. It's funny how Gavin and Dad both came to take my actions for granted. I won't be around forever. Perhaps it's time to wean the men from their dependence on me. As I listen to the voicemails, I realize Gavin is already one step ahead of me. The guy ordered pizza for us and all on his own too. I snort when I realize this glowing feeling is pride in my brother.

Two messages from Dad, the first saying he'll be late and the second reminding me to call if I'll be late. Two from Celia. My heart falls when she finishes her rant—it appears there may be trouble in Jake paradise. I really like Jake. He's good for her. She thinks football is more important to him than she is. I guess I'll need to find a way to prove to her she's dead wrong. Jake worships at the altar that is Celia.

The last message is from Dave who can't drive me to school in the morning, but could I bring his coffee anyway? Since they have an early morning football practice, I'll oblige. I wonder what happened at practice this afternoon to warrant a five a.m. practice tomorrow. The coach must be furious about something.

I ignore the texts for now. Frankly, I'm getting sick of that form of communication. Too many of my friends developed the habit of endless texts. Anyone who knows me well is aware they should leave a voicemail if they actually want me to pay attention.

"Can I give you a ride home?" Logan asks when I look up from my phone.

He's still seated on the sofa next to me, a solid rock at my side throughout the afternoon and evening. If possible I'm even more attracted to him now than before.

"That would be great, thanks," I reply, feeling shy and a touch nervous.

He rises from the sofa and extends his hand to help me up. I take his hand and allow him to pull me from my seat. Logan pulls a bit harder than I was expecting, causing me to stumble and fall into his outstretched arms. My cheeks redden and I jump away as if burned, though I immediately regret my actions. Daniel, having witnessed the whole embarrassing incident, struts over.

"Smooth moves, Romeo," he says snickering.

Logan runs a hand through his golden-brown curls and flashes a sheepish grin. My ire rises and I fail to keep my big mouth shut.

"Bite me," I growl at the pompous ass.

"Thought you'd never ask, kitten," Daniel purrs, wrapping an arm around my shoulder.

"Oh, please," I mutter as I shrug his arm off my shoulder and push him away.

A smirk curls my lip at Daniel's shocked expression. I guess he's not used to being shot down. Logan snickers before he grabs my backpack and winds the strap over my shoulder.

"We should head out while there's a lull in the rain," he says. His gaze drifts from the windows back to me.

I nod my head and follow him without sparing a glance for Daniel. As we pass through the door, several people shout goodbyes which we both return before allowing the door to close behind us. After bounding down the three flights of stairs, I'm dismayed when the shower of water picks up again just as we open the door leading outside.

We walk through the darkened campus, sticking close to the building to avoid the downpour. When we reach the side facing the parking lot, we pause for a moment and watch the rain fall. It's almost empty, only a few cars remain. Fat raindrops are reflected in the lights illuminating the parking lot, creating a beautiful, glittery wonderland. Who knew a vast expanse of blacktop bathed in yellow-orange light could be so enchanting?

"Do you want to wait and see if the rain slows or make a dash for the car?" Logan asks, gazing down at me in the dim light.

"A little rain never hurt anyone. Lead on," I say, a bit breathless. He gives me a bright grin that makes my heart flutter. "I am a Pisces after all. I believe that makes me one with the water," I add, averting my gaze in a desperate attempt to stop the flush spreading across my cheeks.

He takes my hand, making my heart race even faster, and we dash across the parking lot toward his car. The raindrops splattering against my face are cool but not cold, making me feel energized. I've always been partial to the rain. So many view the rain as a spoiler of, well, everything. But to me rain is fresh. It washes away the accumulation of grime, wiping the slate clean, renewing and giving life. Normally I watch the rain from the shelter of our covered deck, but every once in a while I enjoy a long walk with the drops falling on my face. It leaves me feeling calm and refreshed.

When we reach Logan's car, I stop in surprise. Water drips from my damp bangs, and I brush them aside to stare at the beauty before me. With a wistful sigh of appreciation, I run my fingers down the side in a light caress. This is one gorgeous car. The Mustang is black, but not just any black, there's glitter in the paint that makes it glow in the floodlights brightening the parking lot. It has been detailed with several chrome accents. Red racing stripes run across the hood to continue over the roof and end at the rear spoiler.

"Logan, it's beautiful," I gasp in a soft whisper.

Okay, I admit it, I have a thing for cars, and this is one fine automobile. Rain all but forgotten, I circle around the car wondering how he managed to nab such a sweet ride.

"Would you like to get in out of the rain? The inside is pretty nice too," he comments with a crooked smile while hitting the button to unlock the doors.

I open the door and dive inside to escape a sudden gust of wind. It roars through the empty parking lot, blowing the rain almost horizontal. Once both doors are shut, we stare out the windshield at the impressive storm.

"Guess we made it just in time," Logan remarks as raindrops pelt the car from all sides. "Probably shouldn't drive in this downpour, my Dad would kill me."

We both take a moment to text our families to let them know we're still at school waiting for a break in the storm to leave. Sitting in companionable silence, we watch the fury of nature as she unleashes an amazing show of water, wind, and lightning. The lightning is close enough to light up our surroundings as if the sun was making a quick appearance through the black clouds.

"I'm so glad we have four rubber tires protecting us from the lightning," I murmur after another loud boom of thunder follows the flash of lightning too close for comfort.

When I glance at Logan, he's smiling—that smile Gavin uses when I say something cute and incorrect.

"What?" I ask ready for a lecture though I'm not upset, I love to learn new things.

"It's simple physics really. It is safer to be in a car than out in the open but not because of the tires," Logan says, eyeing me for my reaction. When I grin at him and nod he continues. "The vehicle acts as a Faraday cage—the lighting will travel along the metal of the car before traveling into the ground through the tires which keeps the occupants protected. If you're touching anything in the car connected to the outside metal cage you could still be electrocuted."

With a shudder, I move from leaning on the door to leaning on the leather armrest between the seats. This puts me very close to Logan who's also leaning against it.

"This effect doesn't work in a convertible or a car made of fiberglass, so no hopping into a Corvette during a thunderstorm."

"I thought rubber didn't conduct electricity," I say, a bit confused by what I always thought to be fact.

"Rubber is an insulator and doesn't conduct electricity, but lightning is so powerful that rubber tires aren't going to protect you," he murmurs.

With every lightning strike I flinch a bit, glad when the time between flash and thunder begins to increase.

"Will Friday night work for you?" At my blank expression he adds, "To check out the inn in the Queen Anne District. We could get dinner first along the River Walk if you'd like."

"Sounds good," I reply, feeling a bit giddy.

Can I consider this a date? No doubt Celia would since we're having dinner together. Ghost hunting seems a bit odd for a first date. But what about my life has ever been normal? I don't think most girls have to put up a barrier to keep from seeing dead people on a regular basis. Nor do they have to politely ask the spirits living in their house to move on to the next plane of existence. The idea of a ghost watching my private moments is disconcerting to say the least. I don't know if I could shower in peace in a haunted house due to past experience.

"You're awfully quiet, what are you thinking about?" Logan asks, brushing my arm with his in a gentle nudge. The brief contact sends shivers down my arms.

"We moved into our house in Cedar Bluffs when I was eleven," I murmur, becoming lost in the memory. "It was already inhabited by a cowboy and several soldiers from Santa Anna's army. They were all tied to the land the house was built on. I had to learn enough Spanish to send the Mexican soldiers to the next plane. Believe it or not that was the easy part. I didn't realize it at the time, but the Mexican soldiers were protecting me from the cowboy. Once they were gone, things got very bad. The cowboy refused to leave and didn't bother to hide his obsession any longer."

I lean my head against Logan's shoulder when he places his arm around me, the comfort giving me the courage to continue.

"I guess back in his day eleven was an acceptable age to marry, though the idea of marrying so young really grosses me out," I say with a dry laugh devoid of any humor.

My body trembles as the memories resurface, unpleasant reminders of something I'd prefer to leave dead and buried. But Logan is the first person I've met who can understand the trauma I endured. I know I'll feel better if I share with him. His fingers rub small circles on my back. Closing my eyes, I focus on the tingles caused by his touch.

"It'll be okay, Kacie," he murmurs just inches from my ear. "You can trust me. You'll probably feel better once you share your story," he adds, echoing my earlier thought.

"He'd watch me bathe," I admit with another shudder. "I could always feel his eyes on me even though he didn't manifest. After a while he became bolder."

Logan's arms encircle my body, pulling me into a hug. I wrap my arms around him, clutching his t-shirt with my fingers. He doesn't rush me, just waits in silence. Drawing strength from his silent show of support, I'm able to continue.

"He started touching me while I was sleeping. It made me feel so violated and scared. I had no one to talk to, no one to help or even believe my story."

"God, Kacie, I'm so sorry," he murmurs, brushing a kiss on the top of my head. "I can't even imagine what you must have felt."

The steady beat of raindrops pelting the car echoes through the quiet interior. Outside the fierce storm begins to die down, but Logan makes no move to leave. He brushes his fingers through my damp hair, distracting me from the unpleasant memories.

"What happened?" he asks, breaking the lingering silence. "You did get rid of him, right?"

"I found a Comanche tribal elder on the internet. He came out and did a smudging with sage," I reply in a flat voice. "It didn't work. The cowboy was a powerful spirit and totally obsessed—a bad combination. The elder returned with reinforcements—six additional elders from several different tribes, and they were finally able to force him to cross to the next plane. But they did warn me that it can be difficult to banish evil permanently. There's always a possibility he'll return. But he hasn't in four years, so here's hoping he's gone for good," I say with a weak smile, looking back up to meet his eyes.

His expression is soft, turning my insides to mush. My cell phone rings, breaking the mood, and reminding me once again why I'm starting to despise the damned thing. A quick glance down shows it to be Dad so I can't just ignore it. I assure him we're on our way, and I'll be home in fifteen minutes or so.

"Guess we better head out then," Logan says, starting the car. The engine comes alive with a throaty roar that vibrates through the interior.

7
Mother

~

Buckling my seatbelt, I lean back against the soft leather seat and try to relax. As Logan maneuvers down rain slick streets, my mind races with the new discoveries of the day. It's hard to believe that in one day my life could undergo such a drastic change. I've felt alone with my ability for so long, it's nice to finally have people who understand. Rain splatters the windshield, the steady rhythm of the wiper blades soothing—kind of like a metronome lulling my heart into a steady beat. When he pulls up to the gate of Cedar Bluffs, I snap awake. My nerves resurface and I drum on my leg with my fingers.

"When did you move to Cedar Bluffs?" I ask, wondering how I managed to miss seeing him around the neighborhood for four years.

"We moved here from the condos down the street right before school started," he explains as we pass through the gate. "Mom is pregnant and we needed more room than the two bedroom condo could provide."

"Where's your house?"

"Rolling Glen, at the back of the neighborhood," he replies. "It's one of the newest houses," he adds as he drives down the dark street. Our community has few streetlamps making the streets pitch-black at night. "My house was devoid of ghosts when we moved in. I was somewhat surprised since the previous owner died on the property."

"Was it a violent death?" I ask though I'm sure gossip would run rampant if that were the case.

"She died of lung cancer, but I don't know how long she lasted or how much pain she was in," he says as he turns onto my street.

When we reach my house, the headlights reveal two cars parked in the driveway, both Dad and Gavin are home. Logan pulls up alongside the curb and stops the car. Someone remembered to turn the outside light on. Our house faces a canyon on two sides and there's no streetlight at our end of the street. When the outside lights aren't on, the property is blanketed in darkness. By the time I grab my backpack and open the door, Logan is already out and on my side of the car holding the door open. He walks with me to the front door, and I decide it's only fair to warn him of what may be lying in wait.

"You may want to reconsider walking me to the door," I murmur, glancing at the windows on either side of the door to see if any shadows are lurking within. "You may get stuck meeting my brother or worse my dad."

"I think I can handle your brother and your dad," he says chuckling. "I'll just tell them I'm a psychic medium. I'm sure they'll love that." I know he's joking but part of me still cringes at the potential scene it would create. "You know most abilities run in families. If you thought your mom saw the ghost you were talking to, I'm guessing she's clairvoyant… whether she wants to admit it or not."

It's something I've considered more than once in the past. Deep down I know it's probably true. It just hurts so much. He doesn't say anything else as we reach the porch. I dig my key out of the front pouch of my backpack. When I look back up he reaches out, running a light caress across my cheek with the back of his fingers.

"Thank you for everything, Logan. I've felt lost and alone for so long."

I can't seem to look away from his mesmerizing eyes like a deer caught in the headlights of a car. He takes a small step forward. His hand moves from my face to my hair then down to rest against the nape of my neck.

"You have beautiful eyes," he says in a husky murmur. "Green with little flecks of gold. I've never seen anything like them before."

My breath catches in my throat as my gaze moves to his full lips, willing him to lean down and kiss me. When he's only inches away, loud footsteps sound from inside the house. Logan groans before stepping away to a more respectable distance. The door flies open, banging against the wall with a jarring *thud*. It's Gavin, not Dad, and I blow out the breath I'd been holding.

"I heard the car arrive," Gavin says, meeting my eyes with a silent apology. "There's a phone call for you, Kacie. It's our mother."

I stiffen at his words. She hasn't spoken to me in six years. Not one single word. Ever. What could she possibly have to say now?

"Be strong," Logan whispers in my ear. "Call me if you need anything, okay? Otherwise I'll see you tomorrow." He starts walking toward his car, and I race over to him.

"Can I have a ride to school in the morning?" I ask, remembering Dave can't drive me tomorrow.

"Sure, I'll pick you up at eight," he replies, glancing at me over his shoulder.

He gets into his Mustang, and I release a heavy sigh, knowing I have to deal with the phone call now. Has she been waiting this whole time? Strange.

Holding my head up, I steel my shoulders and stroll into the kitchen to grab the phone.

"Hello?" I say into the receiver, hoping she hung up since it took so long.

"Kassandra, it's good to talk to you," she says in a saccharin tone making me gag a little. "How have you been?"

"Is this a sick joke?" I ask, unable to believe her gall.

The woman can't even bring herself to call me Kacie like she did before she left. She doesn't speak to me in years and suddenly calls out of the blue and asks how I've been.

Unbelievable!

"What do you mean, baby?" she asks.

How dare she call me baby!

"I'm not your baby," I snarl through gritted teeth. "What do you want?" There's a long silence on the other end.

"I've been having disturbing visions of your future," she says in a theatrical murmur. "I wanted to warn you and to make sure you were okay."

"Wait a minute," I gasp in shock. "You're having *visions?* You're psychic and never told me?"

"It's not something I like people to know about me," she replies in a dismissive tone.

"You abandoned me, left Dad thinking I was a liar or insane for seeing spirits and having visions!"

My voice is high and cracks with emotion. "How could you do that to me and then call one day like nothing happened, only to tell me you're clairvoyant too?"

Dad sits at the table, his mouth hanging open in shock at my words, while Gavin stares wide-eyed from the counter.

"I admit I've made some mistakes…"

I wait for her to continue, to apologize, to beg my forgiveness. She remains silent, waiting for me to say God knows what.

"Mistakes? Sure, we all make mistakes. Leaving my homework at home, forgetting to set my alarm, letting my friend cut my hair… those are mistakes." My tirade tapers off as I'm overcome with emotion. Somehow I manage to continue through the hard lump in my throat. "Abandoning your child is criminal, not some simple mistake. It was a choice you made to protect yourself. Well screw you and your ridiculous visions. I'm fine without your concern, thank you!"

I end the call and slam the phone down on the table. Tears stream from my eyes blurring my vision. I race away from my family to the solace of my room. Six years. She left six years ago and hasn't spoken a word to me since. Why now? Why today? Throwing myself down on the bed, I allow the tears to fall, uncaring as they soak my pillow. The phone rings again, and I know it's her. It doesn't take any psychic power to know. Neither Dad nor Gavin call me to the phone, and I choke out a beleaguered sigh.

When the doorbell rings I almost scream in frustration. Was she calling from a cell? Did she fly here from Arizona? *Please don't let it be her at the front door.* I pass several nerve-wracking moments waiting to see if someone will call for me. Relief floods me when it doesn't happen. A light knock on my door has the fear rushing back full force.

"Kacie, it's Gavin," my brother calls from the other side.

"Go away," I call out in a choked sob." I don't want to talk right now."

I never lock my door. My family always respects my privacy, so I'm astounded when Gavin opens the door. Burying my face in my pillow, I refuse to look up.

"Please go away, Gavin," I murmur into my pillow.

When the door closes, I allow my body to relax, until the bed sags under the weight of a person.

"Kacie?"

That is so not Gavin! Turning my tear-stained face toward the voice, I cringe when I see Logan sitting on my bed. He can't see me like this! My makeup must be running down my face in grotesque smears. I can just imagine how red and puffy my pale skin is.

"Kacie, I felt your distress before I got halfway home. What happened?" he asks, brushing the hair out of my face.

When I don't answer he continues his tender ministrations, tucking the wild strands of hair behind my ears. He grabs the box of tissues from the nightstand and wipes the tears from my face with gentle strokes. When it occurs to me that he's showing more affection toward me than my mother ever did, fresh tears flow, and I fall into his embrace. He sits beside me not saying anything, just stroking my hair and back while I let out six years of pent up sorrow.

"I'm so sorry you had to see me like this, Logan," I mumble when the tears finally stop.

I pull away and glance at him from under my eyelashes. The look on his face is so sweet and tender it makes my heart flutter.

"I must look awful," I say when he takes another tissue and carefully wipes around my eyes.

"No, you don't," he murmurs, his lips curled into a tiny smile. "You're beautiful. A few tears won't change that."

Grabbing a tissue, I blow my nose before rising and braving a glance in the mirror. It's not as bad as I thought. My makeup is gone but at least it's on the tissue and not running down my face. My nose and cheeks are bright red to match my bloodshot eyes.

"Will you tell me what happened?"

"How did you know I was upset?" I ask instead of answering his question.

His gaze meets mine in the mirror. He motions for me to sit down next to him on the bed, and I return to his side. When his arm wraps around my shoulders, I can't help but snuggle up against him. I feel safe in his arms, something I really need right now.

"Like I said, I sensed your distress," he replies, running his thumb along my cheekbone. "I think we connected on a psychic level today and formed a bond. I felt your anguish. It nearly broke my heart."

Leaning my head on his shoulder, I let out a ragged sigh. "My mother called. She was worried," I say, trying to hold the sorrow at bay. "She hasn't spoken to me in six years since she walked out on us. She talks to Gavin on a regular basis but it's as if I ceased to exist after that day in the kitchen."

"When you thought she saw the spirit you were talking to," he whispers into my hair.

"Yes. She called because she's having disturbing visions about me," I murmur, my lips brushing his shoulder. "She was psychic all along and pretended otherwise. Let Dad think I was crazy, called leaving a mistake."

"She couldn't handle her own abilities, then to see it happening to you was too much for her," he says, still stroking my hair.

"That's no excuse to abandon your daughter!" I cry out in pain.

"No it isn't," he agrees in a calm tone. "I'm concerned about her visions though, did she elaborate?"

"No. I yelled at her and hung up before she could say anything about them," I say, pulling away from him to look at his face. "Do you really think it's important?"

"She hasn't spoken to you in six years," he says, making me cringe.

For some reason hearing someone else say it is disturbing. Dad and Gavin always tiptoe around the subject.

"For her to suddenly call today when you just joined the Circle makes me nervous."

"Why?"

"You'll be hunting with us and it isn't always safe," he says, holding my gaze with serious eyes. "If you're in danger it'd be nice to have more information… especially after what happened last night."

"I'm not talking to her!" I insist, pulling away from him in anger.

He gets off the bed and kneels in front of me, meeting my anger with calmness.

"I don't expect you to," he says, placing his hands on my knees. "Do you think she'd talk to me?" Before I can answer there's a loud pounding on my door.

"Kacie, open up," Dad yells from the other side of the door. "Gavin just told me you have a boy in there. That's against the house rules."

"It's unlocked," I call out.

Logan stays on the floor, and I fall down onto his lap, desperate for the comfort he can provide. I don't think I can handle a fight with Dad right now. My body is tense and rigid—a sharp blow might shatter me into a million pieces. As Logan wraps his arms around me, Dad opens the door and walks into the room.

"Nothing's going on. He's just comforting me."

"I can see that," Dad says before turning to leave. "Leave the door open," he adds as he walks into the hall and disappears.

Logan remains silent, holding me in his embrace. My forehead rests against his cheek.

"She must care about you somewhere in her heart," he says, placing a soft kiss on my forehead. "She hasn't spoken to you for six years out of fear and denial, then out of the blue calls 'cause she's having visions. It must've been hard for her."

"Are you defending her?" I gasp.

"Never," he declares. "I just think she cares and perhaps one day you two can reconcile. You never know."

"Maybe," I agree with an ambivalent shrug. "But I kinda doubt it."

"We need to find out what her visions are about," he says, boosting me up to my feet. "We should talk to your Dad or your brother."

"They won't believe any of this," I murmur, already aware of Dad's closed mind when it comes to the supernatural.

"Then we'll have to make them believe." He crosses the room to stand at the door. "Coming?"

Nodding, I follow him out the door and allow him to lead the way down the carpeted hallway to the spiral staircase.

"I have a feeling you're selling your father short, that he'll believe us," he whispers in my ear.

"I hope you're right," I whisper back, watching him start down the stairs. "I don't know if I can handle the rejection."

He smiles up at me, a brilliant grin, making my heart feel lighter. I can't help but smile back, a tentative smile but a smile nonetheless.

"Your smile is contagious," I say with a tiny laugh. He snorts at me and continues down the stairs.

8
Will You Believe?

~

Dad and Gavin are sitting together in the family room. A normal scene except the television isn't on. They must've been talking, and I'm willing to bet it was about me. Only a serious issue would keep them away from whatever sports happened to be on. Dad is sitting in his easy chair but isn't reclined, another hint he's uncomfortable. Gavin's on the leather sofa adjacent to Dad, his posture damn near perfect. Gavin never sits without slouching…

I motion for Logan to sit down at the other end and join him, sitting in the middle, leaning into him a bit. When he puts his arm around my shoulders, I snuggle against him and curl my legs up onto the cushion.

"I'm Logan Finley," Logan introduces himself to my father. "I'm a junior at Cedar Meadows."

A scowl crosses my father's face. "You seem awfully friendly with my daughter," he says in a low voice, a rather comical attempt to appear menacing.

"Kacie and I have been friends for a couple years," Logan answers in a calm tone. "Circumstances today have brought us quite a bit closer. She and I share a very special bond."

"If you're going to start talking about psychic powers or similar crap, I don't want to hear it," Dad says with a dismissive wave of his hand. "Phony, imaginary powers have already broken this family beyond repair."

My eyes fill with tears when I realize he's still closed to the possibility. With supreme effort, I manage to keep them from spilling over my eyelashes. Logan has a calm, agreeable expression on his face, but I can feel his body tense up.

"You still insist your daughter is either a liar or insane?" Logan asks in a careful, even tone. "That must be very difficult for you."

Hot tears trickle down my cheeks at his blunt summation of our issues. I blink several times to keep more from forming.

"You have no right to come into this house and speak to me like you know anything about our family," Dad barks at him. "We have managed this situation just fine so far."

"No, we haven't," I whisper, forcing myself to look at Dad. "You think if you ignore it, it'll go away.

It's not that easy. I suffer in silence every day, while you go around with your head in the sand. If you cared about me at all, you'd try to open your mind and understand."

"I can't just believe in something I can't see," Dad says, throwing his arms in the air.

"We believe in many things we can't see," Logan murmurs while his fingers rub soothing circles on my shoulder blade. "This sofa is covered in dust mites, I can't see them yet I know they're there. Our bodies are made up of billions of atoms we can't see. The universe exists far beyond what we can see with the limited technology we have."

"That's different," Dad insists with a stony glare.

"What if I could prove it to you?" Logan asks as he stares down my father. "Would you believe then?"

"How could you possibly do that?" Gavin asks.

My heart soars with renewed hope. Gavin wants to believe. I can see it in the excitement in his eyes, the way he leans forward eager to listen.

"I'm a psychic medium like Kacie," Logan replies. "Perhaps I can call on one of your deceased relatives and relay a message from them."

"I'll believe it when I see it," Dad scoffs, adding a snort of derisive laughter.

"Who should I try to contact?" Logan asks with a defiant glare.

"Fine, contact my sister Constance. She died last year, and I have a few questions for her," Dad says, radiating skepticism from the sneer on his face to the clenched fist resting on his leg.

"I banished Aunt Constance from the house," I admit in a soft murmur. "She wouldn't leave me alone. Kept saying she needed me to tell some guy named Richie that the treasure is buried under the spider oak. It made no sense and she wouldn't let me sleep, so I finally convinced her to move on to the next plane." When I glance up at my father, his face is pale. "What's wrong, Dad?"

"Were those her exact words?" Dad asks in a hoarse whisper. "The treasure is under the spider oak?"

"Well, spirits don't just talk the way you and I do," I hedge, confused by his sudden change in demeanor. "Sometimes everything comes out jumbled. But, yeah, that's what I remember her saying. Why?"

"It was a game we played when we were kids," Dad says, running a shaking hand through his dark hair. "The cartoon *Richie Rich*. I played Richie and she played Gloria Glad. The spider oak was the largest oak tree on our farm. I can't believe it. I know I never told you this. I had forgotten until now."

"Do you think she actually hid something under the tree?" I ask intrigued.

"I think I'll go check this weekend," Dad says, pulling and rubbing at his chin. "It's still hard for me to accept that you see and communicate with spirits, but after this... There's no way you could possibly know about it. Constance lived in France for most of your life. I have no choice but to at least try to believe."

"I suppose that's all I can ask for now," I say with a heavy sigh, too scared to raise my hopes.

Silence falls over the room. Dad's starting to believe me. Maybe. And yet, I feel lighter, like a weight I didn't realize I was carrying has finally been lifted.

"Mr. Ramsey, earlier this evening your ex-wife called and told Kacie something disturbing," Logan says, concern radiating from his voice. "She told her she's having visions of Kacie's future. Frankly, I'm concerned seeing as she hasn't spoken to her in years and now she's calling out of the blue."

"I still can't believe my mother is psychic," I murmur, leaning my head on Logan's shoulder.

"She never said anything to me about it," Dad says, his face hard and expressionless. I wish I knew what he was thinking. "I couldn't help but listen to your conversation earlier, so I guess at the very least she thinks she is."

"We need to know what those visions are about, sir," Logan informs my dad. "Kacie's life could be in danger."

"I'll call and ask her," Gavin offers with a shrug. "She'll talk to me." The way he seems so sure makes me wonder.

"You knew didn't you?" I ask Gavin. My stomach clenches at his grave expression. "About our mother's abilities."

"She confessed to me a couple years ago," Gavin admits so softly it's almost inaudible. "I can't say I really believed her, but she knew things she shouldn't have known." He looks over at me, his eyes filled with barely disguised anguish. "That's when I stopped going to visit her unless Dad forced me to. I was so angry for what she did to you, Kacie."

"Why didn't you tell me?" I ask, my voice choked with emotion.

"By that time, you weren't showing any signs you still saw the ghosts," Gavin says with a melancholy smile. "Dad was finally happy again, and I didn't want to dredge up the past. I thought maybe whatever made you see ghosts had disappeared. I'm sorry. You hid it so well. I didn't realize you were suffering." He pulls his phone from his pocket and looks up at me. "Are you ready?"

When I nod he looks her up in his contacts. She's not on his favorites list. For some reason that simple fact leaves me feeling a little bit better.

"Mom, we need to talk," he says. His words are followed by several seconds of silence. "She won't talk to you, and I don't blame her. Tell me about your vision and I'll relay the information." He's silent again while he listens to the woman on the other end. "I'm sorry, Mom, this makes no sense to me. Would you consider talking to Kacie's friend, Logan? He's psychic, so he'll probably understand." He hands the phone to Logan.

"Hello, ma'am," Logan says as he gives my shoulder a squeeze. "Please just tell me the entire vision from beginning to end. Don't leave anything out."

I can hear her voice since my head is resting on his shoulder, but I can't quite make out the words. Logan places his index finger against his lips then puts her on speaker.

"...seem like such a nice boy. Kacie can be a strange girl, spends too much time talking to the dead if you ask me. Hopefully it doesn't scare nice boys like you away." She prattles on unaware we're all listening. "My vision is weird, really weird. Kacie's at this huge house with a group of people. There's this evil man in a goat head mask. The goat man is holding thirteen lambs against their will. Kacie is the only one who can save those lambs. But she needs the golden angel or she won't be able to drive away the evil goat man and free the lambs. If the lambs aren't freed, their souls will suffer for all eternity."

She pauses for a moment, and starts humming some unrecognizable tune.

"Is that it?" Logan asks.

"The angel has eyes and hair the same color, a golden-brown... like the whiskey in my glass right now." She stops talking again, probably to drain her whiskey glass. "Even with the angel, Kacie is in danger. The goat man wants to use her body to return to the world of the living. He'll do anything in his power to capture her and wrench her away from the golden angel. The vision always ends with Kacie and the angel fighting the goat man, but I never see the outcome. Oh, and tell Kacie I don't care what her inner critic thinks. That color fuchsia is beautiful on her."

Logan takes the phone off speaker.

"Thanks, ma'am," he says in a polite tone. Just a hint of his Texas drawl comes out in the word ma'am. "Please call Gavin if you have any further information," he adds before he passes the phone back to Gavin.

"Can't talk now," Gavin says into the phone. "Yeah, call if you see anything else. Bye." He ends the call and stuffs the phone back in his pocket.

"That was by far the strangest thing I've ever heard," Dad says, shaking his head. "I hate to say it but I think Jessica is hitting the bottle a bit too hard again."

Fearing Dad is right, I glance up at Logan to see him staring across the room. His body is rigid and he appears deep in thought.

"So Kacie has to save some lambs from a goat man," Gavin says laughing. "Oh and she needs Logan's help to save the lambs."

"Why Logan?" I ask confused.

"Well he must be the golden angel, right," Gavin says like it should be obvious to everyone in the room. "He has golden-brown hair and eyes. Well, thanks to Mom, looks like you get to spend a lot more time with Kacie," he adds with a snicker.

"Can't say I'm complaining," Logan murmurs, his lips curled into a small grin. "The evil man in the mask is most likely an evil spirit, perhaps demonic given the goat head. The thirteen lambs could be other spirits he's holding captive, keeping them from crossing over—probably children. Of course your father may be right and she's been hitting the sauce a little heavily. Who knows? We'll just have to be careful." His cell chirps and he pulls it from his pocket. "That's my mom, I gotta go."

He stands and walks to the front door. When I follow him out onto the porch, he stops and turns back to me. Several moments pass in silence. He continues to gaze at me while I desperately hope he'll kiss me. Right now I want nothing more than to feel his lips on mine, my first kiss. Well first meaningful kiss anyway.

"I'll see you in the morning, Kacie," he murmurs before turning and walking to his car.

Hugging my arms around my body, I watch in silence as he gets in his Mustang and drives away. The chilly breeze cools my warm skin. I walk out onto the wet grass, the cold water on my bare feet forcing my mind to stay rooted in the present. The storm has passed taking the clouds with it, leaving the half moon and stars visible in the darkened sky. Gazing at the stars my mind fills with images of Logan. His citrine eyes, curly brown hair and his amazing smile. My heart flutters a bit as I think of what it would be like to kiss his full lips. With a wistful sigh, I head back into the brightly lit house and make my way to my room, hopefully to some very sweet dreams.

9
Ghost Hunt

~

The days fly by with school during the day and three hour training sessions with Michelle and Logan in the evenings. Two sessions and I've already learned how to raise and lower a psychic barrier that keeps spirits out. I just can't keep it up all the time or it starts to cause problems. By imagining the barrier as a brick wall, I'm able to block out all but the most stubborn spiritual energy. It will take time and practice, I know. But Michelle said I'm a quick learner and it'll be second nature soon.

Learning to control my psychic walls is much easier than I expected. It seems I was doing it subconsciously when I was a child. Each time I yelled, "go away", in frustration, I was actually throwing up a psychic block. If I hadn't been so stubborn a year ago and refused to lower the barrier, I might be even better at this by now.

Every night the visions plague me—barrier or no barrier. No matter what I do, I can't seem to block them out. Fatigue wears at me from lack of sleep. Were it not for caffeine, I'm not sure I'd survive at all.

Drama rehearsal this afternoon was brutal. Mr. Holmes was in rare form... nasty form that is. Nothing was done right, and he forced Daniel and me to stay an extra hour after the rest of the cast left. Between my "lack of anything resembling grace", and Daniel's "caterwauling", I can't help but wonder why we were cast in the first place. On the ride home, I cried—I actually cried in front of Daniel. I'm just grateful I didn't cry in front of that asshat director.

Worst of all, Daniel wouldn't leak a hint about my test tonight. After all we'd been through together at rehearsal, he kept his mouth zipped.

Rebecca, Daniel, and Logan are taking me out tonight for a *test* of my new control. They've all been so tight-lipped about it. I'm back to imagining animal sacrifices in a graveyard.

I drop my backpack and stare at my bed in longing. A glance at the clock shows there's no time to even consider a nap. Daniel said he'd be back in less than an hour. Plopping on the bed, I devour the fried chicken I nabbed from the kitchen downstairs, washing it down with a diet soda. When I'm finished, I peel off my clothes and head for a quick shower. I swear I worked up more of a sweat at rehearsal today than at a cross country meet.

~⊘

"Downtown?" I ask, staring out the window of Daniel's SUV. "Come on, it's time to spill. Where are we going?"

"Oh, here and there," Rebecca says from the front seat. "By the time we're through, I think it will be four or five places total."

"Please guys," I say, close to tears. "I can't take this anymore. The visions are getting worse and I'm not handling life well right now. And after Mr. Holmes this afternoon…"

"Shh, Kacie, it's going to be fun. I promise," Logan says as he takes my hand in his, weaving our fingers together. "You're going to love it."

My stomach flutters. "Really?" I ask, staring at our entwined hands. If Logan plans to hold my hand tonight, then I think I can handle anything.

"Cici, I guarantee you a fun time tonight," Daniel says, glancing at me in the review mirror. "And you were fantastic this afternoon, by the way. I think Mr. Holmes is having boyfriend trouble which is turning him into a monster."

"So I didn't have 'elephant feet'?" I ask, cringing at the phrase the director used to describe my dancing.

"Hell, no," Daniel says laughing. "Dancing may not be your strongest suit, but you're still good. Besides, you have the voice of an angel."

"Thanks, I needed that," I murmur, smiling at his compliment. "And you didn't sound like 'an alley cat in heat' either. You have a very nice baritone."

"Thanks," Daniel says snorting. "We're taking you downtown for a ghost tour. You'll love it."

"Daniel!" Rebecca's shriek makes me cringe. "You weren't supposed to tell her."

"Really? A ghost tour sounds like a lot of fun," I reply, ignoring Rebecca's outburst.

"It was my idea," Rebecca says, turning in the seat to look at me. "I thought you'd have lots of chances to work on your shields with residual energy. Then Logan wants you to meet a ghost he thinks you can help." Her gaze drops to the backseat. "And Logan's holding your hand," she adds in a squeal.

"It's a great idea, Rebecca," I say, trying to sound casual and normal. "I've never been on a ghost tour."

"Forget that," Rebecca says, pushing her glasses up her nose. "Are you two like officially together?"

"I-I don—" I mutter.

"I hope so," Logan says over my stammering.

I glance at him, praying my face isn't as red as it feels. His smile is breathtaking, and I sigh a bit under my breath. He seems to be waiting for an answer, but I don't think my voice will work no matter how hard I try. I nod, giving him a shy smile while gazing at him from under my bangs. He squeezes my hand, caressing my thumb with his. Closing my eyes, I let my head fall back against the headrest, concentrating on the feeling of his hand holding mine. I never want this moment to end…

Opulence drips from every detail in this magnificent hotel lobby. The chandeliers alone are worth staring at. Dangling crystals send beams of colored light dancing all around. Plush red furniture with gold accents that should appear garish just helps create the turn of the century look. Our tour guide describes the grisly history of the Red Majestic Hotel, but I turn a deaf ear. So much tragedy—I can feel the icy tendrils of energy pulling at my mental block.

"Now we'll head to the kitchen so you can see the spot where Chef Andre killed his *sous chef* with your own eyes," the guide says in a dramatic, booming voice as he ushers the tour members to the back of the hotel.

"This is where we leave you, Jeff," Daniel says, passing a twenty dollar bill to our guide. "We're heading up to room 208."

"Always good to see you guys," Jeff says, tipping his cowboy hat. "Y'all be careful up in 208. You never know what might happen in there."

"No need to worry," Logan says. "Keep us up to date on anything strange."

"You'll have to be a bit more specific than that," Jeff replies with a grin. "Did you see that brunette cougar in the group? The one with the chest out to here," he says, gesturing with his hands. "She actually squeezed my ass. Twice."

"Let's keep the reveal to the supernatural, Jeff," Rebecca says through her laughter. "What you do with your tour groupies is your own business."

"Sounds dreadfully dull," Jeff says before heading off to his tour group. "Have fun in room 208, newbie," he says over his shoulder.

"What's in room 208?" I ask, crossing my arms over my chest.

"A very temperamental ghost," Daniel says, in a deep, spooky voice. "Kinda reminds me of that green slime ball in *Ghostbusters*."

"We want you to try to convince this ghost to move on," Logan says, taking my arm and leading me toward a bank of gold elevators. "Okay, now turn around and face the lobby."

I turn and gaze at the empty lobby. Everything is quiet with the tour group gone. My eyes roam across the turn of the century décor. I wonder what Logan wants me to see.

"Now lower your wall," Logan says in an excited murmur.

The moment my barrier is lowered I gasp in amazement. Spirit energy fills the large room—men, women, children, and even a dog. It's residual energy, an imprint left behind all those years ago. I've never seen anything like this... ever. In a way it's so beautiful watching the wispy white forms go about their business, oblivious to the passing of time.

"It's amazing," I murmur to Logan. "Are any of them aware?"

"No, I think it's all residual down here now," Logan replies with a grin. "It's like the Haunted Mansion ride at Disney World."

"I've never been," I reply, watching the ghostly image of a hotel clerk pass through the man at the bell desk. He shivers and his head darts around before he shrugs his shoulders and returns to working. "I can see why so many people have experiences here. How did we manage to walk through the lobby without running into one of the spirits?"

"I didn't," Daniel says, crossing his arms. "I felt one pass right through me earlier."

"I wish I could see them," Rebecca says, her voice filled with yearning.

"Ready for the next surprise?" Logan asks.

When I nod he pushes the up button for the elevator. The car arrives and we step inside the mirrored box. A ghostly form hovers near the control panel. He's wearing what appears to be a uniform with a small pillbox hat.

"Floor two, please," Logan says to the spirit.

"Cool!" Rebecca says as the number lights up. "Did the ghost push it for us?"

"Yep, this one seems to be aware," Logan says, eyeing the spirit. "Are you happy here or would you like help moving on?" The specter tips his hat before disappearing.

"I guess he's happy here," Logan says with a sigh. "I wonder how long he's been operating this elevator."

"Probably since the hotel opened and an operator was necessary," Daniel says, running his hand over the control panel. "Hmm, he's quite content here. I don't think he really notices the passage of time."

"That's good," Rebecca says shaking her head. "I can't imagine spending both life and death operating a stupid elevator."

A *bing* sounds inside the elevator, and the doors slide open. I follow my friends down a long, dim hallway. Each door we pass is painted bright red to match the ornate red and gold carpet. Electric sconces hang on the walls at even intervals. If they flickered just a bit, I could almost imagine it being one hundred years ago. We stop in front of a door with 208 on it in gold numbers. Before Daniel can put the key card in the lock, a maid appears rushing down the hall toward us.

"Oh, I think you have the wrong room," she says, her breathing ragged from running just a short distance.

"Nope, 208 is the room we're looking for," Rebecca replies in a cheerful tone. "We're paranormal investigators. It's been cleared with management."

"Oh, I see," she says, shaking her head as though she disagrees. "I tried cleaning in there earlier and the TV remote flew across the room and hit me in the head." She glances around the hallway. "Where's your camera crew? Am I going to be on TV?" she asks while fluffing her graying hair.

"I'm terribly sorry but we are academic investigators, not entertainers," Logan says with a hard edge to his voice. "These spirits are people just like you and me and don't deserve to be exploited."

"It threw a remote at me!" the maid says with her hands on her hips.

"We're here to try to convince the spirit to move on to the next plane," Daniel says as he swipes the keycard through the lock. "With any luck, you'll never have to deal with her again."

When he opens the door, a musty, stale smell wafts out. After one last fearful glance at the room, the maid scurries away in silence. I take a deep breath, choking a bit on the heavy air. Even without entering the room I can tell a spirit is here. An unhappy spirit based on the vibes rolling out the door.

"Wow, the hairs are standing up on my neck," Rebecca whispers. "Is that the ghost?"

"Yeah, she's not happy to be disturbed," Logan replies before crossing the threshold. "Rebecca, you can stay out here if you prefer."

"No way in hell am I missing this," Rebecca says, her body shaking in excitement or fear, maybe both.

Logan holds his hand out to me. My stomach does a little flip as I place my hand in his. He laces our fingers together and pulls me into the room. Static electricity crackles around us, making my hair fly in all directions. Through the veil of hair, I see an apparition so solid she looks alive. Her yellow sundress is in tatters, torn at the shoulder and hem. Vivid red stains mar the sunny expanse of ripped cloth across her stomach.

Blood.

"Do you see her?" I ask in a breathless whisper.

"Yes," Logan replies, squeezing my hand. "Talk to her. Maybe she'll listen to you. I think you two have something in common."

"Okay," I murmur, my eyes never leaving the girl.

Energy thrums along my arms, raising every hair. Releasing Logan's hand, I walk toward the girl, watching in fascination as her long, dark hair flies around her. Her eyes are inky pools with no white visible. All in all, I think she's one of the most ter-rifying apparitions I've ever seen in appearance. And yet, I sense only intense sorrow coming off her in undulating waves. This spirit is suffering terribly. She watches me as I lower my body to sit on the edge of the king-size bed. I fold my hands in my lap, trying to appear as innocuous as possible.

"Tell me your story," I say to the spirit girl. "You're suffering. I can help. Please share your story with me."

"You would never understand the pain I have experienced at the hands of the woman who was supposed to provide care and nurture," the spirit replies, turning away.

"You might be surprised," I say in a calm, even tone. "Did your mother hurt you?"

"Yes." Though she doesn't elaborate, she does turn back to face me.

"My mother hurt me deeply," I tell the ghost. My nose begins to burn which means the tears aren't far behind. "Maybe not physically but mental anguish can be bad too. Just three days ago she reopened old wounds. My heart hurts just thinking about it."

"Truly?" the girl asks, tipping her head to the side as though she's contemplating my words.

"I know what betrayal feels like," I reply with a deep sigh. "Tell me your story. You don't belong here anymore. There's no need to suffer like this. Please, let me help you."

"My mother wed my stepfather when I was thirteen," she says in a soft voice. The energy in the room spikes then dims when her shoulders sag. "Within a fortnight he was visiting me in the dead of night. He did things to me. Things that should only occur between a husband and wife. Horrible things—"

She shudders, crossing her arms over her chest. I don't say anything... just wait for her to continue her tale. Her eyes meet mine, filled with tears, and I want nothing more than to hold her, to soothe her. She couldn't be any older than I am. Without thinking I reach out to touch her shoulder, but my hand passes through her phantom image. I snatch my hand back, cradling my freezing fingers against my stomach.

"He visited me weekly for two years—threatened me with violence if I ever told a soul. Threatened to kill my m-mother." She chokes the words out through gut-wrenching sobs. "One night my mother walked in while he was using my body..."

"What happened?" I ask when she remains silent.

"He told her I seduced him, that I was possessed by a succubus from Hell," she says, flinging her arms around. Tendrils of icy wind billow from her finger-tips. "She believed him. They locked me up in this very room."

"I don't understand," I murmur, looking at Logan. "Why would they lock her up here?"

"This building was once used as a facility for tuberculosis patients," Logan replies. He closes his eyes and shakes his head. "It was also used to hide the less desirable people from society."

"I was with child."

"Oh, I see. I'm so sorry," I say as tears spill over my eyelashes.

The monster got her pregnant and locked her away where she wouldn't be a nuisance. I look at the red stains all over her dress. There's still more to this story.

"Mother found out about the baby," she says in a whisper. "She screamed that it was demon spawn and must be removed no matter the cost. She stabbed the baby through my belly. Over and over. Screaming. So much pain."

"What's your name?" Logan asks as he approaches inch by inch, like he's afraid she'll flee.

"Maria."

"Maria, you've suffered enough," I say, rising from the bed. "None of this was your fault. You are a victim and did nothing to deserve it. Move on to the next plane."

"Will my baby be there?"

"I don't know," Logan says when I can't find my voice. "But there's only one way to find out. I'm sure whatever you find there must be better than the pain you feel here."

"I can go?"

"Yes," I say, firm and sure. "Rest in peace, Maria."

My heart leaps when a tiny smile crosses her face. She stares off into the distance, perhaps seeing something we can't. Whatever she sees makes her smile grow larger. Her image flickers and begins to fade away. Right before she disappears, she waves goodbye.

"You did it!" Logan says, pulling me into a hug.

Tears flow down my cheeks. Wrapping my arms around his back, I rest my head on his shoulder. I can't help but smile through the tears. Helping Maria was fantastic. She suffered for so long, and I was the one who was able to get through to her. Right now my ability seems more a blessing than a curse.

10
Date Night

I am so happy. I've been walking around with a ridiculous smile plastered to my face all day. Helping the spirit, Maria, move on was so rewarding. To think she suffered for decades, and I was the one who was able to help her rest in peace. For the first time in my life, I feel good about my abilities—like I can really make a difference. Of course it helps that I've learned to raise and lower my barrier with ease. As I step out of the shower, I catch a glimpse of myself in the steamed up mirror. Silly grin? Check. My grin fades when I open the bathroom door to utter chaos.

They say hindsight is twenty/twenty. Right now I'm wishing I had the foresight to see this decision for the disaster it's turning into. When I asked Celia to come over and help me prepare for my date with

Logan, I didn't think it through. While I was bliss-
fully unaware in the shower, Celia managed to empty
half my closet and most of my dresser drawers onto
the bed. I know the bed is somewhere underneath
the massive pile of clothing, but there's no sign of
it beyond the comforter peeking out along the side.
Shaking my head, I enter the room still towel drying
my hair. Celia turns to me with a beaming smile.

"This is so exciting," Celia croons in a melodramatic squeal. It's obvious why she was cast as Juliet in
the drama production. She was made for it—drama,
that is. "You're finally going on your first date and
with a total hottie too."

Rolling my eyes, I drape the damp towel across
the back of my desk chair and stare at her reflection
in the mirror.

"It's not a date, Celia," I remind her while watching her compare two skirts with a critical eye. It *is*
a date, in my mind anyway, but something makes
me downplay it aloud. "It's an investigation for the
club."

I was relieved when Mrs. Kincaid told me it was
okay to tell my trusted friends and family what the
club does. It would be impossible to participate in
investigations if I was forced to lie to Dad about
where I was going.

"What could be more potentially romantic than
a haunted house?" she asks in a dreamy voice. "A

ghost suddenly appears and you jump into his strong arms for protection. Perfect."

Her comment makes me laugh at the absurd image.

"I wouldn't be much of an investigator if I shrieked and jumped on my partner," I choke out through the laughter.

"True. He's taking you to dinner first," she says with a sly smile. "Sounds like a date to me." She gives me her *I dare you to argue* look.

"It's merely a dinner among colleagues before the assignment," I argue, trying not to smirk at her sullen expression.

"You don't really believe that or I wouldn't be here trying to help you figure out what to wear tonight," she says as she tosses her long, blonde curls. When she turns to look at me, I collapse onto the pile of clothing covering the bed.

"You're right, he's all I could think about this entire week," I admit, closing my eyes to see his face dancing in my memory. "I just get lost in his eyes. When he dropped me off last night after our ghost hunt I was praying he'd kiss me but he didn't." A wistful sigh escapes my lips as I recall standing on the porch with him, the soft moonlight glinting off his curls. "Then on the ride to school this morning, I couldn't stop staring at his lips. He held my hand all the way to school."

"Wow, you've got it bad," Celia remarks, patting me on the shoulder. "About damn time. I guess I'd better cross Logan off my list of potentials."

My eyes fly open at her remark. "He's on your list?" I ask a bit shocked.

"He's sexy as hell, athletic, and in an exclusive, secretive club," Celia says waving her hand for emphasis. "I don't know why it surprises you." She reaches down and pulls me up off the bed by the hand. "It doesn't matter anymore now that you're into him. What time is he picking you up?"

"Five-thirty," I reply, looking over to the clock on the nightstand.

"Twenty-five minutes!" she shrieks. "Hurry and dry your hair while I pick out your clothes."

"I was going to leave my hair damp," I admit in a sheepish murmur, taking in her stunned expression.

"If that's a joke it isn't funny," she mumbles, digging through the pile of clothes on the bed.

With a resigned sigh, I plug in the blow dryer and get to work on my long hair. My strawberry-blonde hair is wavy and doesn't do well under a dryer. Sometimes the waves go a bit crazy from the heat. After a few minutes of watching Celia through the mirror, I turn off the dryer and place it on the dresser.

"Jeans and a sweater," I insist in a tone that doesn't invite argument.

Celia stops pawing through my clothes and appears to contemplate my statement.

"You know, just this once, I think you're right," she says as she starts rifling through the pile of clothing again. "I never thought I'd see the day…" She rambles on about my lack of fashion sense while I turn back to the mirror and finish drying my hair.

When my hair is mostly dry, I turn off the dryer, steeling myself to see what revealing outfit Celia put together. She's busy stuffing clothes back into the dresser drawers and hanging dresses back in the closet. When my gaze falls on the clothing she picked out, I'm pleasantly surprised. I slip on the well-worn, faded bootcut jeans, glad I'll have ease of movement.

I've never been on an investigation before. For all I know we have to climb ladders, crawl on the floor, or go up into a dusty attic. Wouldn't that be a riot in a short miniskirt and heels? Celia picked out a plain black and gray striped turtleneck to pair with the jeans. As I slip it over my head, I wonder for a moment what possessed my fashion forward friend to dress me so conservatively tonight.

"You picked out the perfect clothes, Celia," I say, the surprise apparent in my voice.

"You don't have to sound so shocked, Kacie," she says, worry clouding her features. "I figured you might need comfortable clothes, you know, in case you had to run from a ghost."

I start to laugh until I realize she's serious. Celia's afraid of ghosts—it goes beyond normal fear, it's a phobia. My abilities scare her to death. Without responding, I pull on my gray hiking boots and tie the laces.

"I've never met anyone with hiking boots in so many different colors," she remarks as she watches me from the corner of her eye.

Returning to the mirror, I line my eyes with charcoal liner, topped with a sparkling silver shadow. A quick pass with the mascara wand and I'm finished.

"Well?" I ask, turning to face Celia.

The closer it gets to five-thirty, the more my stomach rebels, forget butterflies, I have a full stampede of wildebeests running around in there.

"You look gorgeous," Celia replies. "Don't forget the lipstick."

"I hate the stuff, it tastes terrible," I murmur, pulling out some tinted pomegranate lip balm. "How's this?"

She looks me over from head to toe before throwing my gray pleather jacket at me.

"He'll love it," she says, nodding her head. "You look great without looking like you spent much time getting ready."

"It only took twenty minutes," I remind her. She looks from me to the clock. "He'll be here in five minutes," I murmur, trying to settle my nerves. "Do you need a ride home?"

"Jake's picking me up here at five-thirty," she replies, striking a pose. "How do I look?"

"Perfect as always, Celia," I remark with a smile.

She's wearing what I was afraid she'd try to dress me in, a short black lace miniskirt and matching halter top. Her black boots have three-inch heels. I'd probably fall to my death if I tried walking in those. The doorbell rings causing my stomach to lurch a bit.

"Kacie, your guests are here," Gavin yells from downstairs.

Running to the mirror, I check my hair and makeup one last time. My hair is rather easy to deal with. It's mostly dry, and I run the brush through it again before turning to Celia.

"Remember you can't tell anyone about the Orion Circle," I say, hoping she takes it to heart. Though I trust her, gossip this juicy might be hard for her to keep quiet.

"I promise," she replies, making a zipping motion across her lips with her fingers. "I'm glad you told me, and I won't tell a soul. Be careful tonight okay."

"Don't worry," I say as we head toward the stairs. "Logan will be with me if any ghosts get out of hand." My words have the desired effect. She snorts with laughter. "Besides we're going to confirm the haunting is a hoax. I really don't think any spirits will try to eat me."

She laughs again, but this time it sounds a bit forced.

"Kacie, ever since your problem with the cowboy, I worry about you," Celia says, all laughter gone from her face. "Swear you'll be careful." She pauses at the top of the stairs, turning to face me. "You and I both know the supernatural is not something to play around with."

A haunted look crosses her face, and I know she's remembering what happened six years ago. Her mom started doing séances with a homemade spirit board, not a good idea under the best of circumstances. Unfortunately her mother had no clue what she was doing and invited a rather mischievous spirit into the house. It targeted poor Celia, made her life a living hell. We were both only nine when I helped rid her house of the spirit.

"Celia, I can use my abilities to help people, like I did with you," I say, pulling her into a one armed hug. "You have no idea how happy that makes me. I'm tired of forcing it down to hide behind a brick wall in my mind. It can be so exhausting. I'll be with Logan, don't worry."

She doesn't say anything as she follows me down the stairs. When we reach the first floor, there are voices coming from the kitchen. Jake and Logan are both in the kitchen talking to my brother. All three clam up the moment Celia and I enter the room. My eyes zero in on Logan. He looks amazing tonight in faded blue jeans and a beat-up brown leather jacket. Celia walks right up to Logan and gives him her best glare.

"You keep her safe tonight," she orders, poking him in the chest with her pink-manicured finger.

Logan gives her a serene smile and nods his head. Jake pulls Celia away from Logan and holds her against his chest. He rests his blond head on hers making it difficult to tell where his hair ends and hers begins. When I first met Jake, he didn't strike me as a peacemaker. But being from a broken home he can't seem to stand any strife. All of San Antonio heard about his parents' divorce three years ago, his mother being a prominent news anchor. To call it messy would be a vast understatement.

"Funny, that's just what Gavin was saying," Logan says chuckling. "Though I have a feeling you're both talking about different things."

Jake snickers into Celia's head, and it finally occurs to me what the three guys were discussing. Right now I'm so glad Celia picked out a turtleneck. I hate the way my neck flushes whenever I get embarrassed. It seems I have no control over it, and with my pale skin, it's all too noticeable. Logan takes my arm and leads me to the foyer.

"We're supposed to be at the inn by eight tonight so we should get going if we're gonna have any time to eat," he says when we reach the front door.

Gavin stalks right behind us, and he almost runs into me when I turn to face him.

"I might be very late," I tell my brother. Before he can protest I continue, "Dad already okayed breaking curfew. We'll be with the owners of the inn so he isn't worried."

"Text when you leave the inn, Kacie," Gavin insists, making me sigh in exasperation. "Don't roll your eyes at me. Dad will be worried."

With a nod I agree to his demands. I suppose Dad would be nervous about me being out in the middle of the night.

"Dad called the innkeepers, Mr. and Mrs. Anders. They have separate rooms available for you and Logan if you're there past one. He doesn't want you on the road that late." Gavin crosses his arms over his chest as though waiting for an argument.

I'm about to protest when Logan rescues Gavin.

"Mrs. Kincaid called our parents, and they already planned everything together so don't feel too picked on," Logan says, squeezing my hand. "It'll be fun to stay at the inn tonight. Besides we really should do an all-night investigation. We both know spirits are at their most active between midnight and three."

The statement makes me laugh. Spirits are only more active at night because it's quiet and we can hear them better. At least that's my theory, and judging by the cute smirk on Logan's face I think he agrees.

"Celia, we gotta go," Jake mutters, pulling on her arm. "Game's at eight. Coach'll kill me if I'm late again." Celia nods before turning and winking at me.

"Happy hunting," she calls out as Jake drags her out the door.

Waving goodbye, I watch her disappear into Jake's Jeep before turning to say goodbye to Gavin. I'm somewhat surprised when he's nowhere to be seen.

"Bye, Gavin," I yell out as I follow Logan out the door.

"Stay safe, Kacie," Gavin yells back.

11

Romance at the River Walk

~

Closing the door softly behind me, I pull my keys from my backpack and lock the door. We might be forced to stay the night so I packed a change of clothes and toiletries just in case. My sweet brother brought home a UTSA Roadrunners t-shirt for me to wear tonight. I hope Logan likes it better than the A&M jersey.

The idea of spending the night at an inn with Logan is both exciting and nerve-wracking. As I follow him down the drive to his Mustang, my mind flashes through all sorts of scenarios. I quickly shut down that train of thought when my entire body begins to tingle from my more lascivious imaginings. Logan opens the passenger door for me, bringing a tiny grin to my face. Very chivalrous.

"Do you have any preference for dinner?" he asks as he eases himself into the driver's seat.

"Sorry, I hadn't really thought about it," I reply, glancing at him in the dim light from the dash.

Dinner has been the last thing on my mind. With any luck, Logan will think I'm preoccupied with our assignment and not him. Right now I can't get my scattered brain to focus enough to even name two restaurants along the river.

"I thought the Crooked Cactus on the River Walk would be fun," he says, a hopeful smile on his face.

When I nod my agreement, he pulls from the curb and eases down the street much slower than Jake did.

"I've never eaten there, but I do love Mexican food," I comment as we exit Cedar Bluffs.

"The food is great and they have live music on weekends."

I take the chance to study his face while he's intent on driving. His profile is rather nice, nose not too prominent, a little crooked but it adds character. The way his light brown hair curls down over his forehead and at the nape of his neck is adorable. I just want to tangle my fingers in those curls. He glances over at me and seems to misinterpret my stare as perhaps disbelief.

"Not mariachi music," he says laughing. "The look on your face is priceless!"

He's still chuckling under his breath, leaving me to wonder what my expression looked like. My best guess is dazed since that was how I felt at the moment.

"Mostly San Antonio bands, rock music, but not the hard stuff."

"Sounds good," I manage to choke out through a throat that feels like it's closing on me.

I'm embarrassed and he's oblivious to it. Against my better judgment, my eyes find their way back to study his profile. He sings along with the radio in a rather nice baritone. Deciding I can't continue to sit here and stare at him, I opt to ferret out some answers about this enigmatic organization I'm now a part of.

"I've been dying of curiosity since the meeting Monday. Are Daniel and Yolanda hunting a real werewolf? I thought werewolves were fairy tales."

"They're real enough and can do major damage without a pack," he replies, tapping his hands on the wheel in time with the music. "It sounds like the Austin chapter found a rogue." When he stops tapping to grip the steering wheel with both hands, I realize he's unnerved. "They change with the full moon once a month, which is less than two weeks away. The pack will go deep into the wilderness—Native American reserves are the most popular. That way there's no danger to the general population."

"What about the Native Americans?" I ask worried for the friends I've made with several Comanches.

"They're well-aware of the werewolves. An agreement is normally made with the tribal elders," Logan says, glancing over at me. Our eyes meet since I haven't stopped studying him since we left my house. "When one goes rogue, there's a greater possibility there'll be human casualties."

He appears lost in thought so I look out the window studying the scenery in the waning light. The drive downtown is only about twenty minutes and there's nothing scenic about it. Everything along the freeway is urbanized, strip mall after strip mall and motel after motel. As we pass the airport, a plane flies directly over us to land on the runway just yards from the road. As much as I detest the urbanization, I have to admit I like the planes flying over so low. The vibrations from the powerful jet engines rumble through the car and straight into my soul.

I have so many more questions for Logan but don't feel like bombarding him with an endless supply at the moment. Though I'm curious about the Orion Circle, most of the questions I really want answered revolve around the hot guy next to me.

"How did you get involved with the Circle?" I ask, breaking the long silence.

He glances at me from the corner of his eye appearing relieved. It seems he didn't like the conversation regarding werewolves. I'll need to dig into that at a later date.

"My parents are both well-known sensitives in psychic circles," he replies. "My mom is like Michelle, very gifted with the living but a null with the deceased. My dad is a physical medium and a prolific author. I was asked to join my freshman year. My parents consult with the Circle from time to time."

"Is it nice having parents who not only understand but believe your powers are real?" I ask, recalling the pain I suffered for so long. He turns the radio down low.

"Yes, it is," he says, placing his hand on my leg. "It can be very disconcerting, to say the least, when medium powers start to come online. I can't imagine what you experienced going through it all alone."

His hand caresses my thigh through my jeans, soothing nerves frayed from the direction of the conversation. My heart leaps from his touch, sending tingles throughout my entire body.

"What doesn't kill you makes you stronger," I mutter the tired cliché under my breath.

"Hmm," he murmurs. "It is annoying to have a mother who seems to always know when I'm lying, sometimes before I even do it." I can't help but laugh. He glances at me again with a sheepish grin. "I got into so much trouble for things I never did when I was younger."

The image of a mischievous little Logan being thwarted in every attempt at mayhem has me giggling almost uncontrollably.

"It really isn't that funny, especially when on the receiving end. Just wait until you meet her."

My laughter abruptly stops. He already plans for me to meet his mother? I don't know whether to be overjoyed or nervous. I settle for both. He pulls off the freeway and heads to an office building rather than a public parking lot.

"Mom works here. Free parking after five," he explains as he flashes a card over the electronic reader.

The parking garage is small and cramped. Colorful paint plasters the walls at every turn from cars cutting the corner too close.

"How can you stand to drive through here?" I ask, feeling claustrophobia setting in.

He chuckles a bit. "Would you believe I drive it with my eyes closed?" he asks as he pulls into a parking space on the third floor. When he turns to look at me, I shake my head. "Well my mom can drive through here in her giant Escalade so I refuse to admit it bugs the hell outta me."

"How many of the marks on the walls are from her SUV?"

"None," he says, opening his door. "I think her psychic abilities must help with driving somehow."

Grabbing my bag, I scramble out of the car and follow him over to a stairwell in the corner. After descending three flights of stairs we end up in the dim light of an outdoor courtyard.

"Careful, the stone walkway is a bit uneven," he says, taking my hand. "It's easy to navigate during the day, but without light..." he trails off as we walk farther from the lights of the building.

The path ends, and we hike across a grassy expanse leading to the River Walk. Light from the nearby building filters through the leaves above us creating a speckled pattern on the shadowed grass. Roots from the large oak trees have broken through the ground, almost impossible to see in the darkness. When I trip over one my face flushes, and I mutter a curse at my clumsiness. Logan chuckles before righting me so we can continue. Within seconds he trips over another root from the same tree. We both stumble a few steps then break out in laughter.

"You don't think the tree is out to get us do you?" he asks as he glares up at it.

I giggle when he kicks the root with his hiking boot. He moves closer until he's inches from my face, close enough that I can see his eyes in the faint light under the tree.

"We're almost to the retaining wall. I didn't consider homicidal tree roots when I chose to walk this way. Sorry."

"I love the trees," I comment. He takes my hand leading me through the old tree's maze of roots. "I'm glad these businesses didn't just tear down the old oak trees. How old do you think this one is?" I ask, running my hand along the rough trunk.

"No idea," he says, stopping to gaze up at the tree. "I bet it's been witness to a lot through the years."

As we continue the hike to the river, he puts his arm around my shoulders, and I snuggle against his side. At the bottom of the grassy hill a four foot retaining wall keeps the earth from slipping onto the path running along the river. Logan jumps down then holds his arms up to me, grabbing me around the waist to help me down the wall. My arms fly around his neck as I jump down, and I end up in his arms pressed against his firm chest. As he lowers my feet to the ground, I breathe in the scent of his leather jacket and spicy aftershave. Once I'm back on the ground, I expect him to release me, but his arms stay wrapped around my body holding me against him.

My face is still buried in his shoulder, and I lift my chin to glance at him. He grins at me, a cute half-smile, while his eyes sparkle in the golden light from a nearby lantern. I focus on his lips as he closes the distance between us.

His lips meet mine—soft and warm, the kiss achingly tender. My eyes flutter closed and my hand moves up to those curls I've been dying to touch. He releases a soft sigh as my fingers caress the nape of his neck and tips his head to deepen the kiss. My lips part under the gentle pressure of his tongue, granting him entrance.

His hand moves from my back to my neck, and he buries his fingers in my hair. I let out a breathy moan, completely lost to the sensations. He uses my hair to tip my head back then trails searing kisses down my chin to my neck.

When he pulls his lips away from my neck, he continues to hold me in his arms for several moments while gazing into my eyes. My lips tingle, and I cling to his arms, feeling a bit lightheaded. After a few silent moments, he takes my hand, and we stroll along the river. I feel like I'm floating while my mind replays our first kiss over and over. No matter how I look at it, the kiss was perfect in every way.

Dinner was wonderful, the conversation about everything but our upcoming assignment. Things were going so well that I decided to not bring up the werewolves again even though the desire to know more was boiling like an inferno in my brain.

I mean someone tells me werewolves are real and I have to ignore it?

I'll have to corner Rebecca first thing Monday morning for some more info. Hopefully the subject won't bother her as much as it seems to bug Logan.

We split nachos, and by some miracle I managed to avoid getting them plastered down the front of my shirt. To think I was worried about eating the messy food. I kept hearing Celia's voice in my head telling me to be ladylike. The first time I licked some cheese from my finger Logan stared at my mouth riveted, and I could almost feel the temperature rise. I spent the rest of the meal teasing him off and on, enjoying every minute of it.

The walk back to the car along the river is quiet, especially when compared to the raucous restaurant we just left. This section of the River Walk passes by businesses and lacks the bars and restaurants farther down. Imitation gas lamps lighting the walk are far apart, the light not reaching the bridges we pass under.

As we walk hand in hand, I notice the sparse crowds are gone and we're alone. We pass under another bridge, and Logan pulls me into the shadows. My back rests against the cold stone of the bridge, the damp chill seeping through my thin jacket. His arms surround me chasing away the iciness as I'm enveloped in his warmth. My arms wind around his back beneath his jacket. I press up against his chest and gaze up at him.

Even in the darkness I can see the smile light his face. He leans down to capture my lips with his. I gasp as his fingers entwine in my hair holding me captive against him. This kiss is fiery and passionate—quite different from his tender kiss earlier. My head reels from the riot of sensations coursing through my body.

With a guttural chuckle he nips at my lower lip, pulling it gently with his teeth. He kisses up my jawline, and I clutch at his back, desperately trying to keep my feet beneath me. When he reaches my ear he runs his tongue up the outer shell in a light caress before nibbling on my earlobe.

"That's for the constant teasing at dinner, little nymph," he purrs in my ear.

He pulls back to look down at me, his eyes darkened with passion. My head falls to his shoulder, my breath coming in shallow pants as I wait for my equilibrium to return. His arms tighten around me holding me against his body, his head resting on top of mine. When I finally feel like the world has stopped spinning, I pull away from him.

"Do nymphs exist?"

"I'm looking at one," he says chuckling softly.

"You know what I mean," I say, slapping at his chest.

"I have no idea." He takes my hand and leads me over to the retaining wall. "I'll boost you up. Ready?"

Lacing his fingers together, he holds his hands down for me to step on. When I do, he lifts me up the wall like I weigh nothing. I scramble onto the wall thankful for the hiking boots and jeans. He climbs up the wall with ease, displaying some impressive upper body strength. As he pulls me from the ground, I giggle a bit under my breath.

"What's so funny?"

"What would you have done if I'd worn a mini-skirt?" I ask, plastering an innocent look on my face.

"Had one hell of a view!" he answers, snickering as I chase him through the perilous tree-root-ridden grass.

When I jump at his back, he pulls me up giving me a piggy back ride. Throwing my head back, I let out a sound somewhere between a shriek and a laugh. I haven't had this much fun in ages.

12
King's Ransom Inn
~

As we pull up to park in front of the inn, I take some time to study the building. Rebecca said it had been completely torn down and rebuilt in the same footprint to mirror the turn of the century house that stood before. The original manor was built in 1865 and fell into disrepair in the 1920s. It was restored in 1967 only to burn down in 2005.

The exterior is gorgeous in vibrant shades of blue apparent even in the dim light of the imitation gas lanterns lining the walkway. Every window on the second floor is made of exquisite stained glass in multiple floral patterns. I wish it was still daylight so I could see the designs better. Two massive willow trees flank the long walkway in the front yard. The trees appear very old, must have survived the fire somehow.

A colorful wooden sign hangs near the street: *King's Ransom Inn – A Haunted Good Time*. As we wander up the slate path, I open the part of my mind that can sense the dead. This area is alive with residual energy from lives long gone. The wind blows, rustling the leaves of the willow, and I can hear the laughter of long forgotten children as they run and play around the tree trunks. Several spectral forms move down the sidewalk in front of the manor, their energy locked in a never-ending repeat of a previous moment in history.

"There's lots of residual energy," Logan whispers. "Intriguing really. I wonder if it's because everything still appears as it did back in the 1800s."

"Interesting hypothesis," I murmur, watching two ghost horses pull a phantom carriage down the street. "I've never seen anything like this before. You think we're looking at a residual haunting here?"

"No," Logan says, his gaze meeting mine. "The team would have picked up something if it was residual energy. My guess is that whatever energy was here faded with the fire and the reconstruction."

"Makes sense."

For some reason, I feel the need to whisper. As we near the wrap-around front porch, the door flies open and a couple appears to greet us. The woman is short and thin with shoulder-length brown hair flipped up at the ends. She's wearing baggy, dark blue jeans and an embroidered Halloween sweater featuring bats, ghosts, and pumpkins.

Mr. Anders looks every bit the literature professor described in the brief dossier we received. He's even wearing a tweed jacket with suede patches on the elbows. His glasses are slightly askew on his thin face as if he's too immersed in his thoughts to notice. Really all he needs is a pipe to complete the stereotypical picture of the absent-minded professor.

"You must be Logan and Kacie," Mrs. Anders chirps as she rushes down the three porch steps. "Welcome, welcome. We're both so glad you could make it."

She attempts to usher us forward, and my gaze flies to meet Logan's. Is this behavior of hers genuine? I've always been rather bad at reading people—too wrapped up in ignoring the spirit world to waste my energy. He shrugs his shoulder at my confused expression. Her behavior seems odd to him as well.

Mr. Anders is silent as he watches his wife flit around us cooing about how adorable we are. When she tries to push us inside Logan finally speaks up. He has to throw his hand out to catch the doorjamb to keep from being shoved inside. This goes way beyond simple courtesy. Why does she want us in there so badly?

"Mrs. Anders, Kacie and I haven't finished our walk out here," he says with a brilliant smile.

My heart flutters a bit at the roguish expression on his face, and I'm sure many girls have fallen prey to that look. Yet all I see in Mrs. Anders' face is hard eyes and a scary, toothy grin. Now I know what a smiling crocodile looks like...

"We need a while to soak up the information around the outside of the inn. We'll come inside when we're finished," Logan adds when she continues to glare at him.

"Oh, silly me," she says, pushing her husband back inside.

Her attitude is even stranger now. It's as if no longer being in control has shaken her.

"We'll be waiting inside. Hurry up now," she says, sounding a bit panicked. "Don't want to keep the spirits waiting." The strange woman rushes back through the door, slamming it shut hard enough to rattle my teeth.

"This is just creepy," Logan whispers as a shudder wracks his body. "She's watching us through the window, hiding behind the curtain no less."

"Maybe curiosity?" I ask, though frankly I doubt that's the case.

"Something strange is going on here," he murmurs. We walk under one of the massive willow trees, the hanging boughs hiding us from view. "I think we need to get Rebecca out here." He pulls out his phone. "Call Rebecca," he orders the phone. His thumb caresses the back of my hand while he waits for her to answer. "Hey, I think Kacie and I are out of our element here." He wraps his arm around my shoulders pulling me close enough that I can hear Rebecca. "Mrs. Anders is acting very strange, and I mean creepy with a capital C."

"Well she is overly excited about the whole ghost thing," Rebecca answers. "Are you sure you're not just reading something into it that isn't there?"

"Yeah, maybe you're right," Logan admits. "I guess we could just be overreacting, but she's acting crazy enough that I have a strong urge to jump in the car and bail."

"Saccharin," I whisper. "It was all fake, an act. She desperately wanted us inside. I mean Logan had to grab the door frame to keep her from pushing him inside."

"Did you catch that?" Logan asks Rebecca.

"Yeah," she replies. "Look I'm free tonight—the investigation I had planned fell through. I was planning to stop by anyway, set up the equipment again. I'll pick up Carl and be there in about forty-five minutes. Hold out until then."

She hangs up without waiting for a response. Logan shoves the phone into his pocket and glances at me from the corner of his eye.

"I have an idea," I murmur as I take his hand and pull him back toward the front door. "Play along."

He nods once. We stroll up the stairs to the front porch with slow steps. The door opens and Mrs.

Anders appears before we reach the final step. Her brown eyes are wide and glistening in excitement. She almost appears rabid.

"We need to walk around the area," I blurt out before she can open her mouth. "Queen Anne's District is so rich in history. It will help us understand the inn and the spirits within. It should only take about an hour or so."

"Oh, of course, dears," Mrs. Anders says, crinkling her nose in what appears to be confusion. "No rush, we'll be here," she adds in her strange syrupy voice before closing the door.

Logan pulls me down the walkway toward the car at a brisk jog.

"Did you see that?" he asks as we reach the car. "The odd glint in her eyes? Something weird is going on here." He leans against the Mustang and crosses his arms over his chest. "What should we do? There's no way I'm stepping foot in there with that crazy woman 'til Rebecca and Carl get here."

"Let's do what I told her we're going to do," I suggest, hoping to ease his worried mind. "Maybe we can get some information based on the residual energies."

Nodding he takes my hand and we stroll down the sidewalk admiring the stately manors lining the street. As we turn the corner, I'm surprised to see another bed and breakfast. I guess this is a popular tourist area. It's rather close to downtown and the ambience is old elegance. Unlike our neighborhood there are no Halloween decorations gracing the lush lawns or hanging from the ancient trees. I wonder if they are frowned on in this area, or perhaps there are no children to revel in the holiday.

"I'm getting a whole lot of nothing," Logan murmurs. He wraps his arm around my back. "Everything seems very normal for an area this old. If I didn't open my senses, I wouldn't even notice anything at all."

"Yeah, I agree. We should head back and concentrate on the inn itself," I murmur, watching a ghost couple pass us in Victorian era clothing.

A gust of wind blows by, and Logan pulls me closer to his body. My face flushes a bit as I wrap my arm around his waist beneath his leather jacket. Even with the ghosts and a creepy innkeeper, I think this is the best night of my life.

We stroll down the street watching the residual activity all around us. They flicker and flash in silver ghost-like images. These aren't ghosts, but echoes of prior energy somehow stored in the fabric of the universe. I'm enjoying our walk so much that I release a heavy sigh when we round the corner to return to the inn. It looms before us, looking much eerier than it did when we first arrived.

Logan leads me to the largest of the two willow trees in front of the inn. We sit underneath, hidden from view by the dense foliage. Placing his arm around my shoulders, he pulls me into his side. The long branches block out the chilly breeze leaving our haven quite comfortable.

Now that I've closed my senses to the ambient residual energy, all I feel is the heat from Logan's body cuddled up against mine. My heart races as I lean up burying my nose into his neck before lightly kissing the soft skin above his t-shirt. His tiny sigh makes me bold, and I trail kisses up along the exposed column of his neck. When I reach his jawline he pulls me up onto his lap, his lips descending on mine in a fiery kiss.

His hands run up my back under my jacket, massaging and caressing, and I shrug it off to give him easier access. The warmth from his hands seeps through the thin material of my turtleneck, sending tiny shivers racing through my body from his light touch. His arms tighten around me, pressing me against his chest as he tips his head to deepen the kiss.

"Um, thought you'd like to know we're here," a female voice says from the other side of the willow branches. "Carl has the thermal imager trained on you right now, just saying…"

Logan groans and pulls away from me. He gently removes me from his lap so he can stand. I take his outstretched hand and allow him to pull me to my feet before retrieving my jacket from the ground where I had tossed it. After slipping it back on, I glance at him from under my eyelashes to see his golden eyes watching my every move like a predator. He leans in, giving me a tender kiss on the corner of my mouth.

"Are you coming out or do I have to send Carl in?" Rebecca asks as she and Carl snicker.

"No way in hell I'm going in there," Carl says in an indignant whine. "Might scar me for life."

Logan parts the hanging boughs of the willow, leading me out with his hand on my lower back. I desperately try to keep the flush I feel on my neck from spreading to my face as Logan walks up to Carl and snatches the strange looking device from his hands.

"My baby!" Carl wails. "Give her back!"

"It's not a her, you moron. It's just an it," Rebecca snaps at the lanky boy.

When he lunges at Logan to retrieve his treasure, she slaps a hand to his chest.

"Are you baiting Logan on purpose? Perhaps you woke up this morning thinking, 'I wonder what I can do today to get beaten to a bloody pulp?' Of all the idiotic…" Rebecca comments with an evil smirk.

Carl buries his fingers in his mousey brown hair, and for a moment I think he might pull some out in his obvious distress. He shakes his head moaning.

"I didn't do anything!" Carl says, reaching for the device again.

"Using this to spy on me with my girlfriend is kinda sick, Carl," Logan says with a cold stare. "The

Circle did not spend several thousand dollars on this equipment for you to use it in such a way."

"Sorry," Carl squeaks while staring at his feet. "I didn't mean any harm."

He wipes his hands down his jeans in a nervous manner. Logan walks over and claps him on the back.

"It's alright, Carl, I'm not really mad. I don't think Kacie is either," he says glancing at me.

Carl looks at me with forlorn eyes, and I smile and shake my head. Logan just called me his girlfriend! I don't think I could be mad at anyone right now.

Carl's shoulders drop as he breathes an audible sigh of relief. "Thanks, Kacie."

"We have a job here and right now we have an audience," Rebecca says, tipping her head toward the inn. She pushes her glasses back up her nose while staring at the front window. "I see what you mean about weird now. She's been watching the whole time. Probably wondering what the two of you were doing hidden under the tree."

"Why do you think we were hiding? She creeps me out," Logan says with a shudder.

"Surely not to make out with your new girlfriend or anything like that," Rebecca says waving her hand in the air. "You were just having a meaningful conversation about the assignment with your tongue down her throat."

My eyes meet Rebecca's cat-like greenish gaze and she grins at me. The shock and horror I felt at her statement disappears with her smile. I like this sarcastic side of her. It's quite amusing, even if I am the target.

"Hmm, perhaps it would be more apt to call it meditating," I reply laughing. "It's important to clear the mind of all stressors before attempting a walk-through such as this."

Logan grabs me around the waist, pulling me up against his body. "Mmm, I think I need to meditate a bit more then," he purrs in my ear while I struggle playfully in his arms. His breath is warm against my neck as he kisses just under my ear. "Unfortunately, that will have to wait until later. We have a job to do."

He doesn't sound the least bit happy about our current job, but he takes my hand and strides to the front porch. On cue the door opens before we even reach the top of the steps. Mrs. Anders appears with her scary crocodile smile. The smile combined with bright red lipstick makes her appear clownish. A tremor courses through my body. I hate clowns. Rebecca flinches beside me. Her head tips to the side as she regards our host through narrowed eyes.

"Oh, you brought more investigators," Mrs. Anders chirps, though I'm not sure if she's actually as happy about it as she sounds, given her scowl. "Rebecca and Carl, right?" Her lips turn down into a deep frown.

No she's definitely not happy to see them.

"Yes, Mrs. Anders. It's good to see you again," Rebecca says in a fake cheerful voice. "Carl and I are here to tape everything and to assist Logan and Kacie with their walkthrough."

Mrs. Anders steps aside and motions for us to enter. As we cross the threshold I'm somewhat surprised by the warm, inviting atmosphere. I'm not sure what I was expecting, but it certainly wasn't something out of a home decorating magazine. The foyer is bright and welcoming with a gorgeous chandelier casting light onto the many paintings decorating the walls on both sides. I turn my gaze from the pictures knowing they can influence what I sense in the house.

We follow the innkeeper into the large living room. Logan and I settle on a garish floral sofa while Rebecca and Carl set up the camera equipment. Mr. Anders is absent and my eyes fall to Mrs. Anders as she settles in an uncomfortable looking armchair.

"I have tarot cards, spirit boards, dousing rods, and a crystal ball," she says, her eyes sparkling in excitement. "I wasn't really sure what you'd need to do the séance."

"I think you misunderstood our reason for coming," Logan says unable to hide the disgust in his voice. "We aren't here to antagonize any spirits that may reside here. If there are any spirits left willing to communicate with us at all."

He's practically seething and I place my hand on his arm to try to calm him. Mrs. Anders may just be ignorant, not downright cruel or stupid. Perhaps she doesn't understand the potential harm those items pose.

"How often do you use those *things*?" he asks through a clenched jaw, his temper still not quite under control.

"Quite often actually," she answers, appearing oblivious to Logan's anger. "Our guests just love the séances. We've also been doing EVPs now since I saw it on a ghost show on TV." She puffs out her chest and flashes a rather smug grin. "I'm planning to offer a séance special for the month of November. Stay two nights, get a séance and ghost hunt free."

"Do you honestly believe the spirits are here for your amusement?" Logan asks in close to a growl.

She gives him an odd look, like she thinks he's a bit crazy. Before he can respond Rebecca cuts in.

"The equipment's set up, Logan," she says while glaring at Mrs. Anders. "Where do you want to begin?"

"Here's fine," he replies, gripping my arm. "Are you ready, Kacie?" His fingers dig into my arm just short of bruising.

"It'll be okay, Logan," I lean in to whisper in his ear.

The pressure on my forearm lessens. When I glance at him, he gives me an apologetic look while massaging my arm where he squeezed it. After taking a deep breath, I drop the shield blocking my senses from overload. I tense, waiting for the onslaught of spiritual energy.

Strange, there appears to be no residual energy here at all. I pick up something for a brief moment at the edge of my senses, but it's gone as quickly as it appeared. Rising from the sofa, I walk around the small living room searching for any trace of energy.

Nothing.

"It's strange, Logan," I say while circling the perimeter of the room. "The area outside is so alive with residual energy, yet there's absolutely nothing in here at all."

"Could the fire and the rebuilding affect residual energy?" Carl asks as he films me with the camera.

"Yes," Logan replies. "I'm sure that's what's happened here. It makes for a very clean house." He pauses and casts a surreptitious glance at the innkeeper. "Though it must be a downer when you actually want a haunting."

I can see his point. Most hauntings with bangs, creaks, and footsteps are residual energy reacting to the environment. Hauntings with a sentient spirit tend to be rarer, not to mention less predictable. Before Logan can continue, Rebecca's cell phone rings, breaking the awkward silence. She glances at the caller and sighs.

"Go for Rebecca," she says in a cheerful voice. Her face falls at whatever the caller is saying. "What's the address?" She repeats the address while Carl scribbles it down in his notebook. "I've got Logan and Kacie with me now. Don't do anything, we'll be right there, Mr. Kincaid." She ends the call and looks over at us. "We have a situation. Mr. and Mrs. Kincaid were doing a routine interview of a new client in Wooded Acres. Mrs. Kincaid collapsed after it seems she was mentally attacked by something. Mr. Kincaid is beside himself and completely clueless. He has her reclined in the car in the driveway. Dr. Hayes is in surgery and can't help. We need to go now!"

Carl has been packing the equipment he had set up only moments before during Rebecca's ramble.

"You're leaving?" Mrs. Anders asks in a dejected screech. "But I was so looking forward to the séance with two professionals." Logan looks ready to throttle the ignorant woman. "I even have wonderful refreshments for you."

"Mrs. Anders, we will be returning soon," I say in a calming tone. "However, I must ask that you refrain from any attempts to contact spirits until we do."

"Whatever for?" she asks in confusion.

Is she really this stupid or is it just me?

"Your attempts to contact spirits here could be creating a harmful environment." I manage to contain the loud sigh I feel trying to escape. "When we come back, we'll discuss everything in detail. We'll be in touch to set up another visit. I'm sorry."

She seems mollified, but I can't help thinking that toddlers would understand quicker than this dense woman.

"I'll be in contact, Mrs. Anders," Rebecca says after she finishes packing the remaining camera in its crate. "Hopefully we can return within the week."

Carl follows Rebecca to the door carrying the bulk of the equipment. I glance down at Logan who is staring off into space, deep in thought.

"Logan," I murmur, shaking his shoulder. "Are you ready to go?" He jumps then looks up at me startled. "Are you okay?"

"Yeah," he croaks, pushing himself up off the sofa. "I was caught up in a very bad... how do I put this? It wasn't a vision, more like a premonition, a very bad feeling. Something has been set in motion, something monstrous..."

He trails off as I lead him to the foyer by the hand. He still hasn't recovered from whatever happened. In fact he seems more disconcerted now than when I first broke his reverie. We emerge from the inn hand in hand, though I'm more dragging Logan than walking beside him. When Mrs. Anders closes the door behind us he stops and pulls me into his arms.

"Be careful, Kacie," he whispers, laying his cheek on my head. "Whatever is going to happen, I know you're somehow involved." I gasp in dismay and his arms tighten around me. "I'll protect you, I promise."

"Come on you two, we need to hurry," Rebecca yells from the curb. She and Carl have finished loading the equipment into the back of the black van. "You have GPS?" she asks Logan as we walk over to his Mustang. When he nods, she hands him a slip of paper with an address. "We'll see you there."

While Logan stares at the paper in his hand, Rebecca jumps into the van, and Carl takes off down the street.

"Are you ready, Logan?" I ask when he continues to lean against the side of his car.

He nods and unlocks the doors. "Don't worry, we'll still beat them there," he says, starting the engine. "Carl drives like my grandma." He chuckles as he pulls out into traffic, heading to the freeway and Wooded Acres.

13
Foxblood Manor

~

Wooded Acres lies about fifteen minutes north of downtown. Traffic is light and we make good time as Logan drives up the freeway, far faster than he should. Restaurants and motels flash by in a blur giving my mind time to contemplate what happened to Mrs. Kincaid. Though I try to explore various possibilities, running the gamut from food poisoning to demonic possession, my mind keeps circling back to the worst case scenario.

Was she really attacked by an evil spirit? I've run into plenty of mischievous spirits, maybe even some that one would consider downright bad. In all my life though, I've never had a run in with a demonic spirit—hell, I'm not even sure they exist. Though, if TV shows have it right, demons are everywhere, possessing unsuspecting people and requiring a very dramatic exorcism each and every time. As Logan eases the Mustang off the freeway, turning toward the mass of dark trees to our left, my stomach clenches. Just when I'm about to write it off as too much Mexican food, the hair on my arms rises to attention.

"Bad vibes," I murmur, glancing at him to see if he feels it too.

His entire body shakes like a dog sloughing off water. "No kidding."

Enormous iron gates block the entrance to Wooded Acres, guarding the residents within from the common riffraff of the outside world. There's no guard, only a small inconspicuous call box. Logan pulls up next to the box and quickly enters the code Rebecca scribbled on the paper with the address. The massive gates begin to open, making no noise, though my mind hears a raspy grating followed by a long creak as they continue swinging open.

We pass through the imposing entrance. I press my nose against the cool window as the first grand manor comes into view. It's amazing, all lit up with dramatic lighting. Long winding roads are lined with untouched forests—the only sign of civilization the majestic mansions peeking out from within the trees.

As we continue farther into Wooded Acres, even the houses disappear, leaving only periodic driveways disappearing into the veil of trees. A deer darts out in front of the car, and Logan slams on the brakes narrowly missing it. The doe is followed by an eight point buck and an adorable spotted fawn. They race across the road after the doe, disappearing into the oak trees.

Logan accelerates again, but drives much slower now, his attention riveted to the road. At the end of the long, snaky street we arrive at a small turnaround and a single gravel driveway. A wooden sign next to the drive declares this to be Foxblood Manor.

Eww, why would someone name their house that?

"Here we are," Logan murmurs followed by a breathy exhale. "Not very welcoming is it?"

Something about this place feels wrong. Waves of dread wash over me, undulating like a water moccasin slipping through the murky depths of a marsh. Evil has left its mark here. We exchange a worried glance before he pulls into the driveway, creeping along the ill-kept gravel road. Tree branches scrape along the roof of the car, making me wince with not only fear but anxiety.

"Damn trees. If this sorry excuse for a driveway doesn't kill my suspension, the trees will destroy my paint job," Logan mutters under his breath.

The car jostles and jolts as we continue to roll down the pothole-ridden road. Just when I'm beginning to wonder if this winding drive will ever end, the headlights illuminate a break in the trees. As we enter the massive clearing, Logan steers over to the black sedan parked near the tree line where a small group of people gathers around the passenger door. I recognize Devon and Mr. Kincaid from the meeting Monday, but the other man and woman are a mystery. Logan leaps from the car the moment it's parked and races over to Mr. Kincaid.

"How is she?" he asks in a hushed whisper.

The small group parts to allow us access to the car. Mrs. Kincaid is reclined in the passenger seat, eyes closed. She looks asleep, though the expression on her face is anything but peaceful. Her eyes dart around beneath her eyelids like she's caught in a terrible nightmare, trapped and unable to escape. Tiny moans escape her lips every few seconds. When a load moan is followed by a piercing shriek, I jump in fear.

"Mr. Kincaid, tell us exactly what happened," Logan orders in a very calm voice, though given the wild look in his eyes, he is anything but calm.

"We came out here at the request of Beth and Bob Carter. They just bought this place several months ago," Mr. Kincaid says, running his hand through his messy dark hair. "Everything was fine. Anna said things were very quiet, she wasn't picking up any spirit activity on the grounds, not even residual. She figured someone did a thorough cleansing."

He pauses when Mrs. Kincaid moans again, thrashing around in the car seat. Her eyes fly open but the blue orbs appear unseeing, or at least not seeing our world. I hate to think about what terrible nightmare she may be embroiled within. Only when Mrs. Kincaid finally quiets and her eyes close does he continue his narration.

"We hadn't been in the barn around back more than a minute or two before she let out a scream. It was the most terrifying, chilling scream I've ever heard…" he trails off, his face turning ashen from the memory.

Headlights illuminate the area around us as a dark SUV screeches to a halt just feet away. Michelle emerges from the driver's seat, her face pale and pinched with worry. She races to Mrs. Kincaid's side, kneeling in the hard gravel of the driveway. Placing her hands on either side of the comatose woman's head, she closes her eyes and appears to go into a trance. We wait in silence while Michelle rocks back and forth, moaning and whimpering.

Icy tendrils of fear shoot through my veins as the seconds turn into minutes. Numerous emotions race across Michelle's face, one after the other, too close together to begin deciphering. Though, one stands out much more than the others. Terror. Stomach clenching, throat closing, silent screaming panic. When you become aware there'll be no escape—that moment when all hope dies.

Logan pulls me into his arms, and I hide my face against his shoulder. The look in Michelle's eyes is all too familiar, bringing back scores of painful memories best left buried. The roar of an engine breaks the oppressive silence followed by the blinding glare of headlights. Rebecca and Carl have finally arrived. Logan wasn't kidding when he said Carl drove like a grandma. They leap from the van, racing to our side. When I glance at Rebecca, whatever she was about to say sticks in her throat. Her mouth opens and closes a few times, like a grouper, before she slams it closed with an audible click.

"Kacie, you look terrified," Carl says in a high-pitched, shaky voice. "What's going on?"

"We don't know yet," Logan murmurs. "Michelle's still in her trance. It isn't good… not based on her facial expressions anyway."

"But Kacie," Rebecca says, staring at me. "What's wrong with Kacie?"

Swallowing around the hard lump that formed in my throat, I try to speak, to say I'm fine. Logan silences me before I can begin to utter platitudes.

"We need to know what's wrong," he says, nuzzling my hair. "It's important that we don't keep secrets from the Circle during an investigation."

"Even the smallest, seemingly insignificant detail can be important," Rebecca adds. "Anything you tell us is strictly confidential and won't be shared outside the Circle."

"I have a strong feeling of déjà vu," I say in a soft whisper, glancing at the darkened land around us. Taking a deep breath, I try to stop my racing heart from beating right out of my chest. "My mind is screaming at my body to run, to escape before it's too late. It started when I was watching the different expressions crossing Michelle's face."

"Have you been here before?" Carl asks the obvious question.

"No, I'm sure I haven't," I reply, as I fight the familiar sensations, "not in body anyway." Three pairs of eyes stare at me in confusion, waiting for me to clarify my ambiguous statement. "I think I've been here in my recurring nightmare."

The second the words leave my mouth, I'm overwhelmed by intense waves of nausea. Nightmare images flash through my mind. My knees buckle—Logan's arms around me the only thing keeping me from collapsing to the ground. A sharp pain stabs through my head, and I close my eyes in a desperate attempt to banish the blinding agony. Hot tears burn my cheeks as I succumb to the debilitating pain.

"Kacie, stop thinking about your vision," Logan says, his voice sounding like it's far away, down a long tunnel. "Focus on my voice, forget everything else. Ah hell…"

Logan buries his fingers in my hair, pulling my head away from his shoulder. His lips descend on mine in a tender caress, drawing my attention away from my internal demons. Winding my arms around his neck, I cling to him like he's the only thing anchoring me in this stormy chaos. The pain in my head recedes along with all coherent thought. His lips move up my cheeks, kissing away the tears before returning to claim my lips again. He shares the salty taste of my tears as his tongue dances with mine.

"I would've slapped her, but this works too," Rebecca says, snorting in a failed attempt to hide her laughter. "You may want to consider stopping now. Just saying…"

"Hey, Rebecca," Carl says in a choked voice. "You sure you don't need some help too?"

"This really isn't the time for jokes," Rebecca says.

There's a dull *thud* that I assume was Rebecca hitting Carl for his ridiculous suggestion. I pull back a bit, and Logan leans down, resting his forehead against mine.

"You better now?" he asks in a husky whisper.

"Yeah," I manage to reply through my closed throat. Taking several deep breaths, I stop myself from grasping at the lingering wisps of memory. "That was… um… thanks."

"I wish a girl would thank me for kissing her," Carl whines.

"You'd just be lucky if she doesn't hit you," Rebecca retorts, adding a kick to Carl's shin to prove her point.

A shrill scream draws our attention back to Michelle and Mrs. Kincaid. Michelle pulls away from

Mrs. Kincaid, her breath coming in pained gasps. She stumbles backward away from the car, her body bent over as she vomits the contents of her stomach on an unsuspecting bush.

"Crap, crap, crap!" Rebecca cries, racing to Michelle's side. She supports the girl's body, leading her over to lean against a tree. "Don't just stand there, Carl. Help me!"

While Michelle continues to dry heave against the tree, Mrs. Kincaid opens her eyes. She peers around as if confused, taking in the worried faces before closing her eyes once more. It's so quiet. Standing amid the trees I expect to hear insects chirping, perhaps the occasional barn owl, or deer rustling through the forest. There's nothing but the sounds of my companions: Logan's soft breathing, Michelle's quick gasps, and now a low keening from Mrs. Kincaid.

"Demon," Mrs. Kincaid whispers, her eyes still closed.

"Demon," Michelle echoes in a faint whimper.

"Demon? As in Dante's Inferno, Christian Hell, Devil spawn?" Rebecca asks, her voice failing to conceal her doubt.

"Evil takes many forms," Mr. Kincaid says while cradling his wife in his arms. "Labels are merely an attempt to classify something impossible to comprehend. We'll meet at my house tomorrow afternoon to discuss this investigation."

"Um, is it safe for us to stay here?" Bob Carter asks. He and his wife had been so quiet during the entire episode. I almost forgot they were here.

"Do you have somewhere else you can stay?" Devon asks, taking charge when Mr. Kincaid continues to fuss over his wife.

"Yeah, we haven't sold our other house yet," Beth Carter says.

"I'd recommend staying there until we have more information," Devon says, his worried eyes trained on Michelle, still huddled on the ground next to the tree. "We'll contact you tomorrow after our meeting."

Mr. and Mrs. Carter both nod their agreement before walking toward the dark house in the distance. Devon races to Michelle's side, pulling her into his arms and carrying her to the still-running SUV.

"I'll take Michelle home," Devon says, placing the girl in the passenger seat. "Text me with the time of the meeting tomorrow."

We watch in silence as the SUV takes off down the winding drive, kicking up gravel in its wake. My mind races with questions. But worse are the answers hidden somewhere deep within me, tickling my psyche. Each time I pull at the wispy images, my stomach clenches in pain, forcing me to tear my thoughts back to the present. Unfortunately, no matter how hard I try, my mind drifts back to the black and white dream images.

"I told you to stop," Logan says, his arm creeping across my shoulders. "Don't pursue those dream images now. You'll only get sick."

"Yeah, I kinda figured that out on my own," I reply, gasping as another wave of nausea hits. "Easier said than done," I murmur between clenched teeth.

"I'd like you four to go back the King's Ransom Inn and complete the investigation tonight," Mr. Kincaid says, drawing my attention away from my internal struggle.

"But, sir, shouldn't we be doing something about this?" Rebecca asks, waving her arm in a sweeping motion at the property bathed in darkness.

"Not tonight," he replies, his voice thready and weak. "There's something big here. We'll need to prepare before anyone returns to this property. Let's clear up our other investigations so we can all concentrate on whatever is going on here."

"Evil," Mrs. Kincaid's voice floats over from the car.

"I need to get her out of here," Mr. Kincaid says before his eyes drift back to the car. "Meet at my house tomorrow afternoon at four."

"Yes, sir," Rebecca chirps with a two fingered salute.

"Go, now. I'm not leaving until I see the taillights of your cars heading back up the drive," he says, crossing his arms over his chest. "Just in case you have any ideas of investigating without supervision."

Logan takes my arm, leading me to his Mustang. He opens the passenger door, waiting until I'm inside to close it. The act of chivalry is both amusing and sweet. He's treating me like I'm made of glass. Funny thing is, at this moment in time, he may be right. My jaw is clenched, my hands fisted at my sides, and I can't stop shaking. Perhaps a hard blow would shatter me into a million pieces…

14

Freak Show

~

When the Mustang pulls up in front of the inn, Mrs. Anders awaits us at the curb.

"Can you say *freak show?*" I whisper. "The headlights make her look even creepier… as if that's possible."

"I wasn't thinking," Logan says, pulling the car over but keeping the odd woman bathed in the lights. "I should've stayed with Carl. I wonder how far back he is."

"Why is she out here waiting?"

"I assume Rebecca called to let her know we were coming back," he says, turning off the engine.

"Okay, but again, why is she out here in the cold, with no jacket?" I ask after glancing at the green dash display. "It's fifty-two degrees out here, she must be freezing in short sleeves."

"Kacie, if that's the strangest thing we deal with tonight, I'll be happy," Logan says, flashing me a grin. "Let's go talk to the crazy lady."

"All she needs are a few cats to hurl at us…"

"Simpsons fan?" Logan asks.

"What gave it away?"

Logan opens his door, unfolding his lean body from the bucket seat. With a ragged sigh, I throw the door open a little harder than necessary, and push myself out of the deep seat. Mrs. Anders rushes over, a wild glimmer in her eyes.

"I'm so glad you returned," she gushes while bouncing up and down. She looks like a kid waiting in line for the ice cream truck.

"I'm glad we were able to return so quickly," Logan says in a calm tone.

He seems to have a flair for dealing with annoying people. I remain silent since anything I say would be rude. With any luck the bizarre woman will ignore me.

My stomach settled the moment we left Foxblood Manor. But the phantom images left along with the pain. Strange, no matter how hard I try, the images that were so clear while we were there are nothing but a wispy memory now. I try once more to grab at a tenuous image only to have it dart away deeper into my mind.

"So, Kacie was it?" Mrs. Anders asks, turning to face me, her wide eyes unblinking. She looks like a spooky owl. "You seem a bit edgy."

Edgy, really? No way in hell am I explaining the million ways I've been put on edge tonight. This crazy harpy is making a bad night ten times worse. *Oh God! Do harpies exist?* I glance at the manic woman from the corner of my eye, watching her shake and bounce. No wings are visible, so probably not a real harpy. Besides, she's fixated on me, and if I remember my mythology correctly, harpies go after guys.

Just as I'm cursing my never-ending bad luck, I hear the roar of the van pull up to the curb. My eyes haven't left Mrs. Anders for at least thirty rapid heartbeats. She still hasn't blinked. What is going on? Or maybe more apt, what is she on? I whisper my suspicions to Logan, and he regards her with a cold glare.

"Well, Mrs. Anders, I'm so glad we were able to make it back tonight," Rebecca says from behind me. I jump, startled by her voice.

"Oh, Rebecca, you've returned too," Mrs. Anders says, her voice hard. *Now who's edgy?* "Come, Kacie, let's go inside while your friends get together all that strange equipment."

She tries to grab my arm, but Logan moves between us, placing my hand on his arm. Wrapping my arm around his biceps, I smile up at him, relief flooding me. He gives me a big grin followed by a sly wink. Mrs. Anders whips around and takes off toward the front door.

"She really freak you out that much?" Carl asks, peeking his head out of the back of the van.

"It's fine, Carl," Rebecca says with a loud sigh. "Just get the equipment and let's wrap up this circus sideshow."

"You okay with us staying here tonight?" Logan asks after pulling me away from the others.

"Yeah, as long as I don't have to be alone," I reply, refusing to allow that bat-crap crazy woman to keep me from completing my first Circle assignment.

"Hmm, is that an invitation?" he purrs against my ear.

My eyes blink a few times while I process his words. I'm terrified and he's making a joke? Though part of me wants to throttle him, deep down I know it must be his way of dealing with a difficult situation.

"Maybe not the best time for a joke," he chuckles when I glare at him.

"Ya think?" Rebecca says, pushing past us to stomp toward the door. "Oh wait, stupid question."

"Rebecca, aren't you gonna help with all this stuff?" Carl whines from the curb.

"I'm sure Romeo will help you," Rebecca says over her shoulder. "He needs something else to occupy his hands."

Logan freezes at her words, one hand entwined in my hair and the other at the small of my back. I glance up into his shocked eyes, watching the blush spread across his tanned cheeks. My lips curl into a smile, and I lean up to peck him lightly on the lips.

"You look so adorable right now," I whisper against his mouth before pulling away and following Rebecca to the door.

"Way to leave him wanting more," Rebecca whispers as I join her on the porch.

While that wasn't my intention, when I glance back at Logan, my heart leaps at the intense look of longing in his eyes. Celia would be proud. Rebecca snorts her laughter when Carl whines again for help, snapping Logan's attention away from me.

"Damn, girl," Rebecca murmurs. "You need to teach me how to do that."

"I wish I knew myself," I mumble in reply.

My gaze is torn from Logan's tall form when the front door flies open with a loud *creak*. The hallway beyond the door is empty. Maybe the wind blew it open. When I run my fingers along the dark wood, I gasp under my breath. It's a brand new door with inventory stickers still pasted on the inner frame. I wonder how they managed to get it to creak like that.

"Old hinges," Rebecca whispers the answer to my unspoken question. "All the doors in the house have them."

"That's just plain weird," I comment, wondering why someone would go through a remodel just to use old rusty hinges on new doors.

"This is only part of the weird," Rebecca says in a conspiratorial whisper. "Once the bat and her husband go to sleep, I'll fill you in."

"Is it anything I should know before opening myself to the spirits?" I ask, not sure if Rebecca understands the dangers a medium faces. Lack of information is seldom a good thing.

"Oh, no. Don't worry," she says, placing her hand on my shoulder. "It's more about the changes she made during the remodel. Weird secret passages with spy holes looking into the rooms… that sort of freaky thing. Oh, and you'd expect the place to have new wiring, right? Well it doesn't. Makes the lighting a bit erratic at times, not to mention it screws with the EMF."

My curiosity is piqued. It's like Mr. and Mrs. Anders created a haunted attraction rather than an inn.

"They also didn't fix the floorboards before putting in the new carpeting, so the stairs creak a lot," Rebecca adds in a whisper.

Standing next to Rebecca on the porch, I watch Logan and Carl lug the equipment from the van. My pulse leaps when Mrs. Anders appears again. She's like some scary English butler, skulking in the shadows and popping up when needed. We follow the guys into the living room, watching as they deposit the equipment on the coffee table.

"I feel like we just did this," Carl mutters under his breath.

"I'll set up the spirit board on the table," Mrs. Anders says in a dramatic whisper.

She glides from the room, leaving behind a cloud of her cloying perfume. Covering my nose, I glance at my friends, wondering if I'm the only one affected by the eye-watering scent. Carl lets out a loud sneeze. Nope I'm not alone. She breezes back into the room, the board tucked under one arm and a reluctant Mr. Anders towed by the other.

It's odd. Mr. Anders has a look of... I don't know... perhaps fear... in his eyes. I watch his gaze dart between his wife and the tray in his hands. As edgy as I am right now, I know what edgy looks like, and that man in most definitely edgy. Maybe he doesn't like spirits.

He places a tray of lemonade on the table and pours glasses for everyone. I drain my glass in seconds and he pours me another. We watch in silence while Mrs. Anders sets up the board on the dining room table. I keep waiting for Logan to say something. We aren't going to let her use the board, are we? My pulse races at the thought. Nothing good comes from opening a portal. If Mrs. Anders uses the board the same way most people do, we may be in for a dangerous night.

"Okay, it's all ready," Mrs. Anders says in an excited whisper.

We join her around the long, oak table. Our host sits at the end with her husband to her right. The spirit board is ancient, beautiful. It looks like an antique. I wonder how many spirits have been called across the veil with her board. The planchette is light ivory in color, almost white. Marble I hope. My mind whispers *bone*, and a shiver races through my body.

Logan takes my hand under the table, caressing my knuckles. My psychic power reacts to his touch, flaring to life. Though I've never been able to see auras before, I watch my blue aura tangle with Logan's red. A strange fuzziness fills my head, but when I shake it, the feeling disappears as quickly as it appeared.

"Without touching the planchette, tell me how you usually go about using the spirit board," Logan says as his fingers tighten around mine.

I have to stifle a laugh at the grave expression in his narrowed eyes. He's glaring at the board like it might leap from the table and attack. The angry red aura swirls around him in pulsating waves. Mrs. Anders stares at the board for several moments then her hand snakes out toward the planchette, stopping in mid-grasp. She makes a fist then places both hands in her lap.

"Okay, well, uh. Are there any spirits that wish to communicate?" she calls out in a theatrical voice.

"Stop," Logan shouts making the stupid woman flinch. "What you just said should never be said."

"I don't understand," Mrs. Anders says, her eyebrows arching above her bangs.

"You just invited anyone around to invade your home," Logan says, shaking his head. When she still looks confused, he sits back and stares. "Would you waltz into a prison and invite all the convicts to visit?"

"Of course not!" she replies as her cheeks turn red.

"What makes you think that all spirits are good?" I ask, meeting her shocked gaze. "People are good and bad, so it makes sense that spirits would be that way too."

"Not only that, but there are some truly malicious entities out there just waiting for some poor, unsuspecting sap to invite them in," Logan adds. He pulls his hand from mine and crosses his arms over his chest. "Now care to tell us what's really going on here? I may not know you, but I've been doing investigations since I was five. Something isn't right here."

Mrs. Anders stares at the table, her mouth in a thin, grim line. Her husband rises from the table and darts from the room without a word.

Just what the hell is going on here?

Rising from the table, I wander from the ornate dining room back to the comfier living room. The ceilings are low as was the norm a century ago, but it feels stifling now that I'm used to the twelve foot ceilings in my house. As I pass the ugly floral sofa, a strange feeling flows through my entire body.

"Logan," I call out in a hoarse whisper.

"What is it?" he asks when he arrives at my side. I turn my head to glance at him, and he gasps. "My God, you're so pale! Are you okay?"

Unable to reply, I shake my head. Vertigo seizes me from the motion, and I shut my eyes in the hopes that the room will stop spinning. My heart hammers, each rapid beat echoing painfully in my ears. Logan helps me over to the sofa, and I collapse against the garish fabric. Within moments my stomach roils as my nose fills with more of the cloying perfume Mrs. Anders seems to love so much. The entire couch reeks of the stuff. My head reels. Coughs wrack my body, and I clutch at my stomach.

"The EMF is going crazy!" Carl shouts. "How can that be? There was no activity at all last week."

"Logan, what's wrong with her?" I hear Rebecca's voice, yet it sounds so distant, like she's speaking through a paper tube.

"I need to get her outside," Logan says before picking me up in his arms.

He cradles me against his chest and races to the door. Once outside, he lays me down on the ground under the willow tree. I roll to my side, rubbing my fevered cheek against the cool grass. Now that the perfume is gone, I take deep cleansing breaths. Logan runs his fingers through my hair, the gentle strokes soothing.

"I think I know what's going on now," I murmur, my throat raw from coughing.

"It's not paranormal," Logan says, releasing a small growl of frustration. "Other than a raging headache, I didn't sense anything paranormal."

"I found the source of the EMF spike," Carl yells, running from the house. "Mr. Anders was playing with all sorts of electronics and generating the spike."

"Rebecca, call Mr. Kincaid," I say, pushing myself to a sitting position. "That smell I thought was perfume, it made me sick. I think it's some sort of incense she's using to try to make us hallucinate. That and the lemonade. I drank more than the rest of you…"

"Crap," Logan mutters, glancing toward the house. "She was so desperate for a paranormal business rating, she tried drugging us?"

We listen as Rebecca relates our suspicions to Mr. Kincaid, her voice reaching a fever pitch before she's through.

"He said to call an ambulance and the police," Rebecca says as she dials her phone. "We don't know what she may have drugged us with…"

She continues ranting at the dispatcher, but her voice becomes more and more distant. Black spots swim in my vision. A sharp pain lances through my skull, but when I try to grasp my head with my hands, I realize I can't move my arms.

My pulse races as panic sets in. I turn my head to look at Logan, and my vision narrows. Blackness takes over, and my frenzied mind is dragged into nothingness.

15

Nightmares

⌒

Everything hurts. My arms are wrenched behind my back, and I'm curled up in the fetal position on my side. When I try to move, to ease my screaming muscles, I realize my arms are tied together. Panic surges through me as I squirm against my bonds. Shivers race along my body from the frigid cold. A sharp pain bites into my cheek. As I shift my head, I realize a small rock is embedded in my cheek. My eyes open to inky darkness. Though I can hear shuffling and scraping, I can't see anything. My heart races and I choke back a sob.

Where am I?

Light flares to life, burning my eyes and leaving me blind for several moments. When I can see again, I cringe at the ghastly vision. Several spirits surround me in vivid corporeal form. They appear as they did in death—bloody, mutilated, bright images of a horrible tragedy. I recognize the raven-haired girl. I've seen her broken body numerous times in my nightmares. She teeters on legs shattered beyond any hope of repair were she still alive.

Two spirits flank her, both boys around ten years old. Their forms are so solid, they appear alive, but the grievous injuries make it clear these boys couldn't possibly be among the living. No one could survive such extensive injury. One boy's head hangs to his shoulder, only attached by a band of sinew. His blond hair is soaked in blood where it brushes his chest. Bile rises in my throat. I wonder if I can vomit during a vision.

My eyes move to observe the other boy. It's hard to tell anything about him because his face has been destroyed. The right side is concave and his nose is missing. Gulping down a breath of air, I hold it in, willing the overwhelming nausea away.

It's just a vision. I repeat this over and over in my head until I can breathe again.

"Help us," the girl rasps in a voice that sounds like she's gargling gravel. "He won't stop hurting us. You can save us. Please!"

"I'm so scared," the boy with the dangling head whispers. "He's getting worse. What will happen if he destroys our souls?"

"I-I don't—" Before I can continue, an angry voice cuts me off.

168

"You left!" The accusation comes from the boy with the smashed face. His voice echoes all around me, loud, furious. "You were here and you left! You left us alone with the monster. How could you?"

"Where?" I ask in a hoarse whisper, flinching at the raw pain that sears through my throat. "Where are you?"

"Be quiet!" the girl orders in a whisper. "He'll hear us."

"Who will hear you?" I ask becoming desperate. "Where are you?"

"The manor," the girl replies, her head darting around in frantic movements. "He's coming!"

"What manor? Who's coming?" I ask in an urgent whisper.

"Foxbl—" The girl disappears in a flash before she can finish.

"Kassandra Ramsey," a deep male voice says from the shadows. "How nice to see you here. You can't help them, you know. Soon you will belong to me and my reign of terror on the mortal plane will begin."

"Who are you?" I shout to be heard above the sinister cackling. Someone has been watching too many melodramatic old movie villains. "What do you want?"

"You, my dear," the voice says in my ear.

I jump, trying to scramble away from the phantom's breath against my face. With my arms tied behind my back I don't get far. A hoarse scream leaves my throat, but it seems to make my tormentor laugh harder. Pain sears through my ankle, such horrible pressure. I can feel the outline of fingers ending in what feels like sharp claws.

"Soon, Kassandra, soon." The dark voice is hollow in my ears as I slip into blessed unconsciousness.

16

Repercussions

~

Pain lances through my head. Sharp, shooting sensations. Darkness replaced by light, and yet...

Why can't I see anything?

Voices, loud mumbling. I can't understand the words. Shouting... so much yelling. Dad... I can hear him—his voice is soft, muted. But the deep grumbling male voice, the one that hurts so much... who is he and why won't he shut up?

"Quiet," I whisper in a raspy voice. "Hurts..." I want to tell them what hurts but the words won't come out.

"She's awake," Dad says in an urgent whisper. "Call the nurse."

Feet shuffle. More whispers, mumbled words I can't hear. But at least they aren't yelling anymore.

A hand grips mine, so warm on my chilled skin. My throat burns when I swallow. Need water.

"Open your eyes, pumpkin," Dad orders in that tone he uses when he expects to be obeyed.

"Water," I croak out as I try to lift my heavy eyelids.

Something cold and wet touches my lips. A small ice chip slides past my lips to melt on my tongue. As the water drips down my parched throat, I almost cry in relief. Before I can ask for another, one brushes against my mouth.

I manage to crack my eyes open, and immediately wish I hadn't. The light is so bright shining off the white walls and ceiling of the room. *Hospital,* my mind whispers. Blinking against the blinding glare, my eyes focus on the face hovering above mine. I expect to see my dad, but am surprised to see Logan instead. He holds another ice chip to my lips, and I suck it into my mouth.

"What h-happened?" I ask now that my throat no longer feels like sandpaper.

"Don't answer that, Logan," that annoying male voice says. I try to look around for the source, but my neck ignores my command to move. "We don't want you influencing her version of events."

"Look, Detective, you need to come back tomorrow," Dad says in an angry tone. "She's in no shape to answer any questions. She just woke up for Christ's sake."

Before I can ask what's going on, a nurse shows up and tries in vain to shoo the hulking man away. He stands his ground, staring at her with a hard glare. Tall and thin, he's dressed in a rumpled brown suit that I'm pretty sure he slept in. The nurse fusses with the IV while muttering under her breath about annoying detectives.

"Okay, quit your hovering," the nurse orders. Dad and Logan don't move an inch from my bedside. The nurse sighs and shakes her head. "She'll be fine now that she's awake. The doctor has been called and will be here in a few minutes."

"Logan, you can't stay here," the detective says after clearing his throat a bit too loud. "If I can't question her now, you can't be around her unsupervised until I do."

"He can and will stay here," Dad bites back. "While his parents are away, I'm acting as his guardian in this mess."

"Just ask your stupid questions," I murmur with an exasperated sigh. "Get it over with."

"Not until the doctor okays it," Dad insists, crossing his arms over his chest.

"No, Dad, I want to get it over now," I reply, pleased that my voice is stronger. "I don't remember much anyway."

The detective wastes no time after Dad shrugs his shoulders in defeat. "From the time you returned to the bed & breakfast after meeting with Roger Kincaid, what do you remember?"

"I remember Mrs. Anders was acting creepy, like she was on edge," I say, cringing at the pain shooting through my head. After taking a couple deep breaths I continue. "We went inside and there was this cloying smell, like perfume or incense…"

I trail off when Logan's fingers tighten around mine. Glancing at him from the corner of my eye, I notice an almost imperceptible shake of his head. He doesn't want me talking about the smell. I wonder why.

"We, uh, sat down in the dining room, and Mr. Anders brought in a pitcher of lemonade." Logan's grip loosens a bit, and he rubs his other hand along my forearm. "I was really thirsty and drank a glass immediately. Soon after I started feeling weird. Nauseous. My brain was so fuzzy I couldn't concentrate. My head was spinning."

"She collapsed on the sofa, and I carried her outside," Logan says when I don't continue.

"Why did you take her outside?" the detective asks. "Seems strange. Wouldn't you just leave her on the couch and call 911?"

"Normally, yeah," Logan says, his voice steady and sure.

I already know the answer. It was the incense. He was trying to get me away from it. But that seems to be a taboo subject.

"But after our hosts acted so strange, I didn't want to stay in the house," he says shrugging his shoulders. "At least outside we'd be in the public eye. The Queen Anne District is full of tourists that time of night on the weekend, including a ghost tour just down the street. I needed to get my team to safety, and at the time, outside seemed safer than inside."

"You have good instincts," the detective says as he snaps his notepad closed.

"Well, I think you have all you need, detective," a female voice says from the doorway. "Kacie will contact you if she remembers anything else."

My eyes widen when the detective nods his head and exits the room without another word. Dad stares at the new arrival like she's the most fascinating thing he's ever seen. She is quite beautiful. Long blonde hair flows past her shoulders in a mass of large waves. Tiny crinkles frame her blue eyes when she smiles at me. A stethoscope hangs around her neck. The white coat tells me she's a doctor. This is confirmed when she steps closer. Her name badge says Tammy Hayes, M.D. Northern Central Hospital.

Logan leans over and whispers in my ear. "She has the power of persuasion." I suck in a surprised breath. Does he mean literally, like a magic power?

"Ah, Mr. Ramsey, it's so good to see you again," Dr. Hayes says in a sing-song voice. The cadence is odd—musical and mesmerizing. "You should head to the cafeteria and get some decent coffee. That machine sludge isn't drinkable."

"I should go get some coffee," Dad says in a dull monotone. Before I can say a word, he's out the door.

"That's amazing!" I exclaim. "What a great power."

"Not so much, actually," she replies in a normal voice. "Before I learned to control it, I never knew if it was me or my power people liked."

"Dr. Hayes is a member of the Orion Circle," Logan says while his thumb brushes over the back of my hand. The motion seems nervous. Maybe he's afraid of what she might make him do against his will. "Dr. Hayes, this is our newest member, Kacie."

"It's nice to see you awake, Kacie," she says, glancing up from my chart. "How does your head feel? Still fuzzy or hazy?"

"It hurts, but no, it's not fuzzy anymore," I say, rubbing my temples the moment I'm reminded of the pain.

"Good. Look here, follow the light." My eyes blink against the bright light. "I'm sorry, I know it hurts." I follow the light, and she clicks it off several long moments later. "Your pupils are responding normally. That's good news." The scratching of her pen on the chart echoes in the room. "Your hearing and light sensitivity may be a touch more acute for a day or so. It's a side effect of the witch's bane incense she used." At my blank look, she adds, "It's a mixture of herbs and flowers that are especially effective on females of certain talents."

"Why only women?" I ask.

"Something to do with the smell receptors in the brain of males versus females. What bothers me most is that she not only knew how to make it, but she had the audacity to use it." Dr. Hayes snaps the chart closed and hangs it on the end of the bed. "The Circle will investigate this. Though the police aren't aware of the incense due to the supernatural nature, she and her husband spiked the lemonade with flunitrazepam, also known as one of the date rape drugs. You got a large dose. Between that and the incense, you're lucky to be awake. Both can cause coma and death in an overdose."

"Why would she do that?" I ask in a hoarse whisper. It's horrifying to think what might have happened if I drank that second glass of juice.

"They both cause hallucinations in small doses," Dr. Hayes says. She pauses, glancing toward the open door. In a lower voice she adds, "Logan thinks she was desperate enough for the haunted inn rating that she drugged you to get it. He said you figured it out before you passed out."

My jaw drops. "So she wanted me to hallucinate a ghost?" I ask, unable to get my mind around it. What kind of person would drug someone for something so asinine?

"All of us," Logan reminds me. "My head is still killing me, and I only had half a glass. Fortunately Carl didn't drink any and Rebecca only had a few sips. They're both fine."

"I don't remember anything other than that awful incense," I murmur, rubbing my temples with my fingertips. "Whenever I try, it hurts too much."

"The police don't deal in the supernatural. Most cops don't even want to discuss it. I have no idea what their reasoning will be for the Anders' actions," Dr. Hayes says with a shrug. "It's easier to keep it a secret rather than muddying the waters with things they don't comprehend."

She pauses, tilting her head toward the door. My father's voice carries through the open door as he speaks with someone right outside.

"All right, young lady," Dr. Hayes says as my father walks through the door. "We're going to keep you under observation overnight. If you eat your meals and show no signs of vertigo or lightheadedness then I'll discharge you either this afternoon or early evening." She stops in front of Dad before leaving the room. "I wanted to thank you for allowing your daughter to be part of the Orion Circle. Not only will it teach her essential skills such as leadership, but it will look amazing on her college transcripts. The Circle has friends in the registrar of most major universities."

She shakes his hand and walks out the door. Dad stares after her hypnotized. I think he's feeling something beyond her simple compulsion skill. It's kind of cute in a disturbing way.

"I'm going to head out, Kacie," Logan says, squeezing my hand. "The Circle needs to meet tomorrow to discuss some important business. If it's all right with you Mr. Ramsey, we'll meet at your house at four p.m. so Kacie doesn't have to travel."

"Hmm," Dad mutters, still staring at the vacant door Dr. Hayes passed through. "Oh, yes, that's very thoughtful."

His words shock me. I thought he'd be livid about the incident last night… wait was it last night?

"Um… what day is it?" I ask in a tentative whisper.

"It's Saturday, for the last eleven minutes at least," Logan says, glancing at his watch. "You weren't out as long as the doctor feared you might be."

"Oh, good," I say with a relieved sigh. "Where's the control for the bed? I want to sit up." Dad hands me the remote, and I hold down the incline button. The bed *whirrs* as it adjusts to the new position. "So when you say tomorrow, you mean…"

"Sunday," Logan says, kissing my forehead. "I'll see you soon."

"Thanks for taking care of my daughter, Logan," Dad says, placing a hand on his shoulder. "Drive safely and call when you get home."

"You're welcome," Logan says. "It's only a fifteen minute drive. I'll be fine. Thanks." With a wave, he's out the door.

"I mean it, Logan, call me," Dad calls after him.

I settle back against the pillows and turn on the television. Might as well get comfortable until the doctor is ready to spring me. It's not like I'll be getting any sleep. Within a few minutes, my eyelids begin to feel heavy. They drift closed a few times, and I snap them back open. Eventually opening them becomes more effort than it's worth. The last thing I notice before giving in to sleep is the quiet *whirr* of the bed as it returns to a reclined position.

17
Faceless Phantom

~

Gavin places me on the giant chaise lounge at one end of the sofa in our home theater room. After wrapping a leopard print blanket over my legs, he kisses the top of my head. Warmth spreads through my chest. My brother hasn't been this affectionate in a long time.

Dad enters the room carrying several bags full of two liter sodas and plastic cups. Taking his time, he sets everything up on the corner bar. The addicting smell of fresh popcorn fills the room, coming from the antique popper on the far wall. Dad and Gavin are really going all out for our guests. I wonder if it has anything to do with the fact that Dr. Hayes will be here.

"Thanks, Dad," I say, grinning at my flustered father. "The Circle will really appreciate all the trouble you're going through."

"I ordered five pizzas," Dad says, running his hand through his already disheveled hair. "Will that be enough? Maybe I should order a few more."

"Wait," I call out before he can rush from the room. "I'm sure it'll be plenty. Did you find the DVD player?"

Mr. Kincaid is bringing a DVD he copied from old media footage. Unfortunately, we haven't watched DVDs since Blu-Ray came out years ago. Leaning over, I grab the three remotes resting on a sofa cushion.

"Not yet," Dad says with a loud sigh. "Perhaps someone can bring one? I think ours is long gone. Can't we play DVDs on the Blu-Ray?"

"I don't know… I never tried to. I'll text Logan," I reply.

A flush creeps across my face when I realize I smiled as I said his name. After shooting off a quick text, I fire up the Wii. A few Mario Kart races are just what the doctor ordered. My cell chimes as the game is loading. *On it* ♥ *Logan.* Hugging the phone to my chest, I take a deep breath to quiet my racing heart. Somehow I resist the urge to squeal. He texted a heart symbol! I want to tell Celia so bad, but it'll have to wait until later tonight. With a happy sigh, I drop the phone to the sofa cushion just as Gavin reappears.

"Call Bowser," he says, vaulting over the back of the sofa.

"You're always Bowser," I say, rolling my eyes. "He's super slow."

"Yeah, but he flattens your stupid Yoshi," he fires back.

"True, but I'm playing Boo this time."

"He's a cheat character."

"No Wario and Waluigi are cheat characters."

"You're going down, little sister!"

Game on!

I lose four races in a row, my worst streak ever. Covering my ears with my hands, I block out Gavin's noisy victory dance. My hands move from my ears to massage my temples. Perhaps playing video games wasn't such a good idea. The pain has returned with a vengeance.

"Hey, I'll get your Motrin," Gavin says, patting the top of my head.

"Thanks," I reply, leaning my head back against the plush sofa. He returns within moments, and hands me two caplets. "This is it? I think I need more."

"It's a prescription," Gavin says with a chuckle. "Give it a try. Dr. Hayes also prescribed something stronger, but it'll put you to sleep."

I swallow both pills at once with a swig of Diet Coke. The doorbell rings, the Westminster chime echoing through the upstairs. My pulse leaps, and I realize how nervous I am about this meeting.

"Looks like your friends are arriving," Gavin says, rising from the sofa. "Once everyone has arrived, Dad and I will make ourselves scarce." He stares at me for a few moments in quiet contemplation. "Be careful, Kacie. That doctor has Dad convinced that the Orion Circle only has your best interests at heart. But she doesn't fool me. You could've died Friday night. No one can tell me what you're doing is safe. I'm not an idiot."

"But, I need—"

"I know," he says, cutting me off. "I kept my mouth shut because I know you need these people. You're different and I suppose that will make your life more dangerous than normal. Just listen to our mother. Be careful."

"Has she called again?"

"She leaves voicemails on my cell several times a day, every day," Gavin replies sighing. "She's really worried, and I think she has reason to be. She seems to think Logan will save you from this danger. And after Friday night, I say stick close to him. He, at least, seems to have your best interests at heart."

Before I can respond, he disappears out the door. Rolling the red plastic cup between my palms, I wonder about my mother and her sudden interest in me. I've been in danger before. The cowboy made my life miserable.

Gritty memories fill my mind—images of a raven-haired girl and two blond boys. Another nightmare? A heavy pressure around my right ankle makes me cry out in pain. Setting the cup on the ottoman, I hike up my leggings to examine my ankle.

I gasp, gaping at the injury as I try to understand what I'm seeing. Four bruises surround my ankle along with several deep scratch marks. Deep, angry purple marks like someone grabbed... my vision returns full force, knocking the breath from my lungs. The sharp, metallic taste of blood fills my mouth, and I realize I punctured my lip with my teeth. That phantom grabbed my ankle in my vision, but how could that affect me in real life?

"Holy hell, Cici," Daniel says with a low whistle as he plops down on the sofa beside me. "What did that asshole do to you?"

"I-I... who?" I ask, unable to process his words. How did he know about my vision?

"I'll kill Logan!" Daniel says through gritted teeth. "Rebecca and Carl may be singing his praises, but they obviously haven't seen this."

"Logan didn't d-do this," I murmur, my voice breaking on the words.

"Hi, Kacie! How's the head?" Logan asks as he enters the room.

When he sees my ankle, he drops the DVD player he's carrying onto the ottoman, spilling the cup of soda. I watch it run down the side of the furniture, pooling on the light brown carpet. He sits on the chaise next to my leg and runs a gentle caress over my bruised ankle.

"What happened, Kacie?" Logan asks in a choked whisper.

"That's what I'd like to know," Daniel says, glaring at Logan. "I thought you did it."

"What the… we've been friends for five years. How could you… I'd *never* do something like this," Logan says, his eyes filled with hurt.

"Yeah, well Carl said you were making out with her nonstop Friday night," Daniel bites back. "Maybe she didn't like it and you fought."

"And what? I extended my adamantium claws and scratched her?" Logan yells. "What the hell's wrong with you?"

It becomes apparent within moments what's wrong with Logan and Daniel. A frigid cold creeps through the room, settling around me like an icy blanket. He's here. The phantom in my nightmares, my visions is here. Sharp stabbing pain spears through the skin on my ankle. This faceless specter is feeding off the angry energy between the two guys. It probably instigated the entire argument.

"Stop," I cry through a hiss of pain. "Can't you feel it?"

"You're bleeding," Logan says, propping my leg on his lap.

As I stare at my leg, three claw marks appear in the skin along my shin just below my leggings. Grisly images fill my head. Pictures of death, human sacrifice, torture. Whimpering, I close my eyes, trying to stop the deluge of horrifying pictures. The cold permeates my pores, soaking into my body.

"Logan, move," Daniel yells. "Let me touch her leg so I can see what's wrong."

I almost forgot he was clairsentient. Daniel's hand wraps around my ankle, his skin so warm against my chilled body. Shivers course through me all the way from my head to my toes. It feels like something foreign is moving around inside, like insects crawling beneath my skin. When I let out a strangled sob, Logan moves to my side, wrapping his arms around me. I lean against him while Daniel maintains a firm grip on my ankle.

"It's inside her!" Daniel yells, releasing my ankle as though he's been burned. "Somehow the spirit is invading her body. We have to drive it out before it can possess her."

"How?" Logan asks, clutching my shaking body against his chest.

"You could try what you did Friday night," Rebecca says from somewhere behind us. "When we were at the manor and her visions overwhelmed her."

"I don't think a kiss will drive out an evil spirit. I was distracting her to keep this from happening," Logan says as he brushes the hair from my face. "Kacie, look at me." He grabs my chin with his fingers, forcing my gaze to meet his. "Fight this thing. You're stronger than it is."

I stare into his stricken eyes, wondering how to fight this faceless phantom. "I don't…" I try to speak, but the words catch in my throat.

Images continue to flash in my brain, horrible pictures of suffering and grief. When gray dots dance in my vision, I welcome them. My hearing becomes hollow as I call to the darkness to take away the mental anguish. Closing my eyes, I allow my mind to separate from the trauma, to drift away to safety.

"Please, Kacie," Logan whispers in my ear. "Don't give in. Please."

His last plea comes out a choked groan. Logan's in pain. I fight my way back to consciousness, pushing aside the nightmares the demon projects into my mind. Logan needs me. The children need me. I need to be strong in the face of evil. Ugly visions are replaced with fond memories: Logan holding my hand as we walked along the river, opening night of the first musical I starred in, Celia's excitement when Jake asked her out the first time.

With a sob, I throw my arms around Logan, burying my face in his neck. His scent is soothing—leather and spicy aftershave. I concentrate on his ragged breathing, his scent, the feel of his soft hair curling around my fingers.

"The marks on her ankle and leg are gone," Daniel says in a relieved murmur.

"It's going to be okay, baby," Logan whispers as he strokes my hair. "I think the spirit fled. Her skin is warming up."

He runs his fingers up my cheek, and smoothes my hair away from my temple. Though my body is still trembling, the frigid cold is gone. I soak up the warmth from Logan's body, grateful when the tremors begin to die down.

"It was the ghost from Friday night," I murmur, my lips brushing Logan's neck as I speak. "The one from Foxblood Manor. He's been chasing me in my visions these last two weeks. I have to stop him. He's the one—the one my mother warned us about. She was right."

18
San Antonio's Dark Past

A third slice of meat lover's pizza plops down on my empty plate courtesy of Daniel. Eyeing the large slice, I wonder how I'll be able to eat it. Four bites in, I realize I'm still hungry. When Mr. and Mrs. Kincaid arrived right after my near possession, the first thing Mrs. Kincaid told me to do was eat... a lot. Any weakness will be exploited by the spirit, including hunger. Logan hovers at my side, watching for any sign of distress. He hides his worry well as he talks and jokes with the other Circle members. But whenever he glances at me, his smile is weary and his forehead is creased.

I watch Carl set up the DVD player. It should be easy but he's surrounded by wires, too many to plug into the media center. He brought his own box of supplies.

Who does that?

His face scrunches up in aggravation as he digs through his top secret box. No kidding… he wouldn't let anyone see his treasures. I'll never understand techno geeks.

"It's ready to go, surround sound and everything," Carl says, dumping the unused cables back into the large cardboard box. "I didn't need this," he says, holding up the DVD player. "Your Blu-Ray player will play DVDs."

"Then what were you doing for so long?" I ask dumbstruck.

"Whoever set up your home theater system did a lousy job," Carl says shrugging his shoulders. "This baby is too beautiful for a bad wiring job. I fixed it," he adds, puffed up like a strutting peacock. "Shall I fire it up?"

"Perhaps we should finish eating first," Mr. Kincaid says, glancing at his wife. She gives a tiny nod. "It's rather gory."

"How about some background," Daniel says before stuffing another bite of pizza into his mouth. "I'm missing a werewolf hunt for this," he mumbles around a full mouth.

"Michelle and I were up all night doing research," Devon says from his perch on the arm of the sofa, hovering over Michelle.

"Research? Is that what we call *it* nowadays?" Daniel asks with a snort.

"You weren't there, dickwad," Devon bites back, his hands clenched into tight fists. "Mrs. Kincaid, Michelle, and Kacie were all affected by this evil. It's not something to joke about. Especially after what happened to Kacie earlier."

"And what did happen to Kacie?" Dr. Hayes asks, entering the room, with Dad following behind like a lost puppy.

Silence fills the room. No one wants to admit what happened with Dad standing there—even if he is under some kind of persuasion spell.

"Adam, we could use some privacy," Dr. Hayes says to Dad in her sing-song voice. "Would you mind?"

"Actually, yes I do mind," Dad replies, shaking his head as though to clear it. "Kacie is my daughter. I have a right to know what's going on."

"I understand that, Adam," Dr. Hayes says in her normal voice, her lips curled into a smile. She seems elated that Dad fought her compulsion. "It's supernatural, though. Logan made it clear that you aren't exactly a believer."

"It was there," Dad mumbles under his breath.

"I'm sorry?" Dr. Hayes tips her head at Dad in confusion.

"The damn treasure was there, under the tree, right where Kacie said it would be," Dad murmurs, glancing at me with an indiscernible expression on his face. "How can I not believe at least a little after that? Besides, I know my daughter, and I know she's no liar. Logan was right. I either have to admit she's insane or accept what she says as true." His gaze is full of regret. My chest tightens when he gives me a melancholy smile. "I'm sorry I never believed you. It's so hard, you know. To believe in something you can't see, something you always thought a myth. What your mother did was a crime. To think, she believed the entire time and just up and left anyway because she couldn't handle the truth. I'm so sorry, pumpkin. Can you forgive me?"

Handing Logan my plate, I kneel on the sofa while Dad enfolds me in his arms. Tears burn my eyes as I cling to my father.

"I forgive you, Dad," I whisper into his shoulder. "But, can you and Gavin go out for a while. You wouldn't understand any of this and it's something I need to do."

"Okay," Dad says, giving me one last squeeze before releasing me. "We'll disappear for a few hours. I'm sending Kodiak up here when we leave, though."

"Sure," I reply to Dad's retreating form.

"Now would someone please tell me what happened to Kacie?" Dr. Hayes asks while helping herself to the Hawaiian pizza.

I curl up next to Logan and take my plate back, finishing the entire pizza slice, including the crust. I'm so full now I doubt any spirit could fit in my body. With the last bit of my soda, I down the two orange pills Dr. Hayes hands to me. Kodiak leaps up onto the sofa, nosing at my empty plate. He shoots me a forlorn look and snorts before stretching out beside my leg. Reaching out, I run my fingers through his plush fur, basking in the comfort he provides.

Leaning against Logan's side, I listen to Daniel recount the tale with a dramatic flair. The boy was made to act. He brushes his dark hair back while describing what he felt when he touched my ankle. For one brief moment his eyes meet mine. The haunted look within their depths sends a shiver coursing through me. I don't know why, but seeing the fear in his eyes makes it all more real for me.

"Why's he getting through now?" Logan asks when Daniel finishes his tale. "She's been having these visions for a couple weeks. Why is he suddenly able to manifest and attempt possession?"

"I think I have the answer," Michelle says, glancing at me with a look somewhere between fear and pity. "Let's watch the DVD Mr. Kincaid and Carl put together. That will explain some of this."

"No questions or comments until the end," Mr. Kincaid orders as he starts the DVD. "We'll discuss it when it's over."

Gritty news footage appears on the seventy-five inch screen, soundless and bouncy. When the camera stops moving, it focuses on a young brunette woman holding a microphone. She glances over her shoulder multiple times while saying something we can't hear. The plastered smile on her face turns to a grim frown within moments. A male voice blares through the silence startling me. Logan grips my hand beneath the blanket.

We interrupt your regularly scheduled programming for a late breaking news story. Please stand by for a live news feed from our sister station KAPT in San Antonio, Texas.

The camera bounces around some more like the cameraman doesn't know where to focus. Police cars are everywhere. Swat team members crouch behind them, their assault rifles peeking out around fenders and doors. The camera moves back to focus on the dark-haired woman.

This is Monika Alexis reporting for KAPT News San Antonio. I am standing outside this house in the tranquil Wooded Acres subdivision of North Central San Antonio, where the police have finally ended their two day standoff with the members of the Hell's Gate satanic cult. My sources indicate that the cult members participated in a mass suicide rather than face arrest by the authorities. The thirteen children held captive by the satanic cult are also dead. May their souls rest in peace. Wait a minute, there's some kind of disturbance. Gerry, are you getting this? Pan the camera over to the right side of the house! He has an assault rifle! Take cover!

"I am Lucas Yardley," the man yells as he sprays the area with bullets. "*I am the son of our God Lucifer— the new Anti-Christ! Your tiny bullets cannot harm me!*"

Those are the crazed man's last words before a bullet pierces his forehead, forever silencing him. The police swarm over the body like fire ants as the news crews stand in shocked silence.

That was the leader of the Hell's Gate cult shot dead by police. It appears there are several downed officers. As you can see the SWAT team is closing in to make sure the premises are clear. We are waiting for the green light from the SWAT team, and there it is. We have Lt. Jonathan Harvey, the chief investigator into the thirteen missing children, prepared to issue a statement. Lt. Harvey can you give us an update on the current situation?

The detective clears his throat several times and runs a hand through his hair before speaking.

At eighteen hundred hours one of the cult members surrendered to the police informing us of a mass suicide before succumbing to the cyanide she ingested. We have confirmed that the thirteen missing children are on the premises, all deceased. We do not have cause of death for the children yet. Cause of death for the thirty-three cult members was suicide via cyanide except for the cult leader. We are actively investigating the scene and will issue another statement when we have more information.

The detective turns and walks away, ignoring the shouted questions from the myriad of media personalities.

Well there you have it. All thirty-three cult members are dead along with the thirteen children abducted by the cult for their satanic rituals. We will provide updates as we receive them from the SAPD. This is Monika Alexis reporting for NBC KAPT Channel 6 TV.

Silence permeates the room when Mr. Kincaid pauses the DVD. I expected to feel something like a flash of recognition when Lucas Yardley appeared on camera, but there was nothing other than disgust. He was crazy, a raving lunatic. The phantom stalking me seems more controlled, calculated. Could they be the same man?

"This news footage was from October 31, 1969. You'd think with an incident this dramatic, people would talk. Look at Waco," Mr. Kincaid says, pausing for the half-hearted chuckles. "Many people believed he was really possessed by the devil. This incident had a similar effect as the movie *The Exorcist* did. It drove people to church, and the evil was buried under the carpet."

"So you're running with the theory that the anniversary makes him stronger?" Logan asks. He tips his head and narrows his eyes. "Why would this year be any more special than last year or the year before?"

"He's been gaining power for years," I murmur, clenching Logan's hand. "Maybe this is the first time he's had enough power to do anything."

"Perhaps, but I have more news footage for you to see," Mr. Kincaid says, his mouth set in a grim line.

The DVD plays again, this time without sound. Pictures of newspaper footage flash by. Each one highlights an unexplained death: a fifty-year-old man, a teenage boy, a young mother of three, a nine-year-old girl, a twenty-five-year-old actress, and a well-respected newsman. It appears that the only thing connecting the cases is the date, cause of death, and they all happened in San Antonio. It was so violent and odd—the police even made a connection, but the investigation never went anywhere. The only place it could lead was where few cops dared to tread. The supernatural.

"So as you can see, each one of these people died on October 31 over the past ten years of a massive brain hemorrhage," Mr. Kincaid says before pausing on the newsman's obituary. "The author of this obituary suspected foul play. But his pleas to the police to reopen the investigation fell on deaf ears."

"Based on the amount of blood, it appears their brains were liquified," Dr. Hayes murmurs while tapping her chin. "They bled out every orifice in the skull, even the eyes. I'll have to pull the autopsy reports."

"Is there anything other than date and cause of death linking these people?" Daniel asks, leaning forward to study the obituary frozen on the TV screen.

"That's what we intend to find out," Mr. Kincaid says. "We need to scour the medical records and the police files. These are all listed as natural deaths so the police files are officially closed. I'll get in touch with my contact at the SAPD."

"I know where you're going with this," I say a bit louder than I intended. All eyes snap towards me. "These people were in some way clairvoyant and Lucas Yardley tried to possess them. Their brains exploded when they were overloaded. You think I'm next. After today, I can't even argue."

I don't know whether to laugh or cry. Several days ago, I was doing a somewhat decent job of ignoring my powers. Now I'm being pursued by a madman in spirit form.

Is this my punishment for acknowledging everything?

Michelle clears her throat. "In all fairness, Kacie, your visions started before you knew about the Circle."

"Get out of my head!" I cry, whipping my head to glare at Michelle.

"I'm sorry, but you're projecting your thoughts rather loudly," Michelle says, staring at her hands. "It would be like ignoring someone screaming in the room."

Daniel puts his hand on my upper arm. Though I know he means it to be comforting, I can't help but think he's trying to read me too.

"Don't touch me," I say in a hissed whisper.

"I promise I won't read you," Daniel replies with a half-hearted smile. "We're all here for you, Cici. You have something the others didn't."

"Us," Logan says when I continue to glare at Daniel. I whip my head back to look at Logan, and

I can't help but melt a bit from the tender expression on his face. "You have us. The Circle. We'll do everything we can to keep you safe."

With a choked sob, I collapse against his side. He wraps both arms around me, holding me close, and I rest my head on his chest. Gentle fingers stroke my hair. I'm relieved when the waterworks don't start.

"You have every right to cry, Kacie," Michelle murmurs.

"You're doing it again," Logan says, his voice rumbling in my ear.

"I know, sorry," she says in a thin, reedy voice. "I can feel what she's going through and it makes me want to cry. I just..." She trails off with a soft gasp.

"Well, you'll all be happy to know that you're being excused from classes tomorrow for Circle business," Mr. Kincaid says, breaking the uncomfortable silence. "We have a little over two weeks until Halloween, so we need to solve this case. Meet at my house tomorrow morning at eight. I'll be handing out assignments at that time. Anything else?"

"I don't want Kacie left alone, especially at night," Mrs. Kincaid says. "Her visions are strongest when her conscious mind is asleep. We can't let this Yardley fellow get to her while she's sleeping. Kacie, tonight I want you to stay with your brother, and we'll work out a rotational schedule for the rest of the week tomorrow. Will that work?"

Logan nudges me when I don't answer. "Kacie?"

"Yeah, Gavin and I can sleep in here," I reply in a flat tone. "We have several air mattresses so it shouldn't be a problem. I doubt I'll sleep, though."

"You will be sleeping because of the medication I prescribed for you," Dr. Hayes says, shaking her finger at me. "You have to sleep well every night. Lack of sleep also makes you more vulnerable to a psychic attack. Promise me you'll take this medication exactly as prescribed. As an added bonus it should suppress your visions and keep that monster away."

I nod, a weak bob of my head against Logan's chest. It's all been too much—the drugging and incense Friday night, the vision in the hospital, the attack today. Closing my eyes, I take deep, even breaths while I listen to the chatter around me. Mr. Kincaid hands out a few research assignments, and I'm relieved when he doesn't offer one to me or Logan. The Circle members trickle from the room, leaving behind blessed silence. Before long, I can't cling to consciousness anymore, and I drift off to sleep in Logan's embrace.

19

Life Goes on in Spite of the Dead

I awaken with a start, grasping at the hazy tendrils of a dream. It was about the murdered children. That much I know, and yet I can't seem to remember anything else. Just fog and trees, some candles... A hand smoothes my hair away from my face, and I realize I'm not in my bed. As the memories come rushing back, I recognize the plush brown sofa beneath me, which means—the pillow beneath my head must be Logan!

Lurching to a sitting position, my eyes fly around the dimly lit room before landing on Logan. He's reclined on the chaise beneath my leopard print throw. Someone covered me with the blanket from my bed when I sprawled out on the sofa. My pillow is on the sofa beside me. It looks as though I tossed it away in my sleep to curl up on Logan instead. The wall sconces are set to the dimmest setting which makes it difficult to see anything other than his outline.

"Dr. Hayes wants you to keep a dream journal," Logan whispers, handing me a notepad and a pen. "Write down everything you remember while it's still fresh."

"I don't remember anything," I whisper back. "Why are we whispering?"

"Gavin's asleep on the floor," Logan replies, pointing to the dark form of my brother on an air mattress near the TV.

Gavin wasn't kidding when he said that medication would knock me out. I can't believe I slept through so much activity.

"What time is it?"

Logan illuminates his iPhone. "Twelve-thirty."

"I'm sorry I woke you," I say, scooting away a bit. My mouth feels like I ate cotton. No way I'm getting close to him with dragon breath. "Why're you still here? Shouldn't you be home?"

"My parents are out of town, remember? Your dad said I could stay here as long as we aren't alone at night," Logan says with a low chuckle. "Like we turn into hormone crazed monsters once the sun sets."

"Sorry," I mutter, imagining the *talk* Dad and Gavin probably had with poor Logan. My cheeks heat up and I'm grateful for the darkness.

"It's fine. Don't worry about it." I can hear the laughter in his voice. "Dr. Hayes said to have you take one of these pills if you woke up before one."

I take the pill from his fingers. "I'm heading to the bathroom. Be back in a few minutes."

Racing from the room, I dart down the hallway, not breathing until the bathroom door is locked behind me. I flick on the light, grimacing at my disheveled state in the mirror. My hair is sticking up and out in so many different directions, I look like I stuck my finger in a light socket. With a sigh, I brush my teeth and swallow the tiny orange pill. Well, at least I'll know by morning whether Logan really likes me or not. If he doesn't run away screaming at my morning appearance, then nothing will scare him away.

"I feel guilty," I mumble while we wait in line at the bagel shop. "This is dangerous and I just dragged the entire Circle into it."

"Dangerous is kinda what we do," Logan murmurs back. "Besides, we had already accepted this Foxblood Manor case before you even joined."

"Coincidence?"

"More like providence or fate, depending on what you believe." He stops talking when we reach the counter to address the clerk. "We'll take two of the dozen specials plus an assortment of cream cheese."

"I can't help but feel bad anyway," I say when the clerk leaves to fill the order.

"You're bringing breakfast," he replies with a laugh. "The guys at least will love you forever."

"Can bagels really cancel out a ghostly homicidal maniac?" I ask, glancing up at him with a grin.

"You're right," Logan says with a groan. "Should've got doughnuts."

My laughter comes out an embarrassing snort. That's what I get for trying to hold it in. After paying for my bribe to the Circle, Logan and I carry the bags out to the Mustang. My mind wanders as the neighborhood flies by in a blur. We pass an elementary school, and for a brief moment I feel a pang of regret while watching the children race around on the playground. Was there ever a time when I was that innocent?

"Hey, I need to ask you something," Logan says, startling me from my reverie.

"What?" I ask when he remains silent.

"It's kinda last minute and all, but the Southern Texas chapters of the Orion Circle have a Samhain Gala every year," he says while twisting his hands on the steering wheel. "This year it's at the Hyatt on the River Walk the Saturday before Halloween."

"A gala?" I ask when he doesn't continue.

"Uh, yeah, it's like a formal dance. It's a reward for a year of hard work," he says as he pulls into the driveway of the Kincaids' house. "Would you go with me?"

"Yes," I reply, nodding like a fool. At least I managed to contain my squeal of excitement. "It sounds like fun."

"Great," he says with what sounds suspiciously like a relieved sigh. "Are you ready for the meeting?"

"I'm nervous and scared, Logan," I reply, the high I was feeling just a moment ago fading in the face of reality. "But, I doubt we could hide out here."

"C'mon, Kacie," he says, opening the door and unfolding his tall frame from the seat. He grabs the boxes of bagels from the backseat. "You got the cream cheese?"

Without a word, I hold up the bag of cream cheese. Logan sets the boxes on the hood of the car and pulls me into his arms. Wrapping my arms around his waist, I rest my head against his shoulder.

"It's gonna be okay," he murmurs. "I promise."

"I hope you're right."

He gives me a tight squeeze before pulling back and kissing my cheek. "I am," he says, giving me a cocky grin that makes my heart flutter. "Let's go inside."

We are among the first to arrive, and I busy myself by helping Mrs. Kincaid prepare the continental breakfast spread. No one asks how my night went, in fact, the conversation is light and about as far away from the paranormal as possible. I sit on a stool leaning against the granite countertop peeling and sectioning oranges.

Mundane. Normal. Yet the light conversation surrounding me seems forced and wrong.

Without missing a beat, I move on to slicing apples. My ears fill with the sound of the knife hitting the cutting board, blocking out everything else. When Michelle takes the knife from my hand, I jump in alarm.

"God, Michelle," I blurt out in a startled gasp. "Don't sneak up on me like that."

"I called your name three times," Michelle says, setting the knife on the counter. With a shaking hand she runs her fingers through her hair. "I'm sorry. Everyone's walking on eggshells around you. Though they mean well, it seems to be setting you more on edge."

"It is," I reply sighing. "I expected to be bombarded with questions the moment I arrived. When it didn't happen I was relieved, but that relief quickly morphed into something else."

"Anxiety," Michelle says, nodding her head. "I'm picking up tons of anxiety… but also elation." She chuckles under her breath, "Shall we talk about what's causing that?"

"I don't know," I say, unsure if I want to share my feelings.

"Ah, come on," Yolanda says as she bounces into the room and grabs a handful of apple slices. "I just got rid of the guys for a while. I already know I missed a ton when I stayed in Austin instead of returning with Daniel. Spill it."

"If you don't talk, I will," Rebecca says with an evil grin. "And I have so much ammo against you and Logan."

"*Ugh*, all right," I say, rolling my eyes. "Logan asked me to be his date for the Samhain Gala. He was all nervous and adorable."

"What did you say?" Yolanda asks, boosting herself up to sit on the counter.

"What did you say?" Rebecca parrots with a snort. "One weekend, Yolanda, and you miss out big time."

"Yes," I whisper, staring at the fruit sitting on the cutting board. Grabbing the knife, I start cutting the apples again. "I said yes."

"And then she threw her arms around his neck and gave him a passionate kiss," Rebecca says with a squeal.

"That didn't happen," I say, feeling my cheeks heat.

"You should've seen them Friday night," Rebecca says with a sigh. "The way he rescued her with a kiss—totally swoon-worthy."

"Wait, how do you rescue someone with a kiss?" Yolanda asks, crossing her arms over her chest.

"He distracted her enough to keep the spirit from possessing her," Rebecca says, sounding a bit defensive. "It was one of the most romantic things I've ever seen."

"All right, girls," Mrs. Kincaid says as she pushes Yolanda off the counter. "We need to get this breakfast out and start the meeting. There's lots to do today."

"Dress shopping later," Rebecca says with a wide grin. "Ryan asked me."

"Who's Ryan?" I shout my question through the almost deafening squeals.

"Just like the hottest guy in the New Braunfels Circle chapter," Rebecca says, wringing her hands. "I have to find the perfect dress. We only have like…" She pauses, staring at her hands. "Oh God, only twelve days!" she screeches when she looks back up.

The sheer panic in her eyes almost makes me laugh. Almost. Unfortunately, I share both her excitement and nerves. I grab the tray of bagels and follow the others into the family room. Twelve days to find the perfect dress… I better text Celia.

20
Unburying the Past

~

While nibbling on a cinnamon bagel, I try to avoid the knowing smirks from Yolanda and Rebecca. I refuse to let them influence my behavior, so I remain seated beside Logan on the large sectional sofa, our legs touching. As if I don't have enough to worry about, now I have two girls scrutinizing my every interaction with him. A dull ache throbs in my temples, and I flop back against the sofa with a heavy sigh.

Mr. Kincaid has been holed up with Devon and Carl for over half an hour. As much as I enjoy missing school, I wish we could just get the meeting started already. It's not like my life is on the line or anything. That morose thought leads to grotesque visions of exploded brains oozing out all over the place.

My stomach roils, and I devour the remaining bagel in the hopes it will settle my upset stomach. Please don't let Dr. Hayes show up with autopsy photos. I'm pretty sure I'll lose it if I have to see the pictures. Knowing what happened is bad enough.

"All right, we finished putting together the photos and information on Yardley's thirteen victims," Mr. Kincaid says, entering the room with a grim look on his face. Haunted. "I'm warning everyone now—the photos Yardley took of their murders are gruesome, vile, just awful. No one has to look at these." His last sentence is directed at me. Unfortunately I'm the one person in the room who has to look.

"We'll do it together," Logan murmurs. He takes my hand, giving it a reassuring squeeze. "Part of the process to move these spirits on is to acknowledge the awful trauma they endured. To let them know we may not understand, but we care."

"Still, we all don't have to see them," Daniel says, his gaze flying to Rebecca and Yolanda huddled together looking scared and ill. "Logan, you and I should be enough to help the spirits."

"I need to see them too," I say in a hoarse whisper.

"Are you sure, Cici?" Daniel asks with a grave expression. "Mr. Kincaid has seen lots of this stuff, and he looks ready to scream and pull his hair out. No offense, sir."

"None taken," Mr. Kincaid replies in a soft voice. "It's bad, no doubt. Worse than anything I've ever seen before."

"I have to do this," I say, thinking of the trapped spirits. "They need me."

"Okay then, Logan, Daniel, and Kacie will go through these files," Mr. Kincaid says, rubbing his chin with his fingers. "Anna, you Michelle and Devon should go help Dr. Hayes with her research trying to find that illusive connection between our Halloween victims. Yolanda, Rebecca, and Carl, I want you to hit the internet and find everything you can about Lucas Yardley and his cult. I have the other members on call. If you need help contact them directly."

"When are we going back to the manor?" Mrs. Kincaid asks in a low murmur as she wrings her hands in her lap.

"This afternoon I'm taking Kacie, Logan, Daniel, Rebecca, and Carl with me to the manor. We'll be out long before dark," Mr. Kincaid says, pausing to see if anyone objects. "Tomorrow it's back to school, so get as much done today as possible." He glances at his watch. "It's eight-thirty now. We'll meet back here for lunch at twelve-thirty. Sound good?"

No one utters a reply, but there are nods all around. The overall mood has gone from playful to somber since Mr. Kincaid appeared looking so haggard. Everyone gets up and starts moving around, heading to their assignments. I stay rooted to the sofa, unable to move. I don't think I'm ready to face actual pictures of the gruesome deaths of Yardley's thirteen victims. Then again, I doubt they could be much worse than what I've already seen in the visions.

"I think we should take these into the study," Logan says, glancing at the stack of colorful files. "I don't want anyone stumbling in while we have the pictures spread out."

Logan holds out his hand, pulling me up from the sofa when I place my hand in his. He doesn't let go on the short walk to the study, and I'm grateful for the comfort. I watch Daniel's stiff back as he opens the door to the study. It makes me sad to see this carefree guy so upset and agitated.

The study is lined with bookcases. A desk with a Mac sits up against the window, the only furniture other than the bookshelves. Daniel drops to his knees, spreading out the colorful file folders on the floor. They look garish atop the pale cream-colored carpet.

"I want to know why thirteen," Daniel says after Logan and I settle on the ground beside him. "Nutjobs like Yardley have a reason for everything. Why thirteen and why these thirteen. Understanding what makes these victims special may help find his weakness."

"Agreed," Logan says, squeezing my hand. "How should we proceed?"

"This one first," I murmur, reaching for a bright blue folder half-buried in one of the piles. "It's calling to me."

I already know who is inside before I peel back the cover to see the raven-haired girl's face staring at me. It's a school picture, and while her smile is awkward, she's still beautiful. As I run my fingers over the picture, I feel a tiny jolt. I snatch my fingers back, rubbing the burning tips. Logan takes my hand, placing a soft kiss on my aching fingertips. My eyes fly to meet his, and I'm lost for a moment in his gaze.

"This'll be slow going if you two continue to moon over each other," Daniel says with a disgusted snort. "Rule number one, Cici. Never touch a photo of someone you've had visions about. Until you're ready, that is."

Tugging my hand from Logan's grasp, I give Daniel my best hard glare. "Care to elaborate?"

"I keep forgetting you're flying blind," he says, shaking his hair with a dramatic flourish until it falls over one stormy gray eye.

"I keep forgetting you're an emoting asshat," I reply. Tipping my head to the side, I plaster an exaggerated smile on my lips and blink up at him with wide doe eyes.

"Ouch," Daniel says, clutching his chest. "And I paid a fortune for those Captain Kirk Intro to Acting classes," he adds in a great mockery of the illustrious *Star Trek* Captain.

"So why did the picture shock me?" I ask, stifling a giggle at the smirk on Daniel's face.

"Photos can contain powerful psychic vibes," Logan says when Daniel just snickers. "Not only can you get a reading on the person in the photo but also anyone who touched it."

"I'm guessing these photos soaked up enough negative vibes to blind us psychically," Daniel adds, handing me a tissue. "Use this."

I look at the guys, trying to determine if this is some sort of newbie joke. They both look quite serious now. Yet I wouldn't put it past Daniel to try to ease the tension with something ridiculous and inappropriate.

"We wouldn't joke about something like this," Logan murmurs when he notices me eyeing them. "For safety, let's keep a barrier between our skin and the photos."

"What about all the papers?" I ask. "Wouldn't they hold psychic energy too?"

"You've heard about the way some people react to having their picture taken," Daniel says while sorting through the pages of the raven-haired girl's file. "They believe it steals or captures part of the soul in the image. Perhaps it's just the aura or psychic energy that's captured. The paper should be fine. I'll pick up the emotions of people who handled them, but you probably won't. Not unless you can add clairsentience to your list of superpowers."

"Since you seem to have a connection to this girl, start with her file," Logan says.

He picks up a yellow file and moves to the other side of the room. When Daniel moves to another side away from both of us, I look up confused.

"We don't want to influence each other," Daniel says.

After a slight nod, I pick up the photo with the tissue and set it aside before starting in on the first page of the missing persons report.

21

Thirteen Sacrifices

~

Scanning the first page of the police report, I realize it contains nothing but vital statistics:

Name: Ellie Emerson
DOB: September 21, 1956
Age: 13
Race: Caucasian
Hair: Black
Eyes: Brown
Height: 5'2"
Weight: 95 lbs

Last seen leaving Pembroke Middle School at three pm on October 18, 1969, wearing the school uniform. After speaking with friends and family, she was determined not to be a runaway. Ellie was the star volleyball player and her team was on their way to regionals. It seems doubtful she would miss such an opportunity. Handle as kidnapping.

Oh God, she was held captive for thirteen days before her murder. No, that isn't right. Flipping through the pages, I locate a brief summary of the autopsy report. Death occurred roughly seven to ten days prior to discovery. So the authorities discovered her body... but then shouldn't her soul be free? On the last page, I find the records I'm looking for. The body was released to Kleavor Funeral Home on November 6, 1969. She was scheduled for burial at Meadow Dawn Cemetery on November 9, 1969. No notes on whether this happened or not, but I'd assume there would be notes if it didn't. So if her body was found and buried in consecrated ground, then why is her spirit trapped with Yardley?

After placing the reports back into the file, I slip the picture into the folder and move on to the next. A familiar boy stares up from the picture clipped to the report. The platinum blond hair is unmistakable, though the last time I saw it, much of it was coated in blood. This is the nearly decapitated boy.

Name: Michael Johnson
DOB: July 9, 1957
Age: 12
Race: Caucasian
Hair: Blond
Eyes: Blue

Height: 5'0"
Weight: 80lbs

Last seen leaving Langford Middle School at three pm on October 19, 1969, wearing khaki slacks and a white polo shirt. Friends thought it strange when he missed football practice without a word. Determined after speaking to friends and relatives to be a kidnap victim not a runaway.

That's strange. He was kidnapped twelve days before Halloween and he was twelve years old. Ellie was thirteen and taken thirteen days prior to Halloween. Closing Michael's file, I set it aside and look through the other two. Carla, age seven disappeared October 24, 1969. Hector, age three disappeared October 28, 1969.

"I found a connection," I blurt out in my excitement. "We need to compare ages and dates the kids were taken. Grab some paper from the printer."

Logan hands me a few sheets of paper and a pen before flopping on the ground beside me. "I hope this will keep me from having to read more of these files. They're heartbreaking."

"Okay, just read out the ages in your files," I say, scribbling down the ages as they fire them at me. "Look at this." I hold up the paper. Both guys let out simultaneous gasps.

"They're all ages one to thirteen," Daniel says with a low whistle.

"Not only that, but there's one of each age," Logan adds.

"I think the dates they were taken will correspond with the ages—at least mine do," I say, adding the taken dates to my entries.

Without a word, Logan and Daniel sift through their files, adding the kidnap dates to each entry. When they finish, my hunch is confirmed. The victims were aged one through thirteen and each was taken the number of days prior to Halloween that corresponded with their age.

"Okay, but what I don't understand is why they were taken in this order," Logan says as he flips through a file. "According to the autopsy report summaries I have, they weren't killed the day they were taken."

After comparing the approximate dates of death, it's apparent there's no obvious correlation, at least that we can decipher.

"Maybe the dates of abduction have more meaning to Yardley than the dates of death," Daniel says, leaning back on his hands. "Without seeing the autopsy reports, we don't even know how they died. I mean other than murder."

"Ellie had her head bashed in and her legs were shattered," I murmur, recalling my vision. "I think she tried to flee. In my vision there was always a broken doll next to her, but now I'm thinking maybe it was an infant. You think she tried to escape with the baby?"

"Could be," Logan says, gazing at me with an intense look. "But if she was killed in a botched escape attempt, then can we assume time and type of death weren't of importance?"

"I don't think we're ready to make that leap yet," Daniel says, staring at the photo of Ellie. "But, yeah. I'm heading there myself."

"Michael's head was almost completely separated from his body," I say with a shiver. "And the other boy, he was like ten or eleven…"

"Kenny," Logan says, pulling out a green file. One look at his picture confirms his identity.

"His face was bashed in," I murmur, gazing at the happy blond boy in the picture.

"So we aren't looking at ritual sacrificial killings like the media suggested," Daniel says, chewing on his lower lip. "Did he just kill them for fun?"

"Well, he needed something from them," Logan says, stacking the files. "I think when we figure that out, we'll know how he trapped their souls."

"I don't understand," I say, stretching my legs. When I glance at the clock, I'm shocked to see that we've been in here for three hours.

"Well, I'm assuming Yardley did some sort of ritual to trap the souls," Logan says, pulling me to my feet. "Most rituals use an item or something as a binder. We need the detailed autopsy reports to be sure."

"He may have taken a piece of each victim for his ritual," Daniel says at my confused look.

"No," I gasp. Waves of nausea force me back to the ground. "That would trap them here?"

"Unfortunately, yes," Logan says, dropping to his knees beside me.

I wrap my arms around his back when he enfolds me in his embrace. Hot tears spill over my eyelashes, tracing a path down my cheek. *How can anyone be so cruel?* To not only torture them in life but then in death as well—it's revolting.

"Why them," I murmur, sniffing and swiping at my cheeks with my hand. Daniel hands me a tissue, and I bury my face in it. "It's so unfair. He planned this out so carefully, but we still don't know what they have in common. Why did he choose them?"

"There doesn't seem to be any rhyme or reason," Daniel says from across the room.

"There has to be," I argue. "He plotted and planned and stalked these kids. They weren't random. Why them? How did he know who they were? How did he find them? How could he know their ages?" My voice rises with each question until I'm shouting.

"Cici, calm down," Daniel says, moving to Mr. Kincaid's desk. "I'll start looking for a connection."

"What should I do?" I ask, hiccupping on a sob.

"You are going to rest for a while," Logan says, maneuvering my body so my head rests on his legs.

"I can't rest right now," I insist.

"Shh," Logan murmurs. His hand caresses my hair in soothing strokes. "Yes, you can. You'll need your strength this afternoon."

My eyes drift closed, fatigue weighing on me now that I'm no longer fighting. When I roll over onto my side, Logan lies down and curls up behind me. His arms wrap around my body, and I snuggle against him. Right now the floor is much more comfortable than I ever remember my bed feeling. A short nap won't hurt.

22
Back to the Beginning

~

Branches claw at the top of the SUV. A shudder runs through my body—they remind me of the hook man urban legend. When another branch screeches across the top, I jump but manage to stifle the scream in my throat. Logan reaches across the backseat, taking my hand. I lace my fingers through his, clutching him like a lifeline. He caresses my thumb as I try to control my ragged breathing. The SUV hits a ditch in the gravel road, smacking me into the door.

My relief at leaving the gravel road is short lived. In the daylight, the manor looms, a dark castle-like structure worthy of any gothic novel. Two stone lions guard either side of the stairs leading to the front door. The house is three stories, maybe four. It's hard to tell if the top section is an attic or another floor. I assumed it would be dilapidated, but it isn't.

Fresh paint in several different shades of blue does nothing to counter the dreary vibes I feel from the structure. Bright sunlight filters through the oak trees surrounding the manor. But even the sunlight isn't enough to brighten the gloomy house.

Daniel pulls the SUV to a stop in the circular driveway. With a heavy sigh, I open the car door and step out into the warm afternoon. Crows line the railing on the wrap-around porch. The quiet birds watch our arrival, ruffling their feathers. All we need are some bats, maybe a black cat or two and we'd be ready for Halloween. As I gaze at the imposing structure, I try to see what Bob and Beth Carter saw in this place. The light gray stone façade is quite beautiful, and I love the twin turrets on either end.

Logan leads me up the stone stairs to the porch by the hand. My eyes never leave the crazy crows as we approach their roost. I expect them to attack any minute. They don't. After scaling the last step, I'm so close to several birds, I could reach out and pet them.

"So are the birds like pets or something," Daniel jokes when he joins us on the porch. His laugh is forced as he watches the crows from the corner of his eye.

"Caw," the crow closest to me says. "Caw, caw, caw."

"Sorry, I don't speak crow," I tell the bird who is staring right at me.

The bird hops back and forth on the railing then spreads its wings, flapping in small movements. If I didn't know better, I'd swear this bird was trying to communicate. I look up at Logan, meeting his curious gaze. He squeezes my hand before pulling me away from the line of crows.

"Let's not rile them up," he murmurs, wrapping his arm around my shoulders.

"I think I'm losing my mind," I whisper in his ear. "I swear that bird is trying to tell me something."

"Maybe it is," Logan says, but doesn't elaborate.

After everything I've seen, it shouldn't surprise me that there could be people who can communicate with animals. Right now I think it'd be a boon. The black van appears at the end of the gravel road, kicking up small stones in its wake. Logan pulls me closer, giving me a tight squeeze before moving away.

"It's time to prepare," he says, scanning our surroundings.

"Logan, I'm scared," I whisper back, running my hands up and down my arms in an effort to banish the goosebumps on them.

"Be strong, Cici," Daniel says from his perch on the only bare spot of railing. "Those kids need you. If your mom's vision is accurate, you might be their only hope."

"You told him about my mother?" I turn an accusatory glare at Logan.

"I had to tell everyone," he says, shrugging his shoulders. The guilt reflected in his eyes manages to make me angry and remorseful at the same time. "We can't keep secrets during an investigation. It can be disastrous."

"Why me?" I cry out, feeling like a petulant brat the moment the words leave my mouth.

The crows react to my outburst, but not the way I expected. Not one takes to the sky. Instead they ruffle their feathers, and make some soft cooing noises. The one who talked to me earlier hops along the railing until it's beside me. When it brushes its head against my arm, I jump back. It continues to stare at me, its head tipped to the side. The behavior should scare me, and yet I find it oddly soothing.

"Sorry. I'm ready to start now," I murmur, still watching the bird.

I wait for the guys to comment on the bird's strange behavior. When they remain silent, I ease the wall blocking my psychic abilities down just a bit. Pain. Sorrow. Fear. Agony. Terror. Hysteria… I slam the wall back in place. I'm not even an empath and the surge of emotions was overwhelming. Thank goodness Michelle isn't here.

When I glance at Logan, his face is pale and his breathing ragged. I hear a pained gasp and spin around to see Daniel clutching a window ledge with a look of sheer terror on his face. Racing over, I wrench his hand away from the wooden ledge. The worn wood scrapes against his palm leaving behind bloody scratches and several long splinters. He throws his arms around me, burying his face in my hair.

"I can't, I can't," he murmurs over and over while shaking in my arms. "Too much… just too much."

"Clairsentients tend to pick up a lot of emotions. It can be overwhelming at times," Logan says while inspecting Daniel's injury. "Let's get him to the van—we need a first aid kit for his hand."

After a rather rocky start, I ascend the stone steps leading to the manor for the second time. Carl has a camera set up on the porch which scared off all the crows but my large friend. He stares at me with beady black eyes that should look menacing but don't. I must be losing it, taking comfort in a crow's presence. Logan wraps his arm around my shoulders, pulling me away from the crow. We decided to take turns opening our barriers so we can support each other. Physical contact makes that much easier.

Daniel walks beside us, his hands encased in black leather gloves. Every inch of him is covered, only his face and neck exposed. He won't have to worry about brushing up against anything by accident. As we walk through the front door, I can hear Rebecca's voice echoing from somewhere down the hall. She and Carl are lucky they don't have to worry about psychic overload. Though, when we enter the elaborate sitting room, both appear ashen.

"This place gives me the creeps," Rebecca says after jumping in fright when we entered the room. She collapses down on a plastic covered floral sofa. It squeaks beneath her as she fidgets. "I've never heard so many creaks and moans. No wind can make that much noise without ruffling something."

"The EMF is off the charts," Carl says, scanning the room with the handheld device. "We haven't ruled out wiring issues yet, but my guess... this is the real deal."

"This will be a quick investigation," Mr. Kincaid says, rubbing his hands together as though trying to get warm. It makes no sense since the heat is almost stifling in this room.

A chilled breeze blows by, winding around my body before darting away. Air conditioning?

"Whoa! Major EMF spike," Carl yells, moving the detector towards Mr. Kincaid.

"Do you wish to communicate with us?" Rebecca asks, holding out her recorder. "Do you need help?"

A bloodcurdling scream echoes through the house. I freeze in fear, my heart pounding so hard it hurts. My eyes dart around, looking for the source of the scream. Wrapping my arms around Logan, I lean into him. It takes everything in my power to keep from burying my face in his shoulder. Some investigator I am. Daniel's hands are on my shoulders, his body pressed against my back.

"Oh, that's just great," Rebecca says in a sarcastic tone. "The pretty girl gets two guys protecting her from the *scary* ghost. And what do I get? Nothing but this lame-o who'd feed me to the ghost if it would get him physical proof ghosts exist."

She points an accusatory finger at Carl who is so preoccupied in his gadgets, he doesn't notice.

"You're very pretty, Rebecca," Daniel says. He pats my shoulder and moves away. "Cici just happened to be there. If she and Logan were reversed, I would've been hugging him."

"You think I'm pretty?" Rebecca asks in a soft voice. Her cheeks flush pink, and she stares at the carpet.

"People, we just heard a ghost. A ghost!" Carl yells, flinging his arm through the air. "And you're worried about girls being pretty? We got that scream on tape. This is awesome! Focus on what's important."

"Jeez, Carl, calm down," Rebecca says with a snort. "That's hardly proof. Any of us could've made that noise."

"Girls before ghosts," Logan says with a smirk.

"Is that like bros before hos?" Daniel asks, chuckling behind his hand.

"Yep, it's the Circle's new motto," Logan adds as he and Daniel both double over in laughter.

Mr. Kincaid clears his throat. "I'm going to let this all slide since you're blowing off steam."

"I think you're being far too nice, Mr. Kincaid," Rebecca says, glaring at them with her hands on her hips.

"Originally I planned to split up to cover more ground in this house," Mr. Kincaid says, rubbing his hand over his chin.

"I call Daphne," Daniel says, draping his arm over my shoulders.

"Yeah, not happening," Logan says, narrowing his eyes.

"I am so not Velma!" Rebecca yells.

"Shut up, shut up, shut up!" Carl shouts, stomping his foot on the floor. "Can't you take this seriously?"

"Carl, some people deal with stress and fear like this," Mr. Kincaid says as he paces the small room.

"Yeah, Scooby," Daniel says in a stage whisper. He and Logan share a glance and start laughing again. By now I've had enough.

"Please, guys, let's try to get this investigation over with," I plead, grabbing Logan's arm. "I don't want to be here when the sun sets."

"What do you suggest, Kacie?" Mr. Kincaid asks, pausing his restless pacing.

"In most of my visions, Ellie is already outside. I've never seen this house in a single vision, though I have seen the barn several times. Maybe we should go out there."

"I was avoiding the barn since that's where Anna was attacked," Mr. Kincaid admits. "There's one area in the house we need to check out before heading out to the barn. There's a secret passage located at the back of the house. Let's head there. The Realtor who listed the house for sale found the secret entrance but was too afraid to explore."

"A secret passage?" Carl says, clapping his hands together. "Could this day get any better?"

I wish I could be excited like Carl, but the moment Mr. Kincaid mentioned the passage, my anxiety rose. My gut tells me this passage leads someplace horrible, someplace I'm better off avoiding. I have to resist the urge to flee down the hall and out the front door.

"Caw!" A crow's cry echoes down the hallway from the open front door. "Caw! Caw! Caw!" More crows join in. They shriek together for several seconds then stop.

A warning… I'm sure of it.

23
Dark Rituals

We follow Mr. Kincaid down several twisting hallways. This house is one of the strangest I've ever seen. The downstairs is a sprawling series of halls and small, dungeon-like rooms. I wonder if it was ever a boarding house. That might explain the layout. Or maybe Yardley designed it specifically for his cult members. We pass through a monstrous kitchen that would be at home in any restaurant. Gleaming stainless appliances, some I don't even recognize, line the walls.

Behind the kitchen we traverse a narrow hallway before coming to a blank wall. A dead end. Mr. Kincaid twists two candleholders on either side of a lackluster fruit painting. I jump in surprise when the wall next to me moves revealing a hidden passage.

He turns on his flashlight and disappears through the opening.

"Awesome," Carl squeals in a high-pitched voice.

"That," Rebecca says, patting his shoulder.

"Huh?" Carl asks

"You wanted to know why girls run from you," Rebecca replies with a sincere smile.

"But it's a hidden passage," Carl says, pointing at the open door. "It's freaking awesome!"

"I agree with Carl on this," Daniel says as he ducks into the dark tunnel.

His flashlight beam bounces off the dusty walls, illuminating cobwebs covering the walls and low ceiling.

"I don't know," Carl says, backing away a couple steps.

"That too," Rebecca says before ducking in after Daniel. Carl follows behind her, his flashlight bobbing all around.

"Our turn," Logan says, turning on his flashlight. "You ready?" He takes my arm, wrapping it through his when I nod. "Stay close."

As we duck through the small opening, I realize I won't be able to hold onto his arm. Placing both hands on his shoulders, I move as close as I can get without tripping us both. The dust tickles my nose, and I hold my breath to keep from sneezing. Cobwebs grab at my hair as we inch forward through the narrow tunnel. I just hope no spiders are still hanging around this dark place.

"Almost there," Logan says over his shoulder.

I lean closer to his body, resting my cheek against his back. With my eyes closed, the tunnel isn't quite as terrifying. Shudders wrack my body. It feels like spiders are crawling all over me.

"Get 'em off, get 'em off!" Carl shrieks as we exit the narrow passage.

"Shit, Carl, there's nothing on you but cobwebs," Daniel says with a loud sigh.

"Please tell me whatever's clinging to my hair is only a cobweb," I whisper, terrified if I speak any louder it will come out a scream.

Logan runs his hands through my hair while I keep my eyes closed. He brushes my back and shoulders, then I feel his fingers on my cheek.

"You're clean," he says. I open my eyes, glancing up at him with a shy smile. "Nothing but cobwebs. What about me?" he asks, shining the flashlight on himself.

"Not too bad," I say, picking out the sticky webs from his golden-brown waves. "It looks like our friends took the brunt of it. And I basically cowered behind you."

Logan lets out a low chuckle while he watches Carl dance around as though covered in bugs. Every time Daniel tries to grab at the webs, Carl dances away. Rebecca strides up and slaps Carl across the face.

"Get a grip!" she yells before backing away from the awestruck boy. "There weren't any spiders left in there. It's been sealed too long."

"Uh, thanks," Carl murmurs, rubbing his hands up and down his arms. "Um… are you sure there's nothing on my back?"

"Carrll," Rebecca growls, making him cringe.

Lights flicker on all around us, illuminating the large stone room. The room is circular, lit by numerous electric candelabra lining the walls. I guess Yardley wasn't old school when it came to electricity. A black stone altar sits in the middle of the room. Before I realize it, I'm walking toward that menacing structure. Grooves are carved all over the rectangular structure. Better to drain you with…

"This isn't for…" I trail off, my finger shaking as I point at the offensive altar.

"Maybe not human, but yes, I think the grooves are to drain blood from a sacrifice," Mr. Kincaid says in a soft voice that echoes in the silent chamber.

"I think I should lower my barrier, see if anyone wants to communicate," Logan murmurs while circling the altar. "My guess is something awful happened here."

"I need to do it, Logan," I say, cursing my sudden bravery. But the fact remains, the victims came to me in a vision, not him.

"Are you sure?" he asks, brushing my hair from my shoulder. When I nod, he sighs. "Okay, but let me hold you. Physical contact should help keep you grounded."

I bite my lip to keep from smiling. Yeah, like I'd ever turn down an excuse to be held in his arms. He takes my hand, leading me over to a bare wall. We settle on the cold stone floor, and he pulls me between his legs. Once his arms are wrapped around me, I lean back into his chest and close my eyes. With a gentle push, I lower my mental barrier, allowing the psychic energy of the room to waft over me. Fear. Euphoria. Agony. Betrayal. Utter hopelessness. So many strong emotions invade my mind at once.

"It hurts," I whisper in a raspy voice. "So much."

"Stop thinking of your mental barrier as one big dam," Logan says, rocking me in soothing motions. "You have different powers. Block your empathic abilities."

"How?"

"Imagine a hallway with lots of doors," he murmurs. "That door at the end of the hall, the one on your left. Can you see it?"

"Yes," I reply, moving down the imaginary hallway in my mind. My body trembles from the influx of emotion.

"The door is slightly open and shouldn't be," he says as his arms tighten around me to quell my shaking. "That's the door to your empathic ability. Close it and lock it."

Focusing on his words, I slam the door shut, breathing a sigh of relief when the tide of emotions wanes.

"Ellie, are you here?" I call out. "Please, Ellie, tell me what happened here."

I'm in the same room, but seeing it through the eyes of someone else. My arms are wrenched behind my back, held in an iron grip. Figures in black hooded cowls chant in low tones. My eyes dart around the room looking for help, some means of escape. But there is none.

Hot tears trail down my cheeks as my captors drag me toward a stone platform in the center of the room. The faceless monsters chain me by the wrists and ankles to the table. Black and red candles are placed all around my body. I struggle in my bonds, but it has no affect other than to cut the iron shackles into my skin.

Toneless chanting increases in fervor and volume as the hooded figures pace around the table in some strange ritual dance. My heart hammers, every beat painful. A figure garbed in a red cloak moves forward wearing a mask resembling some sort of demonic goat. My struggles renew when I see the long dagger clutched in his hand.

Oh God! No! Please, God, protect me from evil!

I yank on the shackles holding my wrists, but even slick with blood, I can't slip free. The chanting is nothing but screams now as the goat man raises the dagger over my body. I clench my eyes shut when the dagger descends toward my torso. Sharp, unbearable pain! My head reels and my stomach rolls with wave after wave of nausea. Tearing. Agony. Then blessed darkness.

"Come back to me, baby," Logan whispers in my ear.

He continues to call to me in low murmurs, coaxing me back from the nightmare vision. I latch onto his voice—concentrate on the feel of his hands smoothing my hair, his lips on my cheek. My eyes snap open, and I throw my arms around him, clutching his t-shirt in my fingers. I gasp out a choked sob when I try to describe what I saw in my vision. My ribs hurt. It feels as though someone ripped one right out of my body.

"I-I," I stumble over the words, my mouth not obeying my brain's commands.

"Shh," Logan murmurs, kissing my forehead. "Give yourself some time to recover. You gave us all a good scare."

"Scare?" I manage to squeak out the one word.

"You were in that vision for a long time," he says. "I was getting really worried."

A bottle of water appears in my line of vision. I take the bottle from Rebecca with a muttered thanks. She had the foresight to open it, and I take several long gulps. The cold liquid feels like heaven on my raw, parched throat.

"Was I screaming?" I ask after several more sips of water.

"Yeah, a lot," Rebecca says in a shaky voice. "Do you remember what you saw?"

"Can't forget," I whisper, trembling from the memory. "I can still feel the pain. It was awful."

"Tell us what you saw," Mr. Kincaid says from across the room. "Take your time."

"The cult did some sort of ritual here," I murmur.

The water bottle falls from my limp fingers. It rolls across the room, spilling on the stone floor. I watch the liquid run across the stones, seeping into the seams.

The liquid should be red.

"Did you hear that?" Logan asks, his eyes darting around the room.

"It was Ellie," I reply, closing my eyes. "They did something awful to her here. To all of the children. In my vision, I was Ellie. I... she was chained to the stone table in the middle of the room. The cult members were all wearing black cloaks and chanting."

A keening wail fills the room, stopping my words. Poor Ellie. She suffered so much in life and is still a prisoner in death due to that dark ritual.

"I'll free you, Ellie," I call out to the restless spirit. "I'll do everything I can. I promise."

"What happened?" Logan asks, coaxing me to continue the story.

"The head guy, Yardley I guess, appeared. He was in a red robe and wearing a demonic goat-like mask." My head falls to Logan's shoulder as I gather the courage to continue. "He raised this curvy dagger over me… her. There was a shooting pain in my side followed by this awful wrenching sensation and a loud pop. He took one of her ribs. I think that's what Yardley used to seal the spirits here."

"A bone would be ideal to seal a spirit," Mr. Kincaid says. He crosses the room and pulls me to my feet. "We need to get out of here. I may not be psychic, but I'm getting a bad feeling. I learned a long time ago to trust my gut."

Mr. Kincaid ushers us through the secret passage before turning off the light and trapping us in inky darkness. Flashlights flare to life. I race behind the others, focusing on Rebecca's retreating form. Hurried footsteps echo on the hardwood floor as we run from some unseen force.

The closer we get to the front door, the more I believe Mr. Kincaid is right. Pressure builds around us—crackling energy that sends my hair flying around my body. Logan grabs my hand, and a jolt of static electricity jumps from his hand to mine. He gives me an apologetic glance before lacing his fingers with mine. We burst through the doorway out into the bright afternoon sunlight.

24
The Barn

~

As I gasp in deep breaths of fresh air, the immense pressure on my chest begins to fade. I collapse onto the porch steps, holding my head in my hands. Was that Yardley? Maybe he didn't like us poking around his inner sanctum.

"What the hell was that?" Rebecca asks, hugging her arms around her body. "It was so cold. I can't stop shaking. Was that Yardley's ghost?"

"Whatever it was, it didn't want us in that room," Daniel says while pacing back and forth.

"Caw, caw, caw." Several crows screech as they take flight from the railing.

A gust of frigid air blows from the house through the open front door. It hits me in the back, sending me flying across the gravel drive. Tiny stones scrape into my hands and arms as I shield my face from harm. When my body finally skids to a stop, I stay curled up on my side, afraid to move. I feel frozen. My entire body is so cold. It's as though I'm immersed in a snowdrift. Each breath burns my lungs.

"Kacie!"

"Cici!"

The shouted voices sound so far away, yet I can feel the footfalls on the gravel as they race toward me. I open my eyes, searching for a dose of reality to drive back the frigid cold. My teeth chatter when I open my mouth to speak. Nothing comes out but a hoarse croak. Logan falls to his knees, skidding to a stop beside me. When he helps me into a sitting position, I blink in surprise. The blast I thought knocked me over, threw me several yards away.

"Kacie, are you okay?" Logan asks, cradling my trembling body against his.

"He's afraid," I say, my lips turning up into a grin. "When his essence plowed into me, I felt intense anger. But at the edges, I also felt fear."

"Your hands are like ice," Logan says when he grasps them in his. "And your arm is all bloody. I'm going to enjoy taking that bastard down."

The anger in his eyes over my injuries warms my heart. As my body thaws, my arm begins to sting from the gravel burn. Logan helps me to my feet, supporting me on the walk over to the van. My jeans have several new holes in the thighs and on one knee. It was rather lucky I was wearing jeans and not shorts, or my legs would be as bad as my arm.

"Set her down here," Carl says as he flings open the back door. "I'll get the first aid kit."

"She needs more than a first aid kit, Carl," Daniel says, helping Logan situate me in the back of the van. He cradles one of my arms. "We need to wash the road rash off."

"Let's head back to my house," Mr. Kincaid says. "We'll get Kacie taken care of and discuss our findings today."

"No!" I shout a bit louder than I intended. Cringing, I glance up at Mr. Kincaid. "Sorry. We need to investigate the barn before we go. When Yardley's spirit hit me, I felt his fear. We're getting really close and he doesn't like it at all."

"That's exactly why we need to leave," Mr. Kincaid argues, crossing his arms over his chest. "He threw you ten yards, Kacie."

Rebecca moistens a towel with some bottled water before handing it to Daniel. He wipes at my forearm with gentle strokes. I hiss at the sharp pain as little pieces of gravel break free from my skin, clattering to the floor of the van.

"His spirit used a lot of energy in that attack," Logan says. He pulls me up on his lap while Daniel continues his ministrations on my arm. "He must be pretty weak right now. It's a perfect time to poke around since I doubt he'll have the energy to attack again soon. As long as you're up to it, Kacie."

I nod then rest my head against his shoulder. Closing my eyes, I return to the vision, trying to see the scene from objective eyes. During the vision I was frantic, terrified. I couldn't think clearly enough to take in my surroundings in any detail. Something about Yardley niggles at my brain but I can't quite figure out what.

"This one's pretty deep, Cici," Daniel warns.

The rag scrapes against the shoulder that took the brunt of the impact. When I glance down, rage bubbles to the surface. This was one of my favorite shirts! Gavin got me this Avenged Sevenfold shirt from a concert I couldn't go to. He was so sweet, and the gift is a happy memory. Now the shoulder and arm are shredded. With tender fingers, I pull on the shredded material. It's beyond repair. Damn.

"Actually, I think the shirt looks cool like this," Rebecca says, noticing my distress over the torn shirt. "We can make the other side match. I'll help you later."

"Almost got it all," Daniel murmurs, running the towel over my shoulder with a gentle swipe. "Yep, I think that's the best I can do for now."

I cry out from the pain when Daniel sprays the entire area with an antiseptic. Logan's arms tighten around me, and I cling to him with my uninjured arm. The entire area stings so badly it reminds me of the time I fell on a fire ant hill.

"We'll have Dr. Hayes take a look at it later," Mr. Kincaid says in a calm tone, though he shuffles from foot to foot, revealing his anxiety.

I start to protest when Daniel winds a gauzy bandage around my arm, but the dark glare he shoots at me leaves the words stuck in my throat. I feel like the subject of a game of doctor. He wraps the bandage up over my shoulder before securing it with paper tape. Maybe a game of Egyptian mummy would be more appropriate. I can't go home with my arm wrapped like this. Dad will flip. He'll decree that the Circle is too dangerous, and no amount of Dr. Hayes' brand of persuasion will change his mind.

"It's only temporary," Logan says, watching me poke at the bandage.

"Do you have any idea how much this is gonna hurt to peel off later?" I fix Daniel with a withering glower. It doesn't have the desired effect.

"Aw, Cici, you can't scare me with your death glare anymore," Daniel says, chuckling under his breath. "It's actually pretty cute the way your bottom lip sticks out in a bit of a pout..."

Hot blood pools in my cheeks. I lean forward a bit, hoping my long hair will hide my blush from Daniel. This is a battle I can't win, so I think I'll just bow out rather than make a fool of myself.

"So are we going to the barn?" Rebecca asks, drawing everyone's attention away from my flaming cheeks.

"Yes," I reply, jumping to the ground from the back of the van.

My hip protests the movement. I rub my fingers along the sore spot on my hip. It extends down the side of my thigh all the way to the knee. I bet it'll be one amazing bruise by tomorrow. My pale skin makes even the lightest bruise rather spectacular.

"Hey, careful," Logan says, rushing to my side. He wraps his arm around my back, supporting part of my weight. "You did just fly down a gravel drive."

"The barn is behind the house. This way," Mr. Kincaid says, heading toward the left side of the manor.

A stone path winds around the house. It looks brand new. The owners probably put it in when they put the house up for sale. In fact the grounds are well-kept. I was expecting something creepy, not some nice pathway through a flower garden. It's still early enough in the season that most of the flowers are in bloom. Perhaps come winter the place will resemble the house of horrors it should. I can't help but wonder about the Carters. Why would they buy a place with such dark history? Kinda like their very own *American Horror Story* house.

"Wow!" Rebecca exclaims as we round the corner. "Look at that barn. And the riding ring. It's perfect!"

The barn isn't the old-fashioned red monstrosity I was expecting. It looks brand new, made of gleaming natural-stained wood slats. Now I understand what attracted them to the property. It's a horse lovers dream come true. We enter through a side door leading into a large office. The sweet woody scent of cedar fills my nostrils.

"The original barn was torn down before the Carters bought the property," Mr. Kincaid says as we pass through the office into the main barn.

The barn is one massive room with at least fifteen to twenty horse stalls. Fresh hay covers the floor, trailing to each stall. It appears the Carters are getting ready for horses.

"Is anything in here original," Daniel asks, running his fingers over one of the stall doors. He never put his gloves back on after treating my shoulder. "I'm getting nothing but forest. It's rather refreshing."

"Is the wood unhappy here?" Rebecca asks.

"Plants don't have complex feelings like that," Daniel says as he moves toward the back of the barn. "I just get glimpses of the forest the wood came from, and any human emotions attached to it. Like here... some guy smashed his thumb while hammering this plank into place. Ouch!"

Daniel snatches his hand back as though burned. He rubs his fingers while glancing around the barn. Above us a large hayloft takes up the back third of the ceiling. No, that's not where Yardley kept the kids.

It was dark.., and smelled of both antiseptic and decay.

The words whisper through my mind. I whip my head around so fast that my hair smacks Logan in the face. With a sheepish grin, I mutter an apology. An image of a symbol on a metal door fills my mind, but I don't recognize it.

"I think Ellie just sent me a message," I say, unable to stop searching for the owner of those whispered words. The speaker sounded like they were right behind me. "Does anyone have a pen and paper?" Rebecca hands both over, and I quickly sketch the symbol.

"That's a radiation symbol," Mr. Kincaid says, studying the paper.

"Ellie was someplace dark, and the door was metal with this symbol," I say, concentrating on the image she projected to me.

"So maybe a fallout shelter left over from the Cold War?" Logan suggests, passing the paper to Daniel.

"How are we supposed to find that without ground penetrating radar or something?" Carl asks, crossing his arms over his chest.

"I need to contact the company that did the reconstruction of the barn," Mr. Kincaid says, heading back toward the entrance. He seems in a hurry to leave. Perhaps the events today were too much. "They should still have the old blueprints and the construction plans. After reviewing those, we'll have a better idea if there is a fallout shelter here and how to access it. It's quite possible they covered the access."

"I hope not," I murmur as my eyes scan the dirt floor. "I think that shelter may be the key to freeing the children."

"Well, there's nothing else we can do here now," Mr. Kincaid says from the office door. "Let's head back to my place and regroup with the others over dinner."

He disappears into the office, followed by Rebecca and Carl. A cool breeze blows by, ruffling my hair. I know it's one of the boys, though I'm not sure which. Just as I'm about to ask for help locating the shelter, the temperature returns to normal. The spirit is gone.

"Come on, Kacie," Logan says, taking my hand. "I don't think there's anything else we can do here today—I mean other than dig up the entire barn."

"You're right," I admit.

There's a heavy pressure in my chest. I feel like I'm letting the spirits down—like I should be doing something other than leaving. After one last glance over my shoulder, I follow Logan out of the barn and into the twilight. Time flew while we were investigating the barn. We pick up the pace to a fast jog, neither of us wanting to be here after dark. Daniel revs the engine in the SUV as we jump into the backseat. Before we can buckle our seatbelts, he takes off down the gravel road, following the van's taillights.

My breath comes out in a relieved *whoosh*.

Why do I feel like we escaped just in time?

25
Slumber Party

~

When no new information turns up from the construction company that rebuilt the barn, grim satanic cult talk is replaced with excited chatter about the upcoming Samhain Gala. It seems everyone is willing to let it go. Everyone but me. Not that I could even if I wanted to.

Dr. Hayes decided several days ago that I need to have more nighttime visions if we are to have any hope of defeating the Foxblood Demon—I hate the name the media coined for him all those years ago, mostly because I get the feeling Yardley loves it. Well, I stopped taking the medication suppressing the visions, but they haven't returned like I expected. Of course, it could be caused by lack of sleep. I think I'm sabotaging myself out of fear. It's hard to go to sleep when I fear *he* will show up.

Nightly slumber parties continue in my home theater room, though tonight is the noisiest yet. The last few nights it was just Gavin and Logan with me. It's no surprise I miss Logan. I felt so safe with him nearby. What surprises me is that I miss Gavin's snoring. Yep, even that foghorn is preferable to the giggle fest going on right now. Girl's night in, they called it. It'll be fun, they said… take your mind off the killer phantom. I've been visionless for three nights now, and I really need one soon.

Halloween is less than two weeks away. What will happen if I can't figure out where Yardley hid the trophies he used to trap the souls? A shudder courses through me. I freeze, caught between hoping it's just the air conditioning and wanting a visitation. Anything to get a little more information. The moment passes, the shiver caused by nothing more than the cool air flowing from the vent in the ceiling.

"You okay, Kacie?"

Raven, our newest addition, plops down on the sofa beside me. She just moved here from Orlando. Her father is high up in the Orion Circle, so Raven and her brother, Mark, were welcomed on arrival. Her fingers wrap around one long strand of black hair, coiling and uncoiling in a nervous gesture.

"Uh, yeah, I guess," I reply, squirming under her scrutinizing stare. Her dark blue eyes never leave mine as her left eyebrow arches above her bangs.

"You seem anything but okay," she comments, breaking eye contact to watch Gavin enter the room.

Gavin stands behind me, his arms crossed over his chest. After several moments locked in a staring contest, he throws his head back with a bark of laughter.

"You've got some visitors downstairs," Gavin says with a wink. "I'm sending them up, but I want them out at midnight." He stops at the door. "Because for some reason Dad thinks teens only have sex after midnight."

"Gavin!" I cry out, my cheeks flaming from his remark.

"I got a lecture before Dad left for the weekend," Gavin says with a mischievous glint in his eyes. "You can't have boys in after midnight and no closed doors. In exchange, I get to be in the same house as a group of teenage girls all night."

"Yeah, Dad didn't think this through," I mutter under my breath.

"Double standard alert," Celia yells from the floor where she's painting her toenails blue.

"Just for that, I won't let Jake up, princess," Gavin says, staring at Celia's bare legs with what looks suspiciously like a leer.

"Jake's here?" she squeals, her hand flying to her hair. "But I'm a disaster!"

"You look adorable, princess," Gavin says, ogling her. "You girls worry too much about looking perfect and together. Guys like that just-rolled-out-of-bed sexy look." He ducks out the door and disappears down the hall.

"Gavin thinks I'm sexy?" Celia asks with wide eyes. I cringe at the tiny smile on her lips. Oh, no. No, no, no! Not my brother. *Eww!*

"Gavin *is* hot," Raven murmurs, flashing me a knowing grin.

"I so don't want to hear it," I mutter, resisting the urge to put my hands over my ears. "He's my annoying brother."

"Well, to the girls here, he's a sexy college guy," Raven says, pointing toward the three enraptured faces.

Closing my eyes, I drop my face into my hands. Celia, I understand, I mean she's boy-crazy. But Michelle and Rebecca too? I almost feel betrayed. My torment is interrupted by the arrival of three noisy guys. Jake races across the room, pulling a squealing Celia into his arms.

"We won, babe!" he shouts over her excited cries. "We're heading to regionals."

"Congrats, Jake," I say but am drowned out by Celia's excited shrieking. Well, at least she forgot about Gavin.

"Got permission from your brother to stay the night," Logan says as he plops down beside me on the sofa.

"But he was just in here saying no boys after midnight," I reply with a skeptical glare.

"Yeah, well, anything paranormal freaks him out," Logan says shrugging. "He's afraid you'll have a vision and he won't know what to do."

"I think I can help her through a vision," Raven says, tossing her hair. "I've been having them as long as I can remember."

"Good to know," Logan says, his tone somewhat icy.

"Don't mind my friend," Daniel says, lowering himself on the sofa beside Raven. He gives her his *come hither* stare which tends to turn those of the female persuasion to jelly. "He has trust issues."

"As well he should," Raven says, giving Daniel a hard glare which he ignores.

If I didn't like her before, I sure do now.

"Sorry, didn't mean to come across so… uh," Logan trails off.

"Neanderthal?" Raven asks, tipping her head to the side. "Or do you prefer alpha male?"

"Oh, sweetie, Logan isn't an alpha male," Daniel says laughing. He places his hand on her leg, right above the knee.

"Don't call me sweetie," Raven bites out as she shoves his hand off her leg. "I'm a second degree black belt in Tae Kwon Do, a black belt in Judo, and a blue belt in Krav Maga. If you like your manly parts, you'll back off."

"Wow, why so many different disciplines?" Logan asks with wide eyes.

"I'm a monster magnet," Raven says, shrugging her shoulders. "Dad started my training when I was four."

"I'm sorry," Daniel says with sad eyes. "For everything but especially the monster magnet part."

"What's a monster magnet?" I ask. Logan and Daniel are quite upset by her remark.

"There's something in my blood that attracts monsters," Raven says, leaning back against the sofa with a loud sigh. "It's like they can smell it a mile away. Vampires, werewolves, all sorts of creepiness will crawl out of the woodwork after me."

"That sounds awful," I say, trying to keep the pity out of my voice. Then one of her words finally registers. "Wait… vampires exist?"

"I'm a vampire hunter, have been for years," she says with a dismissive shrug. "Makes the job easier, I suppose."

Daniel gasps. "You're actually a hunter?"

"My mom was killed by vampires when I was eight. My dad's been obsessed with revenge. He trained my brother and me to hunt as well. The monsters were coming after us whether we liked it or not… better to be prepared."

Her voice is hard, but that edge doesn't reach her eyes. Sadness and regret are reflected in her eyes for a brief moment before she covers it up with a smile.

"I like hunting," Raven says shrugging. "There's something about ridding the world of a dangerous predator that just feels right."

"Hey, on that note, I brought season one of *Supernatural*," Logan says, rising from the sofa. "Who's ready for some good hunting?"

"So, uh, Raven?" Daniel asks, his voice a bit shaky. "The Samhain Gala is next weekend. I don't have a date, and I'm guessing you don't either since you just moved here… want to go together? As friends," he adds in a rush.

"As friends?" she asks in a skeptical tone.

"Promise. As friends," Daniel agrees, smiling. "I happen to like my manly parts where they are."

Raven's reply is drowned out by the booming of the theater speakers. Grabbing the remote, I turn it down from deafening to just loud enough to shake the walls. Cheers erupt around the room at the first glimpse of Sam and Dean Winchester. Yep, the fictional Winchester boys are honorary Orion Circle members. Logan vaults over the arm of the sofa, landing beside me. After he wraps his arm around me, I snuggle into his side for a night of great TV.

As I begin to wake from a sound sleep, the first thing I notice is the stitch in my neck. Sharp pain jolts me awake when I move. My eyes fly open, meeting Logan's sleepy golden gaze. A flush steals up my neck and into my cheeks. I can't believe I just spent the night sleeping in his arms. With a shy smile, I sit up stretching my sore neck and back. Sprawling across a guy's chest all night isn't as comfortable as one might think.

Shaking my head in disbelief, I take in the sleeping forms of my friends, including Jake and Daniel. Gavin did an excellent job keeping the house boy-free. He better hope Dad doesn't come home early and see this.

Dad!

He's supposed to be home late this morning. What time is it? Maybe it's late enough he'd just think they came over this morning. No, can't take the chance.

"Get up!" I call out a bit more frantic and louder than I intended. My command is met with snorts and groans, followed by a shriek.

"No!" Celia shouts, running for the door. "He can't see me like this."

"And that's why I'm not high-maintenance," Raven mutters through a yawn.

Her hair is a wavy, sleep-mussed mass. I'm guessing every guy in the room finds it attractive. My hand creeps to my head, smoothing out my hair. Then I return to my senses—my appearance won't matter if I'm grounded until I turn eighteen.

"Dad could be home any minute," I say while pushing Logan up from the sofa. "You guys all need to clear out!"

"Whoa, sis, calm down," Gavin says, sauntering into the room. "Dad sent an email. He won't be back until tonight."

He's wearing the same clothes from last night, though his t-shirt is on backwards. I wonder if he has a girl hidden in his room. If the smile lighting his face is any indication, the answer is yes. He arches his body backward in an exaggerated yawn.

"Now, I'll be getting back to my room," he says winking. "Try to keep it down, Kacie. Your shrieking kinda kills the mood."

He ducks out the door just as I throw one of the pillows at his head. It bounces off the doorframe. Laughter echoes down the hallway while he walks away. Oh God, he's headed back to his room and his flavor of the week. We have a connecting bathroom… I really hope they're quiet. I don't think my poor heart can take overhearing Gavin in the throes of passion.

26
Six Dress Shops Later

Gavin is not on my good side right now. Between his flame of the week taking up my bathroom for over an hour and his *Spongebob Squarepants* marathon with the guys—which just had to include a cereal fight— I'm ready to end his pathetic existence. What four grown guys see in that yellow sponge is beyond me. Maybe it makes them feel smart by comparison.

Michelle pulls her packed SUV into the parking lot of a huge bridal store, our sixth shop this afternoon. I haven't told my friends, but this is the last store. If I don't find something here, I'll wear jeans. Rebecca found her dress in the second shop we went to. If it had been my decision, I would've bought that pretty blue dress in the first store and been done. But I have five other girls with me who seem to be on the quest for the perfect dress. Like it exists. I've tried on at least eight perfectly fine dresses, yet the search for 'the one' as Celia likes to call it continues.

As we approach the door, my spirits lift. This store is huge! There's bound to be something in here that we'll all agree on. Once we're through the doors, we all peel off in separate directions to root through the endless gowns. After a few racks, I grow discouraged again and plop down on a nearby settee. A loud *whoop* draws my attention to the back of the store.

"This is it!" Celia says in a loud squeal. "Kacie, you have to try this one on."

I follow the sound of her voice and we nearly collide as she races toward me. My eyes fall on the dress cradled in her arms. No. I can't wear that color! It's not hot pink, not quite purple... maybe fuchsia? Fuchsia... why does that sound so...

It hits me hard. Mother and her vision—she mentioned me wearing fuchsia at the end of her rant. Is it a sign? An omen? The dress is exquisite, elegant and simple, something I would pick out were it green or blue.

"Try it on, Kacie," Celia urges, steering me toward the fitting rooms. "I think you'll be surprised by how good this color will look on you."

I glance around, taking in the enthusiastic nods and grins of my other friends. Only Raven looks somber. Taking the dress from Celia with a dramatic sigh, I stomp into one of the large fitting rooms.

"And you better come out and let us see," Celia warns, thwarting my plans to keep this fashion disaster to myself. What if they actually like it?

"Yeah, yeah," I mutter while pulling my clothes off.

As I slip the satin dress over my head, I can't help but notice how nice it feels against my skin, cool and silky. It drapes around my body, falling to brush the floor. I'll need heels for sure with this dress. Sucking in a breath, I turn to face the mirror. My breath leaves my lungs in a surprised gasp.

The dress is gorgeous. I love the way it hugs my body, accentuating the small curves I have. The neckline plunges in a deeper vee than I like to wear, but it makes me look like I have boobs. *Yay!* A satin sash the same color as the dress winds around my waist making it look so tiny.

When I spin around, the dress flares around my ankles. But the color... it's so vibrant, and it makes my pale skin almost glow. It's so much brighter and bolder than I would normally consider.

I step out of the fitting room to startled gasps and squeals. My nervousness turns to something different, something I don't think I've ever felt before. I feel elegant, girly, and pretty. With slow measured steps, I make my way to the raised dais in the center of the room. My image reflects in multiple mirrors, showing the dress from all angles. I feel like a princess.

"This is it!" Celia says, covering her mouth with her hands like she tends to do when she's overly excited. "I never would've picked this one. Raven, you're a fashion genius."

"It wasn't fashion but ESP that made me pick this one," Raven says with a thoughtful look. "When I brushed against it, I had a premonition. It was really hazy, but something tells me that Kacie is meant to have this dress."

"A premonition?" I ask, spinning to see the back of the dress.

"Hmm, yes," Raven replies in a soft voice.

"And you can't elaborate?" Rebecca asks in a rather critical tone.

"No, I'm sorry," Raven says, glaring at Rebecca. "It doesn't work that way."

"Geez, Rebecca, back off," Yolanda says, crossing her arms. "How many times has Mr. Kincaid told you to go easy on the talent?"

"Talent?" I ask, cringing from the rising tension in the room.

"Psychically gifted," Michelle murmurs. Her eyes are closed and her brow is creased. Being an empath, the tumultuous emotions in the room must be painful.

"I'm sorry," Rebecca says, sounding contrite. "It's hard for me to understand and sometimes I get frustrated."

"That's 'cause you're a control freak, Rebecca," Yolanda says.

"I'm pissed off about this Foxblood Demon case," Rebecca says, throwing her arms in the air. "I've spent hours, maybe days researching and have come up with nothing. I guess I got a little jealous when all Raven had to do was touch a dress."

"I didn't get anything useful," Raven says watching me.

"Are you kidding?" Celia asks in a startled gasp. "You managed to get Kacie out of jeans and into a gorgeous dress. You, my friend, are a miracle worker."

The tension lifts with Celia's dramatic delivery. I glance at her and she gives me a knowing smirk. Celia excels at diffusing potential disasters. Maybe she should be an ambassador or something.

"Oh, I wish I had a guy in the Circle," Celia says with a loud sigh. "This Gala sounds wonderful."

"What about Jake?" Raven asks.

"Yeah, he's totally hot," Yolanda pipes in. "Who cares if he's in the Circle or not. He's one of the only starting juniors on the varsity football team."

"It must be something special," I murmur before I can stop myself. Celia sucks in a surprised gasp. "Homecoming was last weekend and you're still together."

"I really like him," Celia whispers, looking at the floor. My jaw drops. Shyness and insecurity? My God, maybe it's true love.

"He adores you, Celia," I say as I walk over and wrap my arms around her. "Don't throw something good away out of fear. Promise me."

"I promise," she whispers before pulling away sniffing.

"So, is this the dress, then?" I ask to draw everyone's attention away from Celia.

"Yes!" they all shout at once.

"Great, then I'm going to buy it, and we're getting the hell out of this store."

⤴

The moment I walk through the door, I'm met by Gavin and Logan who share the same frantic appearance. Taking a deep breath, I wait for the tirade that's about to begin. I'm shocked when Logan pulls me into his embrace, clinging to me like he thought I'd been hurt or something. With my track record of late, I guess that's not unlikely. It's even stranger when Gavin yanks me from Logan's arms, enfolding me in a bear hug.

"I went dress shopping, not to war," I gasp the words out as I'm crushed in Gavin's embrace.

"What happened?" Raven asks from behind me. She remained behind because she feels another premonition coming on and wants to be near me.

"Our mother called," Gavin replies, finally loosening his grip a bit. "Frantic, crazy, *sober*."

"I'm sorry but I don't understand," Raven says as she tugs me away from Gavin. "Let's go sit down and talk."

"No dress?" Gavin asks when he notices my empty hands.

"It's with Celia. She insists I get ready at her house since her supplies are better," I say, curling up next to Logan on the sofa in the living room. "Good thing too, or you guys would've crushed it."

Though my tone is light, I'm terrified inside. What could my mother have said that has the guys acting like this? Logan wraps his arm around my shoulder, pulling me into his side.

"So as you probably guessed, our mother had another vision," Gavin says, wringing his hands together. "I let her talk to Logan since it made no sense to me at all."

"She said her vision has changed for the worse," Logan says, laying his head against mine. "It's darker now, you're lost, frightened. She thinks it may be too late to reverse. She was screaming, Kacie. Shrieking and wailing. It was almost impossible to get anything coherent from her. The best I could surmise is that by suppressing your visions, you've crippled yourself."

27
Restoring the Visions

Raven paces the room. "I don't understand. Why were you suppressing your visions?"

"The Foxblood Demon, Yardley, was tormenting her nonstop in these visions," Logan says with a deep sigh. "The doctor gave her a sleep aid. We thought it best to suppress them since they were taking a huge emotional and physical toll on her. We were afraid he'd try to possess her again."

"Again?" Raven gasps. "How many times has he tried?"

"Twice," Logan replies. "Both times she was awake. We were afraid he'd have better luck when she was sleeping. We wanted to make sure she was protected when she was most vulnerable."

"I haven't had one since," I murmur, clinging to Logan. "Even after I stopped taking the medication last week, they never happened again."

"You have to understand, this demon was attacking her," Logan says. He pulls away and kisses my forehead. "We couldn't allow him to torture her every night."

"But he wasn't the only one I was seeing in the visions," I say as my chest tightens. "The souls of the kids would appear sometimes."

"I think they were piggy-backing on Yardley's visits to try to drop clues," Logan mumbles, dropping his head in his hand. "We screwed up royally. Now we're tapped out on research and are no closer to finding the relic he's using to bind himself and the children to this plane."

"Okay, let me get this straight," Raven says, pacing back and forth. "You suppressed the visions because they were hurting Kacie. But what's this about a relic?"

"Yardley bound the souls of the children he murdered to the ribs he extracted from their bodies," I say, shivering from the memory of that awful vision. "We don't know where he hid them. We've been through the whole house, looked at blue prints and everything. The property is so huge we don't have time to explore it all."

"What's the rush?" Gavin asks.

Logan and I exchange a glance. Should I tell Gavin the truth?

"Don't try to lie to me, little sister. I can see right through you."

"Um, well, I don't know how to put this, I mean it's all speculation until we hear back from Dr. Hayes," I say, staring at my hands to avoid his gaze.

"Stop stalling and spill it," Gavin yells.

"Several people have died on Halloween over the last decade," Logan says rescuing me. "Other than cause of death, we can't find any correlation. They all died of a massive brain hemorrhage. That type of extreme damage tends to be related to supernatural causes. We think the Foxblood Demon's been trying to possess clairvoyants and killing them in the process."

"And you think Kacie is next," Raven says, her eyes wide with fear.

"Halloween is only ten days away!" Gavin says, leaping to his feet. "When were you going to tell me?"

"I wasn't," I reply, cringing from the angry glare plastered to Gavin's face. "We don't know if it's true or not. It's just speculation. And there's nothing you can do about it anyway."

"We need to figure out how to induce the visions," Raven says as she renews her restless pacing. "Have you tried going back to the scene of the crime?"

"We can't take her back there. It's too dangerous," Logan insists. "Last time Yardley attacked her and sent her flying about ten yards. He's gaining strength, and he doesn't like his personal stomping grounds invaded."

"He's panicking," Raven says.

Her pacing drives Gavin to the breaking point, and he grabs her shoulders to stop her. "Please stop that," he says, giving her a little shake.

"Sorry, I think better when I pace."

Happy chimes from the musical doorbell fill the room, completely at odds with the dark energy. Without a word, Gavin releases Raven and stomps from the room heading toward the door. The moment Gavin's hands are gone, Raven paces circles around the sofa like a vulture waiting for its prey to die. I glance up to see her eyeing me with an intense stare.

"Let me braid your hair," Raven says, dropping to the sofa beside me.

I blink at her a few times in confusion. "Uh, why?" I ask, wondering about her sanity.

"The pacing isn't working," she says, reaching for my hair. I turn around to give her better access. "I need to keep my hands busy. It helps me think." Her hands make quick work of my long hair. "Damn, that didn't take long enough."

"Mom!" Logan says in a surprised gasp. "What're you doing here?"

"Can't a mother come by and meet the girl who's stolen away her son?" Mrs. Finley asks in a cheerful tone. She laughs when Logan cringes. "I'm just kidding, hun. Though, I did come to see Kacie."

She floats across the room, the picture of grace. Her light blonde hair is tied back in a neat French twist with several strands artfully framing her heart-shaped face. Intelligence and wisdom gleam in her soft brown eyes. When she smiles, tiny creases appear at the outer edges, stretching to her temples. Reaching out, she takes one of my hands in both of hers. She taps one of her short, pink nails against the back of my hand in a steady beat. Her eyes drift closed, and she hums a melancholy tune under her breath.

"Well, you've managed to stop yourself up good, my dear," she says, making a clucking noise with her tongue.

The first thing that pops into my head makes my cheeks burn—God, I hope she isn't talking about bodily functions. I pull my hand from her grasp with the intention of burying my face to hide my embarrassment.

"Mother!" Logan yelps. I glance up at him to see a flush creep across his tanned cheeks. "Think about things before you say them."

"What?" she asks, tipping her head to the side. I can see the moment his meaning sinks in. Her eyes widen and she throws her head back laughing. "Oh boy, I meant you're psychically blocked. Sorry…"

Yep, just what I needed. I meet my boyfriend's mom and she's busting up over a potty joke. I'm not sure whether to laugh or cry. Fearing I'll do both, I keep my mouth shut in a firm line. When her laughter dies down, she grabs her large black hobo bag from the ground and roots through it while mumbling under her breath. With a cry of triumph, she pulls out a blue velvet pouch. She places it in my hands before making a gesture to open it. After untying the drawstring, I dump the contents into my hand.

"It's beautiful," I whisper, turning the antique silver bracelet over in my hands. "I've never seen anything like it."

The bracelet is covered in strange etchings that look like some ancient runic language. It's lightweight, which is surprising, given the size. The bangle is about two inches wide. A large silver bracelet like this should weigh more, and yet I can barely feel it at all. Near the clasp, several flowers are woven together with thorny braches. *Briars*, my mind whispers. The clasp opens with a tiny *click,* and the moment I place it on my wrist, it closes by itself. Within moments the bracelet shrinks until it's the perfect fit.

"Mom, is that…" Logan seems unable to finish his question.

"It is, Logan," Mrs. Finley says, rubbing her hands together. "The Briar Bracelet finally found a new home."

"It's beautiful, Mrs. Finley," I murmur, tracing the interlocking briars. "I'd like to say I can't accept something this wonderful, but it feels so right on my wrist."

"That's because it was meant for you," Mrs. Finley says with a chirp of triumph. "I had a premonition and in it you were wearing the bracelet."

"How could you have a premonition when you've never met her?" Logan asks, confusion lacing his voice. "I thought that was impossible."

"It is, at least for me," she replies, glancing over at her son. "But her essence was all over your clothes."

"Mother!" Logan gasps, dropping his face into his palm.

"What did I say this time?" she asks perplexed. She waves her hand in the air. "Never mind. When I picked up your clothes to do the laundry, there was enough of Kacie's essence on them for the premonition to come through. I think it'd been trying to for days. Would explain the headaches and my constant need to be near the bracelet."

While playing with the clasp, I realize it won't open. "Um, Mrs. Finley, why can't I take the bracelet off?" I ask, trying to remain calm as my fingers scratch at my wrist.

"The bracelet chose you, Kacie," she says in a nonchalant tone like it's the most normal thing in the world. "It will only come off if it's safe."

I'm not sure I could be more confused than I am right now. Taking several deep breaths, I count to ten before speaking. Logan has mentioned in the past that his mother is scatterbrained but well-meaning. I glance over at her, noting her serene smile. I'm stuck in a strange bracelet and she's calm and happy.

"Safe?" I ask in a squeaky voice. I have so many questions, but I don't think I can voice them without screaming.

"Is it chafing you?" Raven asks with a horrified look on her face.

Good, I'm not the only one who thinks it's strange to be shacked by a bracelet—no matter how pretty it is. It's odd. Whenever I wiggle the bracelet it loosens a bit and moves with my hand. The moment I stop it tightens up again, hugging my wrist. I feel like it should bother me... and yet...

"Oddly, no, it doesn't bother me at all," I say, twirling it around my wrist. "Other than the fact I can't take it off, that is."

"That just means you're in danger, dear," Mrs. Finley says in a cheerful tone that belies her words.

"Mom, please explain in detail," Logan says when she doesn't continue. "You forget, Kacie isn't from a long line of witches."

"You're a witch?" I ask, my eyes widening at the thought.

"Yes, dear," she replies with a small laugh. "I thought you knew. Logan, haven't you told her anything?"

"Wait, if she's a witch does that make you a warlock?" I ask, glancing at Logan with a sly smile.

"Not necessarily, but yes I am," he says with a sheepish expression.

"So you have magic power?" I ask breathless.

"You're reading too much fiction into the term witch," Raven says with a grin. "Modern day witches don't have to have any powers at all, though I suppose some do. Lots of witches are potion makers or spell casters, but don't have any supernatural powers. It's a recessive trait passed down in families. But really anyone can join a coven."

"Are you a witch too?"

"No, but I'd like to be," Raven says. A dark look full of pain flashes in her eyes before she hides it behind a smile. "I was hoping to find a coven here."

"It looks like you've found one," Mrs. Finley says.

"Really?" Raven asks in a gasped whisper.

"Mmm-hmm. Our next gathering is on All Hallows Eve." Mrs. Finley turns to eye me with a knowing look. "You'll be there too, of course."

"I will?" I ask. Pushing up from the sofa, I cross the room to escape that look in her eyes.

"Now that the bracelet chose you, it's obvious you're descended from a line of witches," Logan says, watching me with what appears like awe. "You'll want to learn about your ancestry. Right?"

I nod, unable to put my thoughts into coherent words. "About this bracelet…" I hold up my arm, reminding everyone about my new shackle.

"Yes. It responds to dark energy around us," Mrs. Finley says as she digs through her enormous handbag again. "When dark energy surrounds you, it will help shield you from that power. If my premonition is correct, it will come in handy very soon…"

She trails off into incoherent mumbles while she pulls various articles from her bag and sets them aside. Normal items mix with strange and some things I can't begin to identify. Does she carry all this around everywhere she goes?

"Ah, here it is," she says in a triumphant shout. "I'll need to speak with your father before giving you this." She dangles a few teabags from her fingers.

"Dad's out on a date with Dr. Hayes," Gavin says with a shrug.

"No way!" I say, suddenly glad Daniel went home. Though, I can hear his voice in my head plain as day.

Is Dr. Hayes going to be your new mommy?

"Oh, that's perfect," Mrs. Finley says, pulling out her cell. "I can talk to them both at once."

My lips curl into a melancholy smile as I sit propped up in my bed by five pillows. It's been so long since I've had a mother fuss over me. Did my mother ever fuss over me? Memories flood my mind—constant scolding, drunken cry-fests, and yes nestled among them were moments of affection.

Tears burn my eyes. I bite my lower lip in an effort to keep the tears at bay. After so much time convincing myself I didn't need her, the truth is… I need my mother. Several tears fall from my eyes, and I wipe them away with the back of my hand.

"Sweetheart, why are you crying?" Mrs. Finley asks as she enters the room carrying a small tray.

She sets the tray on my nightstand and cups my cheek with her hand. A lump forms in my throat at the tender gesture, making more tears slip from my eyes.

"I miss my mother," I whisper, biting my lip hard enough to taste blood.

"Oh, sweetie, I'm so sorry," she says, pulling me into a tight embrace. "Logan told me about what happened. It isn't fair, is it? But I want you to know how much your father loves you."

"How do you know?"

"Just a guess, based on what Logan said," she replies, patting my back. "It can be very difficult for someone to make the leap from sceptic to believer."

"I'm not sure he believes," I say, breathing a heavy sigh.

She shrugs. "And yet he supports you all the same."

"Now…"

"Better late than never."

"Cliché," I mumble before my hand flies to cover my mouth. I can't believe I just said that.

"Perhaps," she agrees with a dry laugh. "Though, forgiveness is next to Godliness."

"I thought that was cleanliness," I choke out through laughter.

"Is it?" she asks, raising her brows. "Well, that's just an odd phrase then."

We share a snicker. I feel a pang of regret, a physical ache in my chest. Mrs. Finley enfolds me in her arms again, resting her cheek on my head.

"If you join our coven, I'll be your high priestess," she murmurs, her breath rustling my hair. "Many look to me as a mother figure."

"I think I'd like that," I say, pulling back to smile at her.

"Great," she says as she takes the coffee mug from the tray. "This tea is my proprietary blend. It will not only help ease you into a vision, but also maintain control of the vision."

I take a sip. "This is amazing."

I take a larger gulp of the tea. It tastes of cinnamon and vanilla with a hint of something I don't recognize, an earthy flavor. Before I realize it, I empty the mug. Without a word, Mrs. Finley refills the mug from a small carafe.

"This is your last cup," she says, handing the mug back. "No more than two cups a day of this tea. I mean that literally, by the way. Two normal size coffee mugs or teacups. None of those travel cups. Oh, and only drink it at bedtime or when you're ready for a long nap."

"What will happen if I drink more?"

"The tea also induces sleep," she says while fussing with the tray. "You might be out for a while if you drink too much."

I'm already feeling sleepy, and my head drops back against the pillows before I can finish my second cup. The coffee mug is removed from my grasp by gentle fingers. I try to thank Mrs. Finley, but my mouth can't seem to form the words. As I'm drifting off to sleep, I hear soft laughter.

"Works every time," Mrs. Finley says. Her voice sounds far away. "Sleep well and may the Goddess watch over you."

28
Night Visions
~

My mind wakes from a deep sleep in confusion. I blink my eyes against the darkness. When I wish for light, humming fluorescent bulbs sputter to life, bathing the room in flickering yellow light. What a strange place. Concrete walls, floor, and ceiling with no windows.

Cots line the walls, three high, nine on each side. Old gas masks are heaped in one corner. I push aside a curtain and choke down a scream. A mannequin dressed in a hazmat suit and gas mask stands in silent vigil over the room. I poke at it with one finger, half expecting it to grab me. Nervous laughter bubbles out when the mannequin remains unmoving. Creepy with a capital C.

A metal door with a circular valve handle takes up the majority of one wall. After giving the mannequin one last poke, I walk toward the door. The handle is icy cold, sending a shiver from my finger-tips up my arm.

Righty tighty lefty loosey, echoes in my mind. It's my father's voice from long ago. Back before my mother left and I used to help him with his household projects. Though I use all of my strength, the handle won't budge. I know this is a vision, but I can't help the intense feeling of claustrophobia that grips my chest. My breaths come out shallow and close to panicked.

"Help us," a plaintive voice cries out. It sounds like a young boy.

Gulping, I turn to face ghost Michael with his lolling head. His face is contorted in fear, and his form is much more translucent than last time. The ghost passes through a large metal shelf against the back wall. With tentative steps, I follow Michael. The shelf is filled with canned food. I pick up a can and a layer of dust puffs into my face making me sneeze. There's no date on the can, but I can tell from the label that it's old. Chunky chili with beans. More like botulism in a can...

"Please," Michael pleads in a whisper.

"Where are you?" I ask, my eyes darting around for his ghostly form.

His head peeks out through the lines of cans. "Behind here."

"How do I get back there?" I try to move the shelf but it merely wobbles a bit in place.

"Take the lock off the back wheel then roll it."

On my hands and knees, I wriggle into the small space between the shelf and the wall. The tiny metal lock is stubborn and refuses to turn. Grunting in frustration, I continue to twist it between my thumb and finger. When it finally gives way, I almost cry in relief. My finger is bright red and would be bruised tomorrow if this wasn't some sort of vision or out of body experience. With a gentle shove, I push the metal shelf enough to create a gap large enough to slither through. Crawling forward on my hands and knees, I enter a small tunnel even my dog Kodiak would have trouble fitting through.

At the end of the tunnel, I emerge into a small, round room cut out of the natural limestone. Candlelight flickers off the walls. I rise to my feet, brushing the dust from my legs. For some reason I'm wearing my pajamas in this vision. Jeans and a sweatshirt would've been more suitable. Michael appears before me, hovering next to a crude altar surrounded by numerous red candles. On top of the altar sits an object macabre enough to make my stomach roil in revulsion. A necklace made from thirteen ribs of all different sizes.

A rush of adrenaline surges through my body. This is it—the object binding the children's souls to this plane. All I need to do is destroy it and this nightmare will be over! I reach for it, but my hand passes right through as though it's not real. It doesn't make any sense! I could touch the shelves and the door and the stupid can of chili. Why not this?

"It's protected," Michael says. His voice sounds distant, like he's fading away. "You need to find it and destroy it."

"But where are we?" I ask right as he shimmers and disappears. "Wait, come back!"

A dark presence fills the room, dropping the temperature with its arrival. Wrapping my arms around my body, I shiver, wishing myself awake, or away, or however I can escape. Laughter surrounds me, dark and menacing. Something brushes my hair to the side, and I lurch away with a shriek. Closing my eyes, I renew my efforts to escape.

"Trying to leave so soon, Kassandra?" a deep male voice asks from behind me.

I spin around to face the source of the voice. The Foxblood Demon stands before me looking every bit solid where Michael appeared a ghost. If I didn't know better, I'd think he was alive. His dark eyes leer at me, and his thin lips turn up into a nasty sneer. My heart hammers so hard and fast I can feel each painful beat. He takes a step toward me. I scramble backward, bumping into the altar with my hip. His sneer turns into a gleeful smile, revealing canines filed to points.

"There's no escape, Kassandra," he says with a deep chuckle. "Soon you'll be mine—"

"No!" I scream, cutting him off. "Never!"

I jolt awake with a choked sob. My pulse races as I try to control my ragged breathing. A burning sensation spreads through my chest like I just ran several miles. The vision seemed so real. Light from the hallway bathes my room in eerie shadows. Leaning over, I turn on the lamp by my bed, chasing the shadows away. I fall back against the pillows, flinging my arm over my face. My breaths come out in shallow pants, and I force myself to deepen them before I pass out.

It's over—the vision is over, and I found the relic. I just wish I knew where the underground shelter was.

29
Samhain Gala

~

How hard can it be to find one fallout shelter? Apparently like looking for a piece of hay in a pile of needles. Each time we think we've found it, elation turns to bitter disappointment when we realize we hit another dead end. It's been a week now since my last vision. A week filled with fear, nerves, and frustration.

Dr. Hayes was never able to definitively prove Yardley was responsible for pulverizing the brains of our Halloween victims. But everyone believes it since there's no other logical reason for a brain to suddenly turn to mush. Besides, one of the victims was known to do psychic readings from time to time, and another worked with the police on missing person cases as a consultant. Deep down I know Yardley killed them. Only three days left until Halloween…

Yardley doesn't visit anymore. Perhaps he's building his strength for Halloween, or maybe he's trying to keep those poor tortured souls from providing more clues. Either way I'm both relieved and upset. Yardley scares the crap out of me. I can't help but wonder if I'm blocking the visions somehow. No, I've been drinking Mrs. Finley's tea every single night. The bracelet around my wrist is still stuck tight. Every once in a while it vibrates, reacting to dark energy nearby. Creepy as it sounds I think Yardley is watching me from a distance.

I'm seated at Celia's vanity while she curls my hair with some monstrous device that sucks in the hair and spits out a curl. Any moment I'm sure she'll load it wrong and it will rip out a chunk of my hair. Still as a statue, I continue to sit while listening to the *whirr* of the curler and Rebecca's voice on speaker.

"Will it work on thick hair?" Rebecca asks Celia.

"I'm not sure," Celia says as she guides another small chunk of hair into the machine. "Kacie and I both have fine hair. I think you'd have to use less hair in each curl. You should come over sometime when you don't care if I mangle your hair and give it a try."

"Speaking of mangled hair," I mumble when Celia pulls a bit harder than she had been. "I'd like to keep my hair firmly attached to my head if you don't mind."

"Cute, Kacie," Celia says with a wide smile. "You will be my greatest masterpiece, so stop worrying."

"Should I iron or curl my hair for tonight?" Rebecca asks.

"Could we stick to the topic at hand?" I ask with a frustrated sigh. "Halloween is only a few days away, and we're no closer to finding the fallout shelter than we were a week ago."

"Yeah, are you sure there's a shelter at all?" Rebecca asks. I can hear the hesitation and doubt in her voice.

"Well it was some kind of underground bunker," I reply, picturing the room in my mind. "There was a hazmat suit and some gas masks. Old canned food and cots lining the walls. There were also those radiation stickers on a few of the cabinets."

"That's odd," Rebecca says. "Why would there be radiation warnings inside the bunker? Did you open any of the cabinets?"

"No, I didn't have time," I reply, flinching as the damned machine pulls my hair again. "But now that you mention it... that does seem odd."

"Well, I've gotten nowhere with my research," she says with a loud sigh. "Any ideas?"

A sudden epiphany hits. "Have you located any relatives of his followers?"

"I did," she relies in a glum voice. "Yardley's followers had no contact with the outside world after they joined his cult."

"It's there, I just know it," I say, my voice rising with my conviction. "It would be close to the house or the barn. He wouldn't want to run the risk…" I trail off as my eyes widen and my adrenaline surges. It couldn't be that simple. And yet… "Oh, I think I know where the entrance is!"

"Spill!" Rebecca shouts.

"I think there's an entrance in that ritual room," I say, bouncing in my excitement. Celia berates me after yanking a section of hair.

"Like a tunnel or something?" Rebecca asks. She sounds excited too. I can almost see her leaning forward as her interest is piqued. "It's not on any of the blueprints."

"Was the ritual room or the secret passage on the blueprint filed with the city?"

"No," she admits. "But that room was pretty barren. Where would he hide a secret passage?"

"I don't know, but I have a strong feeling that I'm right on this."

"Rebecca, what time is your date picking you up?" Celia asks while digging through her makeup drawer.

"Six o'clock," Rebecca replies. A sudden shriek comes through the phone deafening us. "That's in half an hour. Gotta go."

"As for you, Kacie, don't flinch or fight while I'm doing your makeup," Celia says, shaking her finger at me. "You should be used to this by now with all the times I've done your stage makeup, and yet I always feel like you might bite my finger any minute…" She trails off, muttering under her breath about colors.

"Just don't make me look like a glamorized clown," I say in a pleading tone.

"Stop worrying," she says while applying my foundation. "When have I ever let you down?"

"Never. Thanks for helping me get ready, Celia," I say, moving my mouth as little as possible. "I'm so happy I can avoid Dad and his camera."

"Too bad I already promised your dad lots of pictures."

"Traitor!"

∽╤

We walk across the grand lobby of the Hyatt arm in arm. Logan looks wickedly handsome in his black tuxedo. Celia blabbed about my dress, or else she helped him shop. His tie and cummerbund match my dress. We must look like a couple on the way to prom or maybe a wedding since it's October and not May.

As we approach the escalator leading to the ballrooms on the second floor I begin to have doubts. The hem of my dress brushes the floor even in my heels. Is there any way I can ride the escalator without getting the dress caught in it? Logan notices my distress and steers me toward the elevator bank. I give him a grateful smile.

Colorful streamers in burgundy and royal blue hang from the ceiling in the magnificent ballroom. Multiple tables covered in matching tablecloths stretch out before us. My arm is wrapped around Logan's, and I clutch it with both hands when my nerves decide to take over. So many people I don't know. Shyness creeps in, a siren song urging me to flee, or I may be forced to make small talk with a stranger. Before I have a chance to decide if I'm going to flee or not, Carl races over, grabbing my arm in his excitement.

"Rebecca told me your theory," Carl says in a booming voice that drowns out the ambient music. "I'm on board. We'll go look for the secret passage tomorrow."

Logan looks at me with his brows raised. "What's he talking about, Kacie?"

"She had a revelation about the fallout shelter," Carl says, bouncing with giddiness.

A strange sight indeed. Carl in a tux is strange enough, but Carl in a tux jumping around like a little boy is too much. He sticks a finger in the neck of his shirt and fumbles with his black bow tie. Watching Carl, I understand why people sometimes call it a monkey suit.

"Why didn't you tell me?" Logan asks.

I glance up at him, surprised by the hurt in his voice. His eyes are guarded as he stares back.

"I got caught up in us," I reply, regretting my words the moment they leave my mouth. Though it's true, I feel like I revealed too much.

"Good excuse," he says winking at me. He extracts his arm from my tight grasp, wrapping it around my shoulders. "I like that I make you forget things," he whispers in my ear.

A bright flush creeps across my cheeks. "While I was getting ready, I thought maybe the fallout shelter has an entrance off the ritual room."

"Interesting theory," Logan says nodding. "Yardley was a crafty planner. If the ritual room led to the fallout shelter, it would be easier to get his prisoners from one place to the other."

"But I still don't know what object he used to bind his soul to our plane," I say with a loud sigh. "I don't think we can exorcise him without it."

"He'll be weakened when we release the children's souls," he says, leading me over to a table laden with appetizers. "Eat. You need to keep up your strength."

"Yes, Dad," I say, giggling.

Logan rubs his chin with his hand. "Please don't call me that."

Still laughing, I fill the plate with an assortment of food I don't recognize. It's all so beautiful. With any luck it'll taste as good as it looks.

"Have I told you how gorgeous you look tonight?" Logan asks in a husky voice as we sit down at an empty table.

"Only about every ten minutes or so," I reply blushing.

He can say it as many times as he wants. I love it.

"I couldn't speak when I first saw you walking down the stairs," he admits, looking away.

"I couldn't breathe while walking down the stairs," I say. His cheeks are red again. "I was sure I'd tumble down."

"You didn't."

"Luck was on my side," I say, glancing down when he turns his gaze to me. "You looked so amazing standing there in that tux. It's a miracle I made it downstairs in one piece. Celia's idea for a grand entrance was—"

"Inspired," he says cutting me off.

"I was going to say fraught with danger," I say laughing.

"Hey, Logan, Cici," Daniel says from behind us.

Turning around, I swallow a slight gasp. Daniel looks good. I mean he always looks good but messy, or maybe casual. Tonight he looks like a movie star in his black tux. His hair is combed and styled instead of the normal careless disarray style he favors. He strikes a dramatic James Bond pose. Yep, there's the Daniel I know.

"I have to say, Cici, you look absolutely stunning tonight," Daniel says in a low purr. He stares at me with his *come hither* pout.

"Where's your date," Logan asks in a brusque tone. "Lost her already?"

When I glance at Logan from the corner of my eye, I see his jealous glare. Misplaced. Daniel isn't my type, no matter how handsome he looks tonight.

"I get the feeling our little Raven is annoyed with me," Daniel says with a casual shrug.

I follow his gaze to the appetizer table across the room. Raven is talking to Rebecca. When she glances at us from across the room, I can feel her annoyance without being an empath.

"What did you do to her?" I ask, rising from the table.

"Nothing," Daniel replies with a scowl. "One of my groupies lives next door to her. When I went to pick her up, groupie number three and her minions caused some trouble."

"Which one is groupie number three?" I ask, trying to picture Daniel's annoying entourage in my mind.

"The icy blonde bitch," Daniel replies. "Raven hasn't been around long enough to know I'm not really dating all those girls. Hell, I can't even stand most of them."

"I'll go talk to her," I say, patting Daniel on the arm.

He puts up with a lot of crap from those damn groupies, and as far as I know, he's never encouraged them either. When Logan looks up at me with sad eyes, I lean down and kiss his cheek.

"I'll be right back, handsome," I whisper in his ear, pleased when a broad smile extends across his face.

As I approach Raven, I can't help but notice how pretty she looks tonight. Her black hair falls in large waves around her shoulders. The sides are done up in several tiny braids draped and tied in back. Her full length cerulean gown brings out the blue in her eyes. It's plain, like mine, no rhinestones or frilly lace to detract from the elegant appearance.

Rebecca's dress is adorable—strapless black lace with silver threads woven throughout. While Raven's and my hemline brush the floor, Rebecca's ends midthigh. I've never seen her look so trendy. In fact, I didn't know she had legs.

"About Daniel's groupies," I say when I reach Raven's side.

"Those bitches? I don't care about them," Raven says, tossing her hair in a motion reminding me of Celia. "I guess I just really enjoy torturing Daniel."

"I know what you mean," I reply, biting my lip to hide my smirk. "He always reacts so well. Maybe it's the acting."

"Drama king?" Raven asks, glancing over at Daniel.

"Something like that," I say, following her gaze. "You can really see what the groupies see tonight."

"I like him a lot," Raven says. I gasp and whirl around to face her. She laughs. "I mean as a friend—only as a friend. He's not my type at all. I hope I didn't give him the wrong idea when I kissed him in front of Queen Bitch. She was treating him like a slab of beef. Pissed me off. So I guess I kinda marked him as mine."

"Um, how did he take it?" I ask, now worried about Daniel's feelings.

"We laughed about it all the way here," Raven says, waving her fingers at Daniel. "I think we'll end up good friends."

As she's laughing, she pats my bare shoulder with her hand. The second her hand makes contact with my skin, she freezes. Her eyes glaze over as her fingers dig into my skin. Small tremors wrack her body. It's obvious she's having a vision or a premonition or something. I don't know what to do. She snaps out of it after a few nerve-wracking moments, saving me the agony of coming to a decision.

"What did you see?" I ask in a whisper.

"This is bad," she says as her eyes dart around the room.

When her gaze lands on Logan, cold dread seeps through me. She stares at him for several moments, her head tipped slightly to the side as though she's deep in thought. Lips in a grim line, she turns her gaze back to me.

"What is it?" I ask in a tentative murmur. "What did you see?"

"I saw Logan stabbed with an athame," she says, closing her eyes. "I don't know if he dies or not…"

"No!" I shriek, slapping my hand over my mouth. "Where? When? Who? What's an athame?" My questions come out an almost incoherent babble.

"A ceremonial dagger," Rebecca answers in a shaky voice.

Memories surface from my vision in the ritual room. Yardley was holding a dagger with a long, curvy blade. Sharp pain lances through my side. My hand flies to my ribs as my breath comes out in a pained *whoosh*. The pain disappears as quickly as it appeared, leaving me reeling a bit in its wake.

"What happened?" Rebecca asks, clutching my arm.

"Phantom pain from that vision I had last week," I reply, shaking my head in an attempt to clear my muddled thoughts. "Raven, what did you see?"

"Logan was stabbed in the stomach," Raven says, lowering her head. "He was dressed all in black. I think he was wearing a Halloween costume. But that's not the worst part…"

"What could be worse than Logan being stabbed?" I ask when she remains silent.

"The person who stabbed him…" She stares at me for a few moments without blinking then she closes her eyes. "Was you."

30

The Search

Darkened landscape flies by in a blur of lights and shadows. My eyes don't focus on anything as I gaze out the passenger window of Daniel's SUV. Car thieves. That's us. Never thought I'd be a party to grand theft auto except on my PlayStation. Yet here I am, squirming in the passenger seat while Raven races down the freeway toward Foxblood Manor.

Raven's premonition frightened me. I would never hurt Logan, so I don't know what to make of it. Though I don't know her all that well, I can't think of any reason why she'd lie about such a thing. Besides, she saw me wearing a fairy costume when I stabbed Logan. I hadn't even told Celia about the risqué costume hidden at the back of my closet. I was saving it for a surprise. I doubt Raven dug through my closet on the off chance she could present a fake premonition.

"You know this is how girls always die in movies," Rebecca says from the backseat. "Leaving the guys behind and rushing into danger alone."

"This is so far from a movie, it's not even funny," I say while trying to keep the tears at bay.

If Raven's premonition is right, then Yardley must possess me. Sure it's possible he possessed Logan, but I don't think I could stab him even if he was possessed. No, I'd try to help him and probably get myself killed in the process. There's little doubt—by Halloween, Yardley will possess me unless I take him out first.

"But Raven's vision happens on Halloween," Rebecca argues. "That's three days away. We should've brought the guys with us."

"The future is always in motion," Raven says as she steers down the off ramp. Silence permeates the car while we wait for the red light to change. "There's always the possibility the time of the attack could change if all the players are present."

"It's so confusing," Rebecca says with an aggravated sigh.

"Agreed," Raven says.

Raven gasps as we pass through the monstrous wrought iron gates of Wooded Acres. With shaky movements she pulls the car to the side of the road.

"What's wrong?" I ask when she drops her head to the steering wheel.

"Bad vibes," Raven whispers. "Really bad… and I've seen some bad things before…"

"Can you still drive?" Rebecca asks, leaning forward from the backseat.

"Not safely," Raven mumbles.

"Guess it's up to me then," Rebecca says in a cheerful tone.

"You're only fifteen, like me," I say, rolling my eyes. "You can't drive."

"I'm not supposed to drive," Rebecca says, pushing open the car door. I watch in silence as she helps Raven into the back. She smiles at me after she slides into the driver's seat. "Shouldn't and can't are two different things. We already stole a car—I may as well drive without a license."

She takes off at a nice, slow pace down the winding road. I'm guessing Carl taught her to drive based on her style. My palms sweat from nerves. I'm about to wipe them on my legs when I remember the beautiful satin dress I'm wearing. Closing my eyes, I let my head fall against the headrest with a sigh. It's obvious we didn't give this endeavor enough thought considering we're all wearing formal attire. Won't we look cute nosing around secret passageways in formal gowns.

"Maybe we should've gone home to change first," I murmur.

"That would give the guys time to figure out what we're doing," Rebecca says as she turns down the gravel road leading to Foxblood Manor.

"Fate is a funny thing, Kacie," Raven says with a loud groan. "God, my head hurts. This better pass soon or I'll be useless in there."

"My head hurts too," I say, pulling a travel size bottle of ibuprofen from my clutch. "Every time I come here I get a headache. Must be the dark energy or something."

"Thanks," Raven says when I hand her two pills and a water bottle. "Anyway, we can't have Logan showing up or the premonition may come true tonight."

"I'm confused," Rebecca says as she slows the SUV to a crawl along the pitted road. "Why would you have the premonition that it occurred on Halloween if it could also occur tonight."

"It is confusing," Raven admits. "Look at it this way. When I had the premonition, the key players and variables were going to be met on Halloween. If Logan shows up here tonight instead then that could change everything."

"The guys aren't stupid," I say, taking the water bottle back from Raven. I swallow the two pills in one gulp. "They'll figure out where we went."

"Then I guess we should hurry," Rebecca says, parking in front of the house. "Man, this place is spooky at night."

Gulping in a quick breath of air, I open the car door before I can lose my nerve. Rebecca's right. This place is scary. Though it's not the rundown, stereotypical haunted house in the movies, something about it feels... evil. Shadows dance across the brick exterior, and my eyes track the movements. My brain tells me it's the moonlight and clouds causing the shadows, and yet that deeper part of me, the primitive drive to run from danger, doesn't agree. A cold breeze blows by, sending my hair flying around my body. Goosebumps rise up along my arms, part from the cold but also from fear.

"This house is beautiful," Raven says, walking toward the front porch. "But the negative vibes are enough to send anyone running."

"Are you coming, Kacie?" Rebecca calls from the front door. How I wish I was a psychic null like her right now.

"Yeah," I say, grabbing Logan's leather jacket from the front seat. After wrapping myself in a little bit of him, I feel not only warmer on the outside, but stronger inside. I'm glad he left it in the car the last time we were out with Daniel. Gathering my long skirt in my hands, I climb the stairs to join my friends on the porch.

"All right, here's the plan," Rebecca says as she fits the key into the lock. "We stick together at all times. Never lose sight of each other, ever. Strength in numbers and all that. We head straight to the ritual room. Ready?"

When Raven and I nod our agreement, she unlocks the front door. It swings open on silent hinges. I can't help but chuckle.

"What's so funny?" Raven asks in a whisper.

"The un-haunted house had squeaky hinges and the haunted house doesn't," I say with a high-pitched giggle. "Ironic."

My laughter betrays my nerves. If I wasn't so scared, I'd be mortified that such sounds were emanating from me.

"Long story," Rebecca tells Raven. "Fill you in later."

Rebecca clicks on her flashlight, shining it on the walls lining the foyer. My body trembles as the small beam of light dances around, leaving most of the room in darkness. Fear grips me, closing my throat and making it difficult to breathe. I just know Yardley is lurking around here somewhere. Maybe he's watching our every move right now. Swallowing around the lump in my throat, I follow Rebecca down the hallway towards the kitchen. Raven is so close behind me, I can hear her breath. She gasps as something scurries across the floor next to us.

"A mouse," Rebecca whispers as she shines the light on the cute little white mouse staring up at us with beady red eyes. "I think he's someone's pet. Wild mice normally aren't white."

The mouse scampers off back the way he came, and I breathe a sigh of relief. I'm not afraid of mice, but I also don't want to be alone in a dark hallway with one. With my nose buried in the neck of Logan's jacket, I breathe in his lingering scent and my nerves calm. Maybe coming here without him was a mistake. Our powers seem are stronger when we're together, especially when we're touching.

No. Raven's vision can't come to pass. He'll be furious when he realizes what we've done. My cell is lying on the front seat of Daniel's SUV. I bet I have multiple voicemails and texts by now. It's been forty-five minutes since we left, he knows by now.

"Wait," I say as we creep past the sitting room.

Rebecca shines the light into the dark room, illuminating the fireplace I remember from our last visit. With careful steps, I cross the room and grab the poker from the stand next to the hearth. I swing it in large arcs a few times, nodding in satisfaction.

"Cold iron," I say in a loud whisper.

"Does that really work?" Raven asks while staring at the poker in my hands.

"Most of the time spiritual energy is repelled by iron," I reply shrugging. "I feel better holding it, that's for sure."

"We'll get some salt from the kitchen," Rebecca says as we continue down the hall. "I wish I had a shotgun with rock salt like Sam and Dean."

"Why do I think you'd just end up shooting one of us?" Raven asks with a dry laugh.

"I'm an ace shot, just so you know," Rebecca says, turning to glare at Raven. "Born and raised Texan here."

"So why don't we have shotguns with rock salt?" Raven asks while Rebecca digs through the pantry looking for salt.

"Mr. Kincaid thinks they're too dangerous..." Rebecca's voice is muffled, and the rest is drowned out by my laughter.

"Too dangerous," I choke out through giggles. "Like chasing homicidal ghosts is safe."

Why I always get uncontrollable giggles when I'm nervous is beyond me. Makes acting on stage a challenge. Raven joins my laughter, though hers is wry and cynical where mine is just hysterical. After a few more moments, Rebecca emerges with a bag of salt. She hands the salt to Raven, then motions for us to follow her down the narrow servants' hallway.

"What about you?" Raven asks.

"This flashlight has a high concentration of iron," she replies, holding up the long flashlight. It looks like something a security guard would carry. "Not that I'd actually see the ghost to use it."

"You've never seen a ghost?" Raven asks, sounding dumbstruck.

"Psychic null here, remember," Rebecca replies, swinging the light around the walls. "I can see their impact on things around us but not the ghost itself."

When we reach the end of the hallway, I'm surprised to see the secret passage open, almost in welcoming. A shudder courses through me.

Is Yardley waiting for us on the other side?

Rebecca leads the way through the narrow tunnel. The cobwebs are gone. It's nice to walk without sticky strands grabbing my hair.

"Who cleaned?" I ask.

"Devon and Michelle," Rebecca answers but doesn't elaborate.

When we emerge into the circular room, Rebecca flips on the lights. The light is blinding, and I blink rapidly trying to adjust.

"If there's power, why did we just sneak through the house in the dark?" Raven asks with a scowl.

"We're not supposed to be here, remember?" Rebecca replies with a snort of disgust. "I didn't want to announce our presence."

"That would make sense if we weren't out in the middle of nowhere," Raven bites back.

"Stop!" I yell a bit louder than I intended. "Let's find this secret passage and get moving. Who knows how long we have before *he* shows up."

"Noted," Rebecca murmurs, moving to the black stone altar. "Remember to stay within sight of each other. We aren't going to be human fodder like in the movies."

Raven and I nod our agreement and begin the search.

31

Nothing Can Shelter Me from this Fallout

~

The ritual room isn't very large, nor does it have much in the way of décor. So finding the secret passage I'm sure is here should be easy, right? What's that phrase… if wishes were fishes… yeah, whatever. After inspecting every inch of the black altar, we move on to the walls. Logic says it must be behind the massive bookcase filled with dark occult books. Well, maybe not logic, but popular culture. Over one hundred dusty tomes later and still nothing.

"It's a great theory, Kacie," Rebecca says after a series of sneezes. Her last sneeze sends more dust flying around us. "But don't you think we'd have found it by now?"

"I can't give up yet," I say as tears fill my eyes. Though I try to convince myself they're from the dust, I know better. "If the passage to the shelter isn't here, then I don't know how we'll find it by Halloween."

"Well, Scooby and Shaggy would goof off and stumble into it," Rebecca says with a half-hearted laugh.

"Maybe I should've brought Kodiak. He's a giant klutz," I mumble while trying to wedge my fingers behind the bookshelf. For a brief moment, I feel a cool breeze on my fingertips. "Hey, I think I felt a breeze from behind here. Keep looking!"

"It is odd that this shelf seems to be affixed to the wall," Raven says, squatting beside the bottom shelf. "You'd think we could move it, or at least topple it."

"The switch doesn't have to be on the bookcase," Rebecca says, brushing the dust from her hands.

We must look ridiculous—three girls rooting around for a hidden passage in formal gowns. I spin around, taking in every rounded wall in the room. Most are bare stone, no help there. We already searched every inch of the altar in the center of the room. What's left? Sconces line the walls, so one of those could be a switch. But that's so obvious. I watch Rebecca and Raven fan out to check each individual light fixture. It couldn't be that easy. Then the passage might open anytime someone changed a light bulb. I just don't think Yardley would make it that easy to find his inner sanctum.

While thinking, I trace the inverted pentagram carved into the back wall with my finger. The stone is cool and smooth beneath my finger until I reach the point on the right. It feels different than the rest of the design. My heart leaps in excitement as I poke around the stone until I feel a small click beneath my finger. A loud grinding noise fills the room. I whip my head around looking for the source. The entire stone altar shifts to the side, revealing a stone staircase descending into darkness.

As I approach the opening in the floor, the silver bracelet around my wrist begins to vibrate—short bursts of energy. Glancing down, I'm surprised to see it move in a steady beat, like a pulse. Blue light flashes with every other beat. I stare at it in confusion as it continues to pulsate.

Mrs. Finley should've given me an instruction manual.

Rebecca shines her light down the set of stairs leading underground. When she looks back up, I'm not at all surprised to see fear reflected in her eyes. Gathering the skirt of my gown in my hands, I step down onto the first stair. Nothing happens, and I exhale the breath I'd been holding. I don't know quite what I was expecting, but images from Indiana Jones movies were flying through my mind. Another step and it's become almost too dark to see.

"I guess this is it," Rebecca murmurs, taking the first step. "Kinda cramped, huh?"

"At least we won't lose sight of each other," Raven says as she follows behind us.

With careful steps, we descend into a small tunnel. Eight steps. I counted each one, expecting a trap to spring at any moment. The stone walls of the tunnel are lined with red candles. We pause while Rebecca shines her light around, checking out the walls, floor and ceiling. This tunnel was carved out of the limestone the house was built on. Warm air with a musty smell makes each breath difficult. We inch down the hallway until we come to a metal door with a radiation symbol on it.

"This is it," I say in an excited whisper. "The fallout shelter."

"But how do we open it?" Rebecca asks, eyeing the door with a wary look.

"Let's try the easy way first," I murmur, grasping the valve-like door handle. It spins beneath my hands with ease, and the door swings open on silent hinges.

"This tunnel has been cleaned, and the door maintained," Rebecca says, taking several steps backwards. "Ghosts can't do that. So who did?"

"We have to keep going," Raven says, patting Rebecca on the shoulder. "We came this far. We're not running away scared."

After taking several deep breaths, I step over the threshold and enter the shelter. It looks just like it did in my vision. Cots with army green blankets line the walls, three high. Cabinets that stretch from floor to ceiling span the small distance between each set of cots. On the back wall I see the metal shelf filled with old canned goods. I'm about four steps in when I realize the electricity is on. The room is lit as bright as day. Did Rebecca or Raven turn on the light? No, it was already on when we entered.

"I don't think we're alone in here," I murmur over my shoulder.

"Maybe we should leave," Raven says, her eyes darting around the empty room.

"No!" a frantic male voice cries from behind the metal shelves. "Don't leave!"

"Oh my God! Who is that?" Rebecca asks, the light from her flashlight bobbing with her tremors.

"You heard it?" I ask, gasping at the implications. She nods her head. Her grip on the flashlight is so tight, her knuckles are white. "Then it couldn't have been a spirit."

"Let's go," Raven says as she passes me to examine the metal shelves. "Whoever it is might need our help."

I admire her bravery. My feet don't want to move. When I try to tell Raven how to move the shelving unit, the words never make it from my brain to my mouth. Instead, I crouch down, releasing the wheel lock with fumbling fingers. A short tunnel appears, leading to another brightly lit room. The ceiling is low enough that we have to bend over to make it through. At least it's bigger than it was in my vision. With one hand I gather my skirt to keep from tripping. The other hand trails across the cool limestone. By the time I've counted to twenty in my head, I emerge into a small room.

A wooden desk covers about half the room, with a bookshelf behind it. Limestone walls are covered with white bed sheets. Affixed to the sheets are hundreds of photos, grouped together by person. I recognize Ellie almost immediately. She has a lot more pictures than the others. It seems Yardley was watching her for quite a while before she was abducted. Pictures of her at school, at the pool, and the mall dominate an entire section. She's not alone. Pictures of other girls surround Ellie. Were they other potential victims, future victims?

Posted next to the pictures is a long list of names with dates of birth written beside them. Most have been crossed out—all but thirteen anyway. At the top of the paper is the name and address of a pediatric clinic. So that's how he found his victims. They all went to the same pediatrician. One of his followers must have worked in that office. Sorrow settles over me. Fate can be so fickle. A trip meant to keep a child healthy ultimately led to death.

"Uh, Kacie, you need to see this," Rebecca says in a shaky voice.

I cross the small room to stand by Rebecca. My eyes widen as I take in the array of photos before me. A whole montage dedicated entirely to me. And not all recent either. Some of the photos are from last year. How is this possible? My throat closes, making it difficult to breathe. Black spots dance across my field of vision. Terror squeezes my heart in a vise-like grip. I can hear my friends calling to me, but their voices are hollow in my ears.

"How?" I croak, falling to my knees on the limestone floor.

"That would be me." It's that same male voice again.

He sounds quite pleased with himself. I know I've heard the voice before, but I can't seem to place it.

"Who are you?" Raven asks in a harsh tone. "Why are you here?"

"I live here," he says, closer this time. "I do my father's bidding. Since he's been building up power, there's little choice in the matter. Not that I mind."

"Your father?" Rebecca asks as she pulls me to my feet. "Who's your father?"

"Lucas Yardley, of course," he replies in a haughty tone.

Once the world stops spinning around me, I turn to look at the owner of the voice. He's a man, maybe fifty. The man preens under our scrutiny, a proud smile plastered on his face. Sunken eyes dart all around the room. A shock of silver hair crowns his head, cut short but erratic, as though he cut it himself without a mirror. He's a walking contradiction. His body looks as though it's falling apart, but his attitude is larger than life.

"You look so familiar," I murmur, watching the strange man caress the photos of me in a loving manner. "Uh, what's your name?"

"Bob," he says, nodding his head. "Bob Carter."

It suddenly hits me. This is Mr. Carter, the owner of the house. The one who called us to investigate in the first place.

"Why are you in here, Mr. Carter?" Rebecca asks, creeping closer inch by slow inch.

"Scared," he replies, his voice tinged in anguish, his hands fisted in his messy hair. "My head hurts." His proud arrogance is gone in the face of his pain.

"Did you take these pictures, Mr. Carter?" I ask, pointing to the images with my face staring back.

Mr. Carter's face lights up at the mention of the pictures. "Yes!" he says with enthusiasm. "Good, right? Father was so proud of me."

"Yes, they're lovely," I reply, confused by his abrupt mood swings. "Why did you take these pictures?"

"Father told me to," Mr. Carter says, his face darkening again. "He wants you."

"For what?" I ask, my voice rising with my fear. "Why does Lucas Yardley want me?"

"To live again, of course." A chill courses through me at the new voice coming from Mr. Carter's mouth—deep, male, and ethereal.

"Holy crap! He's possessed," Rebecca says in a high-pitched squeal.

"What gave it away?" Raven asks in a shaky, yet wry tone. "The maniacal gleam in his eyes or the freaky voice change?"

"What do we do?" Rebecca asks as she backs away from the laughing man.

A chill permeates the room, cooling it enough that I can see my panting breaths in small white clouds. Help has arrived. Wind gusts around Mr. Carter/Lucas Yardley turning into a fierce whirlwind within moments.

"Quick, while he's distracted!" I yell over the raging wind. "Find the relic."

As I dart around Mr. Carter, he makes a grab for my arm but is thrown backward by an unseen force. He hits the wall with a loud *thud* before sliding down and crumpling to the ground. For a moment I can't see anything as my once perfectly coiffed hair whips around my body. I can almost hear Celia cry in frustration. Once my vision clears, I move to the desk and rifle through the drawers. Nothing. I know from my vision that the rib bones were made into a macabre ritual necklace. It just has to be here!

"Back here," a tiny voice says from behind me.

Turning around, I'm surprised to see a small child holding a battered plush bear. She hugs the bear to her chest while biting her lower lip. The girl is translucent, silvery white in appearance. With a shaky finger, she points to the back wall next to the bookcase. I'm about to ask her why she's pointing when her image crackles and disappears. The only thing on the wall is one of those old velvet paintings. This one is a skull with roses and barbed wire. Ripping it from the hook on the wall, I stagger under the weight. It drops to the floor, barely missing my feet.

Part of me expects to find a safe, like in an old mystery movie. There's always a safe behind the painting. Instead there's a dark hole about a foot wide. I don't want to stick my hand in there. With shaking hands, I push the end of the long poker into the hole and move it around. It seems to snag on something, but when I pull the poker out, whatever it was stays behind.

Loud groaning forces me to give up my tentative search and do what I was trying to avoid. Mr. Carter is coming around, and we're running out of time. Cringing, I stick my hand into the hole, praying there are no spiders or scorpions within. My fingers brush against satin, and I grab the bundle, yanking it from its hiding place. With shaking hands I unwrap the package, breathing a relieved sigh when I find the rib bone necklace.

"I've got it!" I yell to my friends, holding my prize in the air. "Now what?"

"Toss it to me," Rebecca says, holding out her hands. "There's a burn barrel by the barn."

"How are you gonna make the fire hot enough to burn bones?" Raven asks, her eyes never leaving Mr. Carter's groaning form.

"Daniel has a hunter's pack in the SUV. There's lighter fluid," Rebecca replies, shaking her hands in her urgency. "Come on, toss it here. You'll have to deal with him."

I throw the necklace to her, and she takes off running once she has it. When Mr. Carter moves to sit up, Raven bashes him over the head with an odd looking statue. He crumples back to the ground, but it's not enough to knock him out.

"We have to find the relic tying his spirit here," I say, reaching back into the black hole. After groping around, I realize it's empty now.

"I've got his athame! This must be it," Raven says, holding the ceremonial dagger in the air. "Let's get out of here!"

32
Free at Last

~

She doesn't have to tell me twice. My bracelet is pulsing so fast, it's like a second heartbeat. The rapid beat spurs me into action. I leap over Mr. Carter's flailing legs, thankful Celia let me get away with wearing my character shoes from drama. If I can dance on stage in the shoes, then I can run through a creepy mansion in them as well. Raven follows, a bag of salt cradled in one arm and the black athame brandished before her. We race through the shelter and into the dark tunnel. It's only then I realize we don't have a flashlight. I slow down in the shadows only to speed up again when several crashes sound from the shelter behind us.

As I pass the black stone altar, my bracelet pulses a frantic beat. I stop to stare at it, and Raven gives me a gentle push forward. She's right. There's no time to worry about it now. The bracelet is probably reacting to the evil emanating from that insidious structure. When we reach the longer tunnel, I enter with my eyes closed, running my hand along the wall to guide me. I'll have to remember to bake a cake or something for Michelle and Devon as thanks for cleaning this awful thing.

At the end of the secret passage, I gather my skirts in my free hand and run through the kitchen toward the front door. Bursting through the open door, I come to a dead stop when I see Logan's Mustang parked behind the SUV. Raven comes to a halt beside me.

"Crap, they found us," I murmur, looking around for Logan. "We'd better go find Rebecca before your premonition has a chance to come true."

"You stab him with this athame," Raven says, clutching the dagger close to her chest. "Don't touch it for any reason."

I nod before running around the side of the manor toward the barn. Rebecca is in the front next to a barrel with flames leaping from the inside. My heart soars when I see Logan and Daniel standing beside her. The moment Logan's eyes meet mine, we race toward each other. I drop the poker to the ground before throwing myself at him. He catches me in his arms, holding my trembling body in his tight embrace.

"I was so worried about you," Logan murmurs, leaning his forehead against mine. "Why did you run?"

"No time for that now. Look!" Rebecca shouts.

Large silver orbs shoot out from the burn barrel, careening through the air in swooping arcs. One flies so close to our heads that Logan and I both duck away from the odd ball of light. Some fly off into the night, while others merge together, forming a silvery image that slowly takes shape before us. Ellie steps forward from the silver light holding a small wispy infant in her translucent arms.

"You did it," Ellie says with a brilliant smile while watching the orbs flying around her. "We're finally free. Thank you all so much. We can finally move on, away from the unending sorrow and pain."

"Goodbye, Ellie," I call out as her form begins to fade away. She lifts her hand and waves before fading into a silver orb that shoots up towards the heavens. "Rest in peace," I whisper to the starry sky.

"Now to take care of Yardley once and for all," Raven says, holding up the athame.

"Wait, let me hold that before you destroy it," Daniel says, taking the dagger from Raven. Closing his eyes, he holds the dagger in both hands for several moments. "His soul is not bound to this athame."

"What?" I cry, pulling away from Logan. "It has to be. We decided this was the only thing it could be bound to."

"I'm sorry, Kacie, but this is just an ordinary athame with a very evil vibe," Daniel replies, dropping the dagger to the ground. He brushes his hands together as though trying to rid himself of the taint. "I'm sure I'd feel it if his soul was attached. This athame was used in some heinous rites but that's it."

Despair creeps into my soul as I stare at the athame lying in the dirt at my feet. How will we stop Yardley now? I bite my lip when my eyes start to burn. Crying won't solve anything. Leaning down, I pick up the object I was so sure would set me free from the Foxblood Demon. How could we have been so wrong?

"Kacie, don't—" Raven yells, but it's too late.

My fingers close around the warm hilt. The silver bracelet around my wrist reacts with violent shocks and pulses. I try to drop the dagger, but my right hand refuses to release it. With a pained cry, I grasp the dagger in both hands trying to wrench it from my grip.

"It's stuck to my hand!" I cry out in alarm. "How is this possible? Help!"

"Logan, get away from Kacie!" Raven shouts when he reaches out to help me with the demonic blade.

Her warning is once again too late. The athame acts all on its own, slashing down Logan's arm, tearing through the sleeve of his tuxedo jacket.

"No!" I scream, shaking my hands in an effort to dislodge the blade.

"I'm okay, it's just a scratch," Logan says, backing away from me.

"What's happening?" I manage to choke out through the terror gripping me. "You said Yardley wasn't attached to this thing."

"A spell maybe…" Raven says, her eyes never leaving the curved, black blade. "It would be the darkest magic."

Daniel grabs the blade and rips the dagger from my hands, slicing open his hand in the process. Without hesitation, he throws it into the raging fire. Blood gushes from the deep wound on his palm.

"Logan, take off your jacket," Raven orders in a calm voice that belies the wild look in her eyes. After he drops the jacket to the ground, she grabs his torn sleeve and rips it from his arm. "Crap this isn't going to be enough. Rip off your other sleeve."

A loud ripping sound fills the air as Logan yanks off his other sleeve. I stand rooted in place, staring at Daniel, perhaps in shock, unable to move or offer help—just watching the blood gush from his injured hand. Raven balls up part of one sleeve and presses it to the wound while winding the other pieces around his hand. By the time she's finished, Daniel's hand is mummified beneath several layers of Logan's shirt.

"This should stop the bleeding," Raven says, staring at her bloody hands.

Logan peels off his shirt, handing it to Raven, and she wipes her hands on the white cloth. My eyes move from Daniel's hand to Logan's rather nice torso. The sight jolts me out of my stupor.

For a brief moment I'm torn. Part of me wants to run to him and lose myself in his embrace... to pretend none of this hell around us exists. The other part wants to get as far away as possible before I hurt him. My eyes move from his chest to meet his forlorn gaze. With a choked sob, I fall into his arms, resting my head on his shoulder.

"It's going to be okay, Kacie," Logan whispers against my hair.

"How?" I ask, pulling back to look at him. "I have no idea what he tied his spirit to... I should've listened to my mother."

"Your mother..." Logan trails off, a thoughtful look on his face. "That's it!"

"What?" I ask, perplexed at his sudden excitement. "What's *it*?"

"I think I know what his spirit is tied to," he says, placing his hands on my upper arms. "This is important. I need you to distract his spirit. He can't know what I'm up to."

"But how can I—" Before I can finish my question, the air around us grows frigid.

"Trust me," Logan says. He kisses my forehead then runs off toward the house.

"He's here," Rebecca screams as she spreads the salt on the ground around Daniel in a large circle.

"Cici, run!" Daniel shouts, shooing me away with his uninjured hand. "If you keep moving, it'll be harder for him to possess you."

"I'm going to go help Logan," Rebecca says, darting away with a frightened look on her face.

Gathering my long skirt in my hands, I jog around the side of the barn, relieved when the fierce cold I was feeling moments earlier fades. I'm stopped in my tracks when a misty figure appears in the darkness before me. Without a second thought, I run back the way I came, towards the flickering light of the fire. Daniel has collapsed to the ground, most likely from blood loss. Behind him Raven hovers, brandishing the iron poker at some misty wisps of… something. Whatever it is fails its attempt to cross the salt circle.

Not wanting to draw Yardley's ghost to them, I run over to the house where the porch lights are blazing. As I round the corner, I realize the entire manor is lit up. It looks as though Logan flipped on every light switch he passed. I run past the open front door, out onto the gravel driveway. My lungs burn, and even with my cross country training I don't think I can keep up this zigzag running much longer. After passing the parked cars, I stop to lean against one of the columns lining the wrap-around porch.

Several crows touch down on the railing next to me, staring at me with beady black eyes. The air grows cold, signaling the arrival of Yardley's spirit. Frigid wind spirals around my body, rooting me to the spot. Panic seizes me when I realize I can't move my limbs. One crow, the largest of the bunch, hops over next to me then lets out a loud *caw*.

Flapping black wings fill the air as the crows take flight. They swoop and caw, attacking the silvery outlines of Yardley's phantom presence. I watch in amazement as the wispy shadow flees, heading toward the barn. Several crows chase it while the rest settle back down on the porch railing.

"Kacie!" I hear Logan shout behind me. "Are you okay? What happened? What's with the crows?"

It takes several tries before I can speak. "I-I think, I mean... the crows... they—I think they just saved me from Yardley." Logan takes my hand, leading me away from the porch and my unusual saviors. Glancing over my shoulder, I'm unsurprised to see the remaining crows watching my departure. "Thank you," I call out to the birds. Several ruffle their feathers and spread their wings.

"That was weird," Logan says, pulling me towards the barn. "Do you have a natural affinity with animals?"

"I love animals, but that's about it," I reply still confused about what just happened.

"Aren't you gonna ask me if I found it?" Logan asks with a brash grin.

My heart leaps. "I take it by your expression, you did."

"Thank your mother for this one," he says holding up a hideous goat mask. I reach out to touch the strange looking thing. "I never would've thought of this mask if she hadn't mentioned it. I think the hair on it is Yardley's."

"Eww, gross," I say, pulling my hand back in disgust. "I almost touched that *thing!*"

"Hair is technically a body part," Logan says, holding up the goat mask. "See it could only be the athame if it had his blood on it or was made from his bones."

My spirit soars when the burn barrel comes into view. Only a few more steps and this nightmare will be over for good. One moment Logan is beside me, running toward the barn, the next he's gone. I turn to see him fly through the air, skidding to a rough landing in the gravel. The mask flies from his hand as he hits the ground and is snatched by a white wisp of smoke. Yardley!

"Logan, are you okay?" I ask when I reach his side.

He groans and sits up. "Crap—that hurt like hell!" He groans, massaging his shoulder.

"You're covered in road rash," I murmur as I look him over.

He landed on his right side, and his entire shoulder, arm and upper back are covered in gravel. When I try to tend to his wounds, he knocks my hand away.

"I'm fine," he says, pushing himself to his feet. "We need to get that mask back."

"Yardley took it," I say, allowing Logan to pull me back to my feet.

"Where?"

"I don't know. At the moment I was more worried about you."

A loud cacophony of *caws* echoes all around us. I look up and my jaw drops. Dozens of crows fill the night sky. Black feathers rain down around us from the fighting birds. They take turns swooping at Yardley's wispy phantom image, battering what seems to be an invisible shield. Silver mist wraps around the goat mask protecting it from the birds. Logan and I stand transfixed, confused and unsure what to do.

Though the phantom mist puts up a fight, it isn't long before the unending stream of birds knocks the mask from his spectral grip. It falls to the ground several feet away. Before I can get the message from my brain to my legs to run, Logan snatches the mask from the ground and tears off toward the barn.

The spectral mist abandons its fight with the crows and descends on Logan. Yardley's spirit plows into him, sending him skidding toward the barn. I watch in horror as he slides along the ground on his back, losing his grip on the mask when his arm slams into the gravel. It flies through the air, landing just a few feet from me. Yardley's spirit races toward the mask, but I snatch it up, hugging the foul thing against my chest. Logan rises from the ground, shouting at me to get the mask to the burn barrel.

After only two or three steps, something grabs my arm, stopping me. Silver mist winds around my body, squeezing the air from my lungs like some ghostly boa constrictor. I fight against it, but my hand passes through the mist. There's nothing to grab, no way to stop the phantom as the mist tightens around my entire body. The crows swoop around me, but even they realize there's nothing they can do to stop this ghost from squeezing the life from me.

Glancing up, I see Logan running toward me. Yardley will not get this mask. He can kill me, but he won't exist afterward to harm anyone else. Drawing on the last of my strength, I curl my arm toward my body and throw the mask to Logan like a macabre Frisbee. He catches it in one hand, his gaze darting between me and the fire. *Go*, my mind urges him. After one last look at me, he turns and races toward the burn barrel.

I fall to my knees, gasping for breath. Black spots dance in my vision until I see more black that anything else. When I suck in a tiny breath, the phantom tightens his hold. It's a vicious cycle repeated over and over. Tears fill my eyes, spilling over my eyelashes. My hands scrape against the rough gravel as I fall forward. I try to call out to my friends, to anyone, for help. My plea comes out a raspy wheeze as I collapse to my side.

I lift my head in time to see Logan throw the mask toward the dancing flames. Blue sparks fly and loud crackling *pops* fill the air as the fire engulfs the demonic relic. The Foxblood Demon roars in fury, and his hold around my neck tightens. Darkness washes over me. I give in to it, floating away to a safer place within myself.

33

Reflections & Revelations

~

My latest brush with death put Gavin into overprotective mode again. It's been three days since that awful night. I was told I almost died, that Logan saved my life with CPR. My memory is patchy at best, and I think it's better that way. I remember saying goodbye to Ellie and watching the children move on… but everything after that is foggy. Black feathers, silvery smoke, and pain. Crushing agony. A shudder courses through me, and I shut down that train of thought. Every time I try to remember, it's the same torment, like my brain is melting or something.

Sweet Gavin has hovered over me for the last three days, acting like a mother hen. The theater room is just down the hall from my room, maybe twenty or thirty steps. And yet Gavin insists on carrying me like I'm some sort of invalid. Arguing accomplishes nothing so I keep my mouth shut. He places me on the chaise end of the sofa and fusses with my blanket. Rolling my eyes, I allow him to tuck the blanket around my legs. I have no intention of rocking the boat in any way.

It's been two days since I last saw Logan. I was in and out of consciousness—I remember him holding me in his arms but that's it. I know Gavin snuck him into my room against doctor's orders. That alone is reason to put up with my brother's hovering.

"You comfortable?" Gavin asks in a muted tone.

"Gavin, I'm fine," I reply with a bright smile. "Really. I promise," I add when he stares at me with a raised brow.

Kodiak jumps up on the sofa and settles at my side as Gavin leaves the room. My faithful Goldendoodle hasn't left my side for more than a few minutes since I returned from the hospital Sunday morning. That includes trips to the bathroom. Between him and Gavin I'm beginning to feel stifled. Kodiak's behavior doesn't help my case with Dad or Gavin either. They assume the dog is overprotective because he can sense something they can't.

Dr. Hayes explained in detail what happened to both Dad and Gavin, but not to me. I haven't seen anyone from the Circle since I regained consciousness yesterday—doctor's orders. This afternoon, everyone is coming here for a meeting. So many questions are circling my mind like hungry vultures.

Kodiak lifts his head a bit, and his tail thumps against my leg. Moments later Logan enters the room with a relieved smile on his face. He flops down on the sofa beside me as Kodiak wiggles out of the way. His arms wrap around me, pulling me against his chest. The hungry look in his eyes makes my stomach flutter. He captures my mouth with his, parting my lips with a gentle sweep of his tongue. I throw my arms around his neck, burying my fingers in his wavy hair.

"God, you scared me, Kacie," he murmurs against my lips. "I've been so worried."

"I'm fine," I reply, leaning my forehead against his. "Thanks to you I hear."

"I'm so sorry," he says as he pulls away to gaze at me with serious eyes. "I knew you were fighting Yardley's possession, and I left you to do it alone."

"You kn-knew?" My voice catches in my throat. His words bring a sliver of memory to the surface, but it dances away before I can remember anything.

He nods. I stare at him while trying to process this new information. Tears burn at my eyes, but I refuse to break eye contact.

"Why?" I ask.

"You know the answer," he replies with a sad smile.

It suddenly hits me. "You had to destroy the mask."

"It just about killed me to leave you like that," he whispers between kisses along my cheekbone. "I had no way of knowing if the mask was the right object. His spirit was so strong. I kept picturing the others he tried to possess…"

"You did the right thing, Logan." I pull him into another kiss—slow, tender, and sweet.

"I have something for you," he says, brushing the hair from my forehead. "Close your eyes, I didn't have time to wrap it."

"You didn't have to get my anything."

"Just close your eyes already," Logan says, putting his hand over my eyes.

Grabbing his hand, I push it away playfully. Kodiak thinks we're playing a game, and he jumps to his feet. The dog sticks his face between us before giving Logan a big lick on the nose. I try to keep my laughter at Logan's shocked expression in, which turns out to be a very bad idea. My unladylike snort makes Logan double over with laughter.

I push at him, knocking him over on his back. Before he can move, I pounce, pinning him to the sofa. His lips beckon me, and I close the small gap between us. A warm, fluttering feeling starts in my stomach, spreading like flames through my limbs. I tilt my head to deepen the kiss, and he responds with a deep moan. He cups my face in his hands as his tongue tangles with mine. When he pulls away, I whimper.

"Don't you want your present?" he asks with a lopsided grin.

I nod. His fingers brush a caress along my cheek before he reaches into his pocket and pulls out a small black velvet bag. I dump the contents into my hand, gazing in awe at the beautiful silver medallion. On one side there's an image of an angel etched into the silver. The other side features an image of a crow.

"Michael the Archangel," he says, pointing to the angel side. "I also brought a card with the prayer for you to memorize. It could help in the future if any other spirit tries to possess you."

"What about the crow?" I ask as he clasps the medallion around my neck.

"Hmm, you haven't looked outside recently have you," he remarks, pulling me from the sofa. "Come on."

He leads me to the next room and to the window overlooking the canyon on the side of the house. Dozens of crows sit in the trees watching the house.

"It's not uncommon for a witch to have a familiar," Logan says as we head back to the theater room. "It seems you have not just one crow but a whole murder of them."

"Can we just call them a flock?" I mutter, exasperated by his word choice.

"Well yeah, but that kinda takes all the fun out of it," he jokes, nuzzling my neck with his nose.

"So I really am a witch?" I ask, though I already know the answer. "I don't know the first thing about being a witch."

My fingers play with the silver bracelet on my left wrist. It comes off now, meaning the danger has passed, but I feel wrong without it, like something's missing.

"Don't worry, you have a great teacher," Logan says, lacing his fingers with mine. "We postponed the coven meeting until tomorrow night. Mom already okayed everything with your dad. She's really looking forward to teaching you everything about our history, and also looking into yours as well."

"You postponed the Samhain coven gathering just for me?" I ask, a bit awed that Mrs. Finley would do that.

"Everyone is looking forward to meeting you and Raven," Logan says, kissing the back of my hand. "After what you've been through, one day won't make any difference. It's not like we were planning any spells or rites. Some of those need to be performed on certain days."

"It's all so confusing," I murmur, leaning into his shoulder. "I can't wait to learn everything!"

"Ow," Logan hisses through gritted teeth. He shifts my head to lean on his chest rather than his shoulder.

"You're hurt!" I exclaim. When I try to sit up to inspect him, his arms tighten around me holding me captive.

"I'm fine," he says, stroking my hair. "Just lots of road rash. My right shoulder got the worst of it. Stop squirming," he orders when I try to pull away. "It's still bandaged so you can't see it."

Voices echo from down the hallway as our guests begin to arrive. Kodiak joins the voices with his joyful barks. Daniel is the first through the door.

"Hey, Cici," Daniel says, giving me a one-armed hug. "Good to see you conscious. Did you know you have crows lining the railing on your porch?"

"And in the trees and on the cars in the drive," Raven adds, hugging my other side. I can feel her shaking with laughter.

"What are the neighbors going to think?" I ask, closing my eyes and sighing.

"Some crow outside just attacked me!" Carl screeches as he enters the room.

"What did you do to it?" Rebecca demands, hands on her hips and a scowl on her face.

"Why do you assume I did something?" Carl asks, his face a mask of mock innocence.

"Because everybody else managed to make it inside without a bird attacking!" Rebecca yells back.

"I might've called it ugly and maybe stupid," Carl says, shrugging his shoulders. "But last time I checked birds don't speak English!"

"Carl, these crows are Kacie's familiars," Logan says, biting his lip to keep from laughing. "The bird sensed your hostility."

"God, I'm queen of the crows," I say with a deep sigh.

"I'm sorry I insulted your bird, Kacie," Carl says looking rather contrite.

"It's okay, Carl," I reply.

"No it isn't," Rebecca insists, dragging Carl away to berate him some more.

"That's a match made in heaven," Daniel says, watching them continue to argue across the room.

"You got your afterlife destinations mixed up," Raven comments. "Hell is more appropriate."

"All right, everyone, quiet down," Mr. Kincaid says as he enters the room with Mrs. Kincaid at his side. "Kacie's dad needs to know what types of pizza to order."

Shouts fill the room, and more arguments break out over topping choices. Kodiak thinks it's a fun, new game. He races from one person to the next, adding his barks to the excited shouting.

"Enough!" Dr. Hayes shouts into the deafening din with an extra dose of her compulsion spell. The room falls silent. "Not another word or every pizza will be anchovy and pineapple."

"You aren't pregnant are you, dear?" Mrs. Kincaid asks, her eyes wide. "Strange cravings and all…"

"What? N-no of course not," Dr. Hayes sputters while shaking her head. "I just picked what I thought was the most vile."

"If you say so, dear," Mrs. Kincaid says with a knowing smile.

"I'm NOT pregnant!" Dr. Hayes yells just as Dad enters the room.

"Good to know, Tammy," he says, wrapping his arm around her shoulder.

A broad smile lights his face. As much as I hate the idea of another mother, it is nice to see him so happy. Perhaps it's too early to worry about that. They've only been together for two weeks. And yet the way they gaze into each other's eyes makes them look like two love-struck kids.

"I'll order an assortment," Dad says without breaking eye contact with Dr. Hayes. "No anchovy and pineapple, though. Sorry." He ducks out the door before she can respond to his comment.

"All right, settle down," Mr. Kincaid says, herding everyone to the folding chairs scattered around the room. "Take your seats. Let's get this meeting over with so we can celebrate. Michelle, your report on Sue and Frank Anders."

"They've been charged with eight felony counts including fraud, attempted kidnapping, and drugging a minor," Michelle says with a wicked grin. "They were arraigned last Thursday and will stand trial. Currently they're out on bail but still under house arrest due to the severity of the crime and fear of potential retaliation." I cringe a bit, and Logan pulls me closer to his side, draping his arm over my shoulder. "Their business license has been revoked. The assistant DA will be in touch with us shortly to take statements and decide who will be used as witnesses in the criminal trial."

"Remember this is strictly non-supernatural. No mention of anything paranormal other than our investigation of the house for a potential haunting," Dr. Hayes says. She makes eye contact with everyone in the room before continuing. "Let's keep our 'abilities' quiet. They aren't relevant to the DA's case and have the potential to hurt it. The last thing we need is the defense using our abilities against us."

"What about their source for the witch's bane?" Mr. Kincaid asks.

"Mrs. Anders won't talk, says they'll kill her," Devon replies. "It looks like we may have a new player in the San Antonio paranormal underworld. Signs show it may be a vampire."

"We'll need to tread lightly with this investigation," Mr. Kincaid says, not bothering to hide his worried expression. "Vampires are not something to mess with."

"I volunteer," Raven says, raising her hand. "I have lots of experience vampire hunting. Dad moved us here because he thought the coven that killed my mother fled here when we had them on the run. I have some connections in the vampire community."

"Not alone, Raven," Mr. Kincaid says in a stern tone. "We have a new member, Blake, arriving next week. He's a werewolf and will be very helpful in a hunt for vampires."

"I don't care if werewolves are good against vamps," Raven bites out. "I'd rather not work with one. I've had a, uh… bad experience with a were-wolf in the past."

"I'm sorry, Raven," Mr. Kincaid says. "But we don't allow personal prejudice to get in the way of our ability to hunt. You know that full well. Besides, Blake might be your only defense if the vampires turn on you."

"You're right, sir," Raven says, hanging her head. "I'm sorry. I'll be happy to work with our new recruit."

Though her voice sounds contrite, I notice the hard gleam in her eyes. Whoever this new werewolf is, I pity him. Raven is not one I'd want as an enemy.

"I have good news regarding Bob Carter," Dr. Hayes says, looking up from her iPad. "Just got word from the hospital. He's been officially upgraded from critical to stable, and they've completed the move from ICU to a regular room. I've diagnosed a stroke, although we all know it was a minor pos-session. The damage to the brain is consistent with a major stroke."

"Will he recover?" I ask, remembering the bizarre state he was in at the shelter.

"We won't be able to ascertain the extent of damage for quite some time," Dr. Hayes says, shaking her head. "He may never regain memories or function as an adult again."

"That's so sad," I reply, burying my fingers in Kodiak's fur when he jumps up beside me. "How could Yardley do that to his own son?"

"You can't psychoanalyze a psycho," Daniel says with a snort of disgust.

"I've been reading his journals," Mrs. Kincaid says shaking her head. "I understand the importance of thirteen in some rituals, but he took it to the extreme. The ritual he laid out was so diabolical and complicated. Thirteen children aged one to thirteen kidnapped on each of the thirteen days prior to Halloween. The night of their kidnapping, each child had one rib removed in a dark ceremony."

She pauses, falling into Mr. Kincaid's arms. He wraps his arms around her and coos softly for several minutes. After blowing her nose and wiping her eyes on a tissue, she continues the horrible tale.

"He thought this macabre necklace would grant him immortality," she says with a sad sigh. "Even Halloween was important because not only is the thirty-first an inversion of thirteen, but the veil between the spirit plane and the living realm is the thinnest. He'd been planning this for several years and chose 1969 because of the multiples of the number three. He was truly demonic in every sense of the word, except he wasn't possessed. What he did to those children… well, Yardley was one sick bastard. He loved every minute of it. When the police began their standoff on October thirtieth, Yardley used the rib necklace to trap the children's souls to him and our plane."

"For a while anyway, I suppose he was somewhat immortal," Mr. Kincaid says while stroking his wife's hair.

"He's gone right?" I ask in a whisper. "Truly gone. Banished?"

"Yes," Raven says, her mouth in a grim line. "Thanks to Logan."

"Kacie has limited memory of that night," Logan says, rubbing my arm with his hand. "I thought we could fill her in on what she missed."

"Well, you almost died," Dr. Hayes says, glaring at me. "Logan saved your life. Again. I had to smooth things over with Adam. He wanted to pull you from the Circle. Can't say I blame him. I can't use my compulsion on him anymore either."

"Why?" I ask.

"Because I care about him as a potential… um…"

"Husband," Mrs. Kincaid supplies the missing word.

"Possibly, but way in the future," Dr. Hayes says, waving her hands in the air. "Using compulsion is akin to lying. I won't do that to someone I'm in a relationship with. So stay out of trouble, young lady!"

"Yes, ma'am," I reply, staring at my hands.

"And please don't call me ma'am," she says sighing. "I'm still paying back my student loans. I'm not that old yet."

"On the positive side, your dad and brother think I'm the greatest person ever," Logan says with a proud grin.

"That's 'cause you are," I murmur, kissing his cheek. My face flames when I remember our audience. He pulls me closer and kisses my forehead.

"You are too," he says. "You freed those child spirits and led us to Yardley."

When I try to grasp the hazy threads of memory, they unravel into nothing. "I just can't remember anything after freeing Ellie and the other spirits, no matter how hard I try."

"Yardley possessed you through the athame and you tried to stab Logan," Rebecca offers with an eager expression. Like her revelation would ease my mind or something.

"It was just a scratch because you did a good job fighting him," Logan says, pointing to a long cut on his left forearm that looks like a cat scratch.

"Daniel, grabbed the dagger from your hands, slicing his palm open in the process," Raven says, looking at Daniel from the corner of her eye.

"He needed eight stitches to close the wound," Dr. Hayes adds in her matter-of-fact tone.

"We stripped Logan to stop the bleeding," Rebecca adds with a sly wink.

"Just my shirt," Logan says when I glance at him. "After Daniel threw the athame into the fire, I had a sudden realization. The last time I spoke with your mother, when she was frantic, she kept going on and on about the goat mask. It seemed like the perfect thing to bind his spirit. I remembered seeing it in the ritual room."

"I guess I should call my mother and let her know it's over and I'm okay," I say with a resigned sigh. "I really don't want to talk to her."

"It's the first step in mending bridges," Dad says, entering the room with his arms full of pizza boxes. "But later. Now you celebrate a job well done."

I watch the last of the taillights disappear around the corner while standing in Logan's arms. It was a good evening, and I'm sorry to see everyone go, especially Logan. My arms wrap around his waist, careful to avoid the bandages on his back. We stand in silence, just holding each other, feeling utterly content. That is until a crow lands on my shoulder and starts playing with my hair. It doesn't bother me like I expect it to. When I pet its feathered back, the bird lets out a strange chirping noise I had no idea a crow could make then it flies back to the porch railing.

"I guess I better head home," Logan says, caressing my cheek with his fingers. "I'll pick you up at seven-thirty tomorrow morning."

"I was afraid Dad wouldn't let me go back to school this soon," I murmur, turning my head to kiss his palm. "It'll be nice to get back to drama rehearsals."

"Bye, Kacie," he says as he heads toward his Mustang. "Sweet dreams. Remember, I'm only a phone call away if you need me."

"Thanks," I reply, waving. "See you tomorrow."

After his car disappears around the corner, I turn to head back inside, unsurprised to see both Dad and Gavin lurking in the foyer. I guess after two brushes with death it may be a while before they tone down the overprotective vibes. With a smile, I give both a kiss on the cheek before heading up the stairs to my bedroom. I'm looking forward to a night of uninterrupted sleep and with any luck, some pleasant dreams.

The End

Thank you for reading *Tortured Souls*! If you enjoyed this story, please consider leaving a review on Amazon. Reviews are very important, especially for a newer author. It doesn't have to be long. Short and sweet reviews are wonderful too.

I love communicating with my readers. Please feel free to send me an email if you have any questions or would like to discuss the world of books. I'm recruiting beta readers right now. If you enjoyed this book and would like an opportunity to read my work prior to publication, please contact me.

http://www.kimberleighwheaton.com
https://twitter.com/Cymberle
https://www.facebook.com/KimberLeighWheaton
cymberle1@gmail.com

About the Author

Kimber Leigh Wheaton is a YA/NA author with a soft spot for sweet romance. She is married to her soul mate, has a teenage son, and shares her home with three dogs, four cats, and lots of dragons. No, she doesn't live on a farm, she just loves animals.

Kimber Leigh is addicted to romance, videogames, superheroes, villains, and chocolate—not necessarily in that order. (If she has to choose, she'll take a chocolate covered superhero!) She currently lives in San Antonio, TX but has been somewhat a rolling stone in life, having resided in several different cities and states.

Acknowledgments

There are so many people to thank... I feel like an award winner afraid to forget someone in their speech! First and foremost, I want to thank my husband and son for their constant support. Writing is not an easy task in any way. There are many times when it's an emotional rollercoaster. They have stood by my side through laughter and tears, and I couldn't ask for more. Thanks to my mother and mother-in-law for the help with beta reading. Note to self: remember the two mothers are far too supportive to see problems. Thanks to my father for listening when I needed a shoulder to cry on. And thanks to my father-in-law who always stays positive and that rubs off on me.

I want to thank my cover artist, Amanda, for her amazing vision and work. I have never seen anything she designed that I didn't like, but this cover is truly spectacular. Also thanks to all my writer friends, especially Lisa Temple. Your support has meant a lot to me. Thanks to everyone involved in making this book a reality: my formatters, editor, and proofreader.

And lastly, thanks to you, my reader. Without you there would be no reason to write at all.

Now available
Shadow Fire
Light Chronicles Book 1

Amazon Bestselling YA Fantasy Romance
Amazon * B&N * Kobo * Smashwords * iTunes *
Goodreads

Ashlyn – a free-spirited teenager whose peaceful life
is shattered when the village elders honor her with a
perilous quest to recover a stolen relic.

Zane – a jaded mercenary, torn by his undeniable
desire for Ashlyn and the dark secret that could
make her hate him forever.
Delistaire – a malevolent sorcerer driven by an insatiable lust for power.
All three are bound together by an ancient relic sup-
posedly infused with the power of a Goddess.
Shadow Fire – adventure, passion, secrets, and betrayal
As Ashlyn and Zane race to stay one step ahead of
the evil lurking in the shadows, their passions are
ignited and their bond strengthens. But will they
find the relic before Delistaire? Or has their entire
quest been orchestrated from the very beginning by
a madman in pursuit of ultimate power?
Each installment of the *Light Chronicles* is a standalone story.

Excerpt from Chapter One of *Shadow Fire:*

Every step I take is one step closer to death.

Hiking through the dense underbrush, I try to calm my frayed nerves and control the fear threatening to overwhelm me. Twigs and tendrils of ivy grab at my ankles as I continue to forge ahead, forcing me to wrench away from their skeletal grip. The sunlight is fading, signaling the end of another day, but this is no ordinary day.

A loud *crack* pierces the air. I freeze in my tracks, my breath catching in my throat. Whipping my head around, I try to locate the source of the sound. My heart pounds in my chest, the erratic rhythm painful. These woods are full of predators, some animal, some monster, but the worst... human. Taking a deep breath, I listen to the surrounding woods: birds chirp, insects hum, and small animals scurry about as if they have no care in the world.

Lungs burning, I force myself to continue walking. I didn't collapse three weeks ago when this whole fiasco started, and I won't give in now. My family needs me to be strong.

The trees become sparser as I approach the edge of the forest. My shoulders slump when I pass the tree house we used to play in so many years ago. Any other day when I'm this close to home after a long day of hunting, I'd smile, breathe a sigh of relief, and perhaps look forward to dinner. Today there will be no raucous family meal, no solace in entering the peaceful village, and nothing to smile about.

The villagers will be awaiting my return, skulking in the shadows, desperate to catch a glimpse of the walking dead girl.

I've dealt with the whispers and pointing for three weeks with my head held high, my anxiety hidden behind a mask of indifference. I don't want them to see me like this, trembling in fear, broken. They've taken everything I am, every hope, every dream I've had for the future and smashed them to pieces with little hope of salvation. The townsfolk of Verdane decided my fate and they chose death.

The elders told me being *Chosen* is an honor. Either they are ignorant or apathetic. Every five years for the last twenty, a teenage girl has been chosen by the town, via secret ballot, to undertake this dangerous quest, never to return. Perhaps if the elders had to forfeit their lives instead they wouldn't be so quick to label it an honor, they'd call it what it is… a sacrifice.

Coming in August 2014 from Astraea Press
Stolen Moon
Light Chronicles Book 2

YA Fantasy Romance
A standalone sequel to the Amazon bestseller *Shadow Fire*

Katarina ~ a Royal Knight bound by honor and duty who steals a powerful relic from a sorcerer in a desperate attempt to save her kingdom from the clutches of a madman.

Ethan ~ a mercenary leader trapped between his growing attraction to Katarina and his responsibility to protect his friends from the evil pursuing her.

Zebulon ~ a malicious sorcerer waging war as though it's a game, caring nothing for the lives he destroys in his quest for power.

Drawn together by a moonstone medallion—an indestructible relic with immense magical power.

Katarina steals the medallion from Zebulon and flees in the dead of night. Together with Ethan and his mercenaries, she struggles to stay one step ahead of the sorcerer and his minions in a race against time to save her homeland. Fierce battles, ravenous monsters, and bloodthirsty brigands—those are no surprise. But Katarina never dreamed her greatest obstacle could be falling in love.